I0769034

Also by the Author

The Erin O'Reilly Mysteries

Black Velvet
Irish Car Bomb
White Russian
Double Scotch
Manhattan
Black Magic
Death By Chocolate
Massacre
Flashback
First Love
High Stakes
Aquarium
The Devil You Know
Hair of the Dog
Punch Drunk

Bossa Nova
Blackout
Angel Face
Italian Stallion
White Lightning
Kamikaze
Jackhammer
Frostbite
Brain Damage
Celtic Twilight
Headshot
Vino Blanco
White Lady
Blackjack
Last Round (coming soon)

Tequila Sunrise: A James Corcoran Story

Fathers
A Modern Christmas Story

The Clarion Chronicles
Ember of Dreams

Blackjack

The Erin O'Reilly Mysteries
Book Twenty-Nine

Steven Henry

Clickworks Press • Baltimore, MD

First publication: Clickworks Press, 2025
Release: CWP-EOR29-INT-P.IS-1.0

Sign up for updates, deals, and exclusive sneak peeks at clickworkspress.com/join.

Ebook ISBN: 979-8-88900-035-8
Paperback ISBN: 979-8-88900-36-05
Hardcover ISBN: 979-8-88900-37-02

For Aunt Susan, the librarian,
who has always shared my love of books.

Special Preview

Keep reading after Blackjack to
enjoy a first look at the new series
coming soon from Clickworks Press

The Coventry Adams Mysteries
by Steven Henry

Want a reminder when the new series is out?

Join Steven's list at
clickworkspress.com/join/steven

Blackjack

Combine 1 oz. Scotch whiskey, 2/3 oz. Kahlua, 1/3 oz. orange liqueur, and 1/3 oz. lemon juice in a shaker. Shake with ice. Strain into an old-fashioned glass containing ice cubes and serve.

Chapter 1

"We've got ourselves a misdemeanor homicide," Vic Neshenko said.

Erin O'Reilly wanted to tell him to shut up, but she couldn't disagree. Cops had plenty of darkly funny names for what had happened outside the tattoo parlor: "misdemeanor homicide," "public-service homicide," "pest control," and "street cleanup" were just a few. That was what cops did with bloody violence, in order to cope with it. They made jokes. All of them came to the same punchline in this case: the body at their feet didn't represent a great loss to society.

"I heard that, Neshenko," Lieutenant Webb said. "Don't let me hear it again."

Webb had a sense of humor. But you had to dig for it, and you had to know what it looked like if you hoped to recognize it.

"Copy that, sir," Vic said. "What I mean to say is, this is a heinous crime that deserves and demands the full resources of the Department. Justice must be served, swiftly and impartially."

Vic was a lot of things, but he wasn't subtle. When he laid

on the sarcasm, he used a big shovel.

"We don't dispense justice," Webb said, choosing to give a straight answer. "That's up to the courts. What do we do, Detective Piekarski?"

"Serve the public trust, protect the innocent, and uphold the law, sir," Zofia Piekarski said without hesitation.

"Good answer," Webb said.

"Where have I heard that?" Erin wondered aloud.

"*Robocop*," Vic said, grinning. "The original. That's his primary directives. We watched it last night."

"I knew it sounded familiar," Erin said. "Do you really think you should be learning policing from '80s action movies?"

"Why are we even here?" Vic asked. "We're Major Crimes. This loser is strictly minor league."

"The local Homicide boys are overbooked," Webb replied. "Their Lieutenant asked me to do him a favor. Besides, I thought you looked bored earlier today, and I don't trust you when you're bored. You're like a preschooler with a book of matches."

"Fair enough," Vic said. "So we're in the business of trading favors now? What do we get in return?"

"Satisfaction for a job well done?" Erin suggested.

"Continued employment with the City of New York," Webb corrected. Now, if we could return to the matter of our murder victim? What do we know about him?"

"Gangland tats," Vic said. "And prison ink. He's a tough guy who's done hard time. Check out those scars. There's only one way you get marks like that on your knuckles."

"Fist-fighting," Erin agreed. "Bare-knuckled. Mickey Connor had scars like that."

"Oh yeah," Vic said, grinning again. "You got a real close look at Connor's knuckles, once upon a time."

"Yeah." Erin rubbed the side of her head, remembering. "But he was a lot bigger than our guy here."

"How's the body coming along, Doctor?" Webb asked the woman kneeling beside the corpse.

"Rigor mortis has fully set in," Dr. Levine said without removing her attention from the dead man. "Algor mortis suggests four hours since death, indicated by a five-degree drop in body temperature. Lividity confirms this, further determining that the body has not been moved postmortem. I estimate time of death was approximately eight o'clock in the evening. Decomposition has not become noticeable at the present time."

"Yuck," Zofia said.

"I'm not actually asking about the body's rate of decomp," Webb said. "I was wondering whether you'd isolated a cause of death."

"Your question was nonspecific," Levine said, irritated. "Preliminary cause of death is blunt-force trauma to the base of the skull. The crush pattern suggests a single blow with a semi-rigid implement."

"Semi-rigid?" Erin prompted.

"I hypothesize the impact was made by a bag or sack containing a number of small, hard objects," Levine said. "These objects appear to be round and of a uniform diameter of approximately eight millimeters."

"Translation," Vic said. "Somebody slapped this bozo upside the head with a bag full of ball bearings."

"That hypothesis aligns with available data," Levine said.

"A blackjack," Webb said.

"Those aren't supposed to be lethal," Zofia said.

"A half pound of metal to the back of the head can be plenty lethal," Vic replied.

"I know," she said. "I meant this might not have been a deliberate murder. Maybe it was a botched mugging."

"Yeah," Vic said. "Because we're dealing with an epidemic of muggings of young, tough, tattooed Black men. Our most brilliant mind, Zofia, just solved the case."

Zofia scowled at him. "You're sleeping on the couch," she growled. "Forever."

"What else can you tell me about the victim?" Webb asked Levine, ignoring the lovers' quarrel behind him.

"He was struck from the rear," Levine said. "He probably was unaware of his assailant, since his pistol is tucked into his waistband instead of in hand or on the ground."

"Oh, I'm sorry," Vic said. "Young, tough, tattooed, *armed* Black men."

"What kind of pistol?" Erin asked.

The body had fallen awkwardly, twisting as it struck the curb. The man's legs were on the sidewalk, his torso contorted in the gutter. The handgrip of a pistol was indeed visible. The gun was crammed down the front of the dead man's trousers.

"Ruger American," Vic said. "You can see the brand name on the bottom of the grip. It's the compact version, so looks like a ten-round magazine. Nine-millimeter. Pretty decent handgun. They just introduced them a year or two ago."

Nobody doubted him. Vic pretended to be a dumb thug, but he was an encyclopedia of firearms knowledge.

"An armed convict gets his skull crushed outside a tattoo parlor," Webb said. "I think we may end up kicking this one over to the Homicide boys, or maybe the Gang Task Force."

"Do we know anything about the tattoo place?" Erin asked. The sign on the door advertised it as The Needle X-Change. "Looks like a high-class establishment."

"Good place to pick up hepatitis," Zofia said. "Or HIV."

"You have a tattoo, don't you, Erin?" Vic said. "Didn't you get one right before that power outage a while back?"

"Yeah."

"What is it, again?"

"None of your business."

"It's a tramp stamp, isn't it?"

"No."

"Prove it."

"In your lonely, pathetic dreams. If Zofia isn't going to show you any skin, I'm sure as hell not going to."

"The victim was struck at least three additional times," Levine said. "Possibly more. The weapon does not have a specific shape, so it is difficult to determine exactly how many blows. All of these were delivered to the left temple."

"Our perp kept hitting him after he was already down," Vic said. "He was an unmoving target. Otherwise all those hits wouldn't have been in the same spot on the side of his head. And it's the side that's up. I figure the killer was in that doorway next to the tattoo shop. Our boy comes walking down the sidewalk, the killer comes out behind him and bam! Then bam, bam, bam to make sure and he's on his way."

"That doesn't seem like a mugging to me," Erin said. "It looks more like he was deliberately beaten to death."

"The additional blows were superfluous," Levine said. "The impact to the base of the cranium crushed at least two vertebrae and the skull itself. It was not a survivable injury."

"He was coming out of the tattoo parlor," Erin added.

"How do you know?" Webb asked.

She pointed to the back of the dead man's arm. "See that bandage? I'll bet that's covering a fresh tat."

Webb nodded. "You think this was an ambush?"

"Yeah," Erin said. "I think the perp followed him here, or knew he'd be here. Then he waited outside until our victim came out. Then it went down like Vic says."

"Gang hit," Vic said. "I'd bet twenty bucks on it."

"You might be right," Webb said. He was staring at the dead man's hand. "He's got something there."

"What is it?" Zofia asked. "Some sort of calling card?"

Levine carefully lifted the arm. The hand was clenched, the muscles stiff in death. In it was a single playing card.

"Jack of spades," Webb said. "You're right. It's a literal calling card. O'Reilly?"

"Sir?"

"You may want your partner to get a whiff of this."

Erin looked down. Rolf stood as close to her hip as he could get, his whiskers actually in contact with her leg. The German Shepherd stared back at her with his serious brown eyes.

"You think the killer left it?" she asked.

"Probably," Webb said.

"Gang symbol?" she guessed.

"Or maybe he's part of some freaky cult," Vic said. "Or he's named Jack."

"That'd be remarkably convenient," Webb said. "In my experience, murderers don't usually leave their names with their victims."

"Ooh! I know!" Vic said. "We're dealing with a hardcore psycho who's going to kill fifty-two people and leave a card with each one. No, wait... fifty-four people. I forgot the jokers."

"Fifty-four homicides?" Webb said, raising his eyebrows. "That seems like a lot of trouble to go to for a gimmick. Before we go jumping to ludicrous conclusions, why don't we at least get an ID on our victim and try to zero in on potential motives?"

"We shouldn't have any trouble finding out who the poor schmuck was," Vic said, jutting his chin in the direction of the body. "I guarantee we'll have his prints on file."

"It's awfully late," Webb said. He rubbed his eyes. "I'm too old to be up past midnight."

"Real cops work the dog watch," Vic said. "Isn't that right, Erin?"

"Absolutely," she said. "But the Lieutenant's right, too. We've been on the clock a really long time, counting the earlier shift."

"And we'll be on it a little longer," Webb said. "Don't worry, your overtime is approved. The PC still likes you for catching that pattern killer last month and it helped the whole squad. We got that extra budget allotment."

"Not quite enough for another detective, I can't help but notice," Vic said.

"Something wrong with the current batch?" Zofia asked.

"Of course not. If you ask for more of something, that's usually a sign that you like it."

"So you'd like a few more blondes on the squad?"

Vic considered this. "Hmm. Maybe."

"I want all of us back at the Eightball," Webb said. "I want an ID on our victim. And I'd love to know why he was killed. If it was a gang hit, or a mugging, or something else. Then, once we decide whether it's our case or not, we can get some sleep. Maybe."

Erin was still considering the playing card. "A black jack," she said. "On a guy who got blackjacked. That's a pretty sick joke."

"It's a dad joke," Vic said. "I've been working on some of mine, for when Mina's old enough. Why did the coffee cup call the cops?"

"Oh dear Lord," Erin muttered.

"Because it got mugged," he said. "Why doesn't the DA like to prosecute lamps?"

"Don't encourage him," Zofia said.

"Because they always get a light sentence."

"You're a dad all right," Erin said. "But if I'm going to pull overtime after midnight, it's going to be for actual police work, not to listen to dad jokes."

"We can do both," Vic said. "Let's go find out who our mystery man was."

*   *   *

The victim's identity didn't stay a mystery for long. Zofia had it within moments of loading the fingerprints into the database.

"Kamal Lobert," she announced. "He is most definitely in the system. Orphaned at age nine, went through half a dozen foster homes. Did some time in juvie for boosting cars and shoplifting. Graduated to the big leagues when he was seventeen and went down for armed robbery. Got five to ten, served three. Looks like he hooked up with a gang when he was inside. Since then he's had three narcotics busts, plus two ADW and three counts of aggravated assault."

"Assault with a Deadly Weapon," Vic said. "One of my favorites. Jesus. Why was this guy still walking the streets?"

"He pled out on two of the drug beefs," Zofia said. "One ADW was dropped when the star witness didn't show up to testify. The aggravated assaults didn't go to trial either. Insufficient evidence. He got eighteen months for the other ADW and probation for the drugs. But that's not the bad part."

"By all means, tell us the bad part," Webb said.

"Especially if it explains why a convicted violent felon was walking around Manhattan holding his own balls at gunpoint," Vic added.

"He was recently tried for murder," Zofia said. "Along with his fourth drug charge. Misdemeanor weight of heroin."

"Murder?" Webb repeated. "And he was on the loose?"

"He was acquitted," Zofia explained.

"Details?"

"He was charged with the second-degree murder of LaRayne Shaw," Zofia said. "Age nineteen. About six months ago, a couple gangs had a shootout. Some sort of bullshit dispute over a street corner, apparently. The Trip Sixes and the *Cuchillos Locos*."

"I've heard of them!" Erin exclaimed. "Remember? They were one of the gangs involved in that thing with William Ward in Hell's Kitchen."

"Yeah," Vic said. "The Crazy Knives. What're they doing getting in shootouts? Do they use guns, too?"

"Yes, Vic, they use guns," Zofia said with exaggerated patience. "The Crazy Knives is just their name. Anyway, Lobert was a member of the Trip Sixes. The DA said he was the triggerman who fired the shots that killed Shaw. She wasn't a gang member. She was just a local girl on her way home from work who caught a stray bullet. She died at the hospital."

"Interesting," Webb said. "I assume this girl had family? Friends?"

"Probably," Zofia said.

"People who might be pretty upset her shooter skated?" Erin added.

"He was convicted on the drug charge," Zofia said. "But that was small potatoes. It wasn't dealer weight. He was looking at three months. Sentencing was going to be on Tuesday."

"Less than a week away," Webb said. "Somebody seized their opportunity before he got locked up."

"I'm liking a couple guys for this already," Vic said.

"Is it a gangland hit?" Erin asked. "Gang Task Force stuff?"

"I think maybe we'll keep it," Webb said. "We don't have any proof he was killed because of his gang activity. And there's a couple things about this that seem a little off to me. I don't want it going to some overworked Homicide dick's inbox. He'll just assume the same thing we did and push it to the back of the line."

"What are we assuming?" Erin asked.

"That Lobert was a bad guy who got what was coming to

him," Webb said. "And nobody cares."

"But he was a bad guy," Vic said. "He did get what was coming. And speaking from a deep, personal place, I really don't care that he's dead."

"That's not the point," Webb said. "The only reason we care whether a victim deserved what they got is if it helps us establish motive."

"You really believe that, sir?" Vic asked.

"If you don't, the Captain has transfer request forms in his office," Webb replied. "Because I don't want anybody on my squad who doesn't believe it. Our job isn't about justice. It's about the law. And the law says you don't get to beat a man's brains in with a sock full of ball bearings. You copy?"

Vic muttered something inaudible.

"We copy, sir," Erin said loudly.

"Good," Webb said. "Now let's get to work."

"Can I run home quick?" Zofia asked. "Mom's watching Mina, but it's going on one AM. I'll bring her in. I promise, she won't be any trouble. She sleeps like... well, like a baby."

"Rolf can watch her," Erin said. "He's a natural babysitter."

Chapter 2

The youngest member of the Major Crimes unit lay on a blanket in the middle of a portable playpen. Rolf sat with his chin resting on the railing of the pen, watching Mina Piekarski intently. He never looked away and hardly blinked. Occasionally he made a soft, throaty noise deep in his chest, almost like a cat's purr.

"Don't look now," Vic said to Erin. "But your boyfriend's got a new crush. I mean, I can't blame him. She's the most beautiful girl in New York."

"That's my genes," Zofia said.

"No argument there," Vic said.

"CSU finished cataloguing the victim's possessions," Webb announced. "The deceased was, at time of death, in possession of a Ruger American nine-millimeter semi-automatic pistol."

"Told you so," Vic interjected.

"Yes, good eye, Neshenko. We're all very impressed. The pistol was loaded with a full ten-round magazine, safety engaged."

"Good," Vic said. "If you're gonna be pointing your gun at your own dick, you'd better have the safety on."

"He also had an extra ten-round magazine in his right front pocket. His left front pocket contained a set of keys, including what's probably an apartment key, two keys to either storage lockers or mailboxes, and a decorative fob in the shape of a silhouette of a naked woman. It appears to be a souvenir from a strip club called Hot Kitty."

"Classy," Zofia commented.

"His right hip pocket contained a roll of currency amounting to five hundred twenty dollars," Webb went on. "In twenties, held together by a rubber band. His left hip pocket held a pack of Camel cigarettes, two cigarettes missing, and a disposable plastic lighter. The burnt-out stub of a cigarette was found one meter from the body. CSU hypothesizes he was smoking the cigarette when he was struck. It fell from his mouth, still lit, and burned itself out on the sidewalk. They swabbed the cigarette to match the DNA to the victim, just in case."

"I guess we can rule out robbery as a motive," Erin said. "There isn't a mugger alive who'd take the time and effort to beat a downed man to death, then leave over five hundred in cash."

"Finally," Webb said, "the playing card in the victim's hand is a red-backed Bicycle card, showing no sign of wear. It appears to be brand-new, fresh out of the pack. CSU obtained a thumbprint and partial index and middle prints off the card, matching the victim's hand. The card was otherwise clean. They found no additional playing cards nearby, nor any card box."

"That's not a lot to go on," Vic said.

"If the gun was fully loaded, he probably hadn't used it," Erin said.

"CSU found no gunshot residue on his hands," Webb confirmed.

"I blame the cigarette," Vic said. "Those things will wreck

your night vision. That glowing end right in front of your nose? Forget seeing anything in the shadows. Just one more way they can kill you."

Webb rubbed a thumb and two fingers together, clearly wishing he had a cig at that moment. "Lots of things will kill you," he said. "Most of them are less pleasant."

"What about the fresh tattoo?" Erin asked.

Webb took a moment scrolling through the initial crime scene report. "It's a birdcage," he said. "With the door open and the bird flying away. I don't think we need rigorous psychoanalysis to figure out why he chose that design."

"Because he got away with murder," Vic said. Then he snickered. "For a day or two, anyway."

"According to the proprietor of the Needle X-Change, one Dominic Grinder, Lobert received the tattoo earlier in the evening, paid in cash, and left a couple of minutes before eight."

"And died immediately afterward," Erin said. "Did Grinder see anything?"

"He didn't see a thing, didn't hear a thing," Webb said. "I'm guessing he's learned to be selectively blind and deaf."

"It's amazing how many witnesses are like that," Vic said.

"We can conclude that Lobert wasn't expecting trouble," Webb said. "He was armed, but it's safe to say that was his normal state. On his way out of the Needle X-Change he stopped to light a cigarette once he stepped onto the sidewalk. He had time to put the pack and lighter back in his pocket, but then he got hit on the head from behind. The first blow would have been fatal, according to our Medical Examiner, but our attacker wanted to make sure. The killer delivered several more blows to the downed, helpless victim, then left him there and got away clean."

"Good ambush," Erin said. "If Lobert had just lit a cigarette, his night vision would've been wrecked by that flame right in front of his eyes. And he was probably standing still, or walking slowly. He was vulnerable. He probably never even saw it coming."

"The perp really wanted him dead," Zofia said. "Otherwise why keep hitting him? He was helpless."

"This was a deliberate hit," Webb said, nodding. "But who did it? And why?"

"The Crazy Knives," Vic guessed. "Assuming they use blackjacks along with knives and guns."

"For the last time, Neshenko, that's just their name," Webb said wearily. "They'd probably beat your head in with a brick if the situation required it. And if they thought a brick could make it through your thick skull."

"I'm just saying," Vic said. "If that was my gang name, I'd use knives most of the time. I'd make a point of it. See what I did there? A point of it...?"

Erin and Webb rolled their eyes. Zofia groaned. Mina gurgled and waved her arms in the air, which made Rolf cock his head and only increased his fascination.

"It might have been a family member of the shooting victim," Erin said. "Was the Shaw girl married?"

"Let me check the case file," Webb said. "No, but she had a kid."

"The kid did it!" Vic announced.

"LaRayne was nineteen," Erin reminded him. "How old is this kid?"

"Eighteen months," Webb said. "I don't think he could have reached Lobert's head with a blackjack."

"Underage single mom," Zofia said quietly. "What a shit deal."

"She had a brother," Webb said. "Micheal Shaw. That's Micheal with an E-A, not an A-E. Two years older. And he's got a criminal record."

"Ooh, I like him already," Vic said, smoothly shifting suspects. "What's he done?"

"Drugs and aggravated assault," Webb said. "His record looks a lot like our victim's, now that you mention it."

"He's not in prison right now, is he?" Erin asked. "That'd be a pretty good alibi."

"Not at the moment," Webb said. "He was living with LaRayne at the time of her death. He has a gang affiliation, but it isn't the Trip Sixes or the Crazy Knives. Looks like he's part of... interesting."

"What?" Vic, Erin, and Zofia asked in unison.

"A gang called the Wild Cards," Webb said. "I think we want to talk to Mr. Shaw as quickly as possible."

*   *   *

"This is my kind of talking," Vic said.

Erin rolled her eyes. "I'm still not sure we needed ESU for this," she said.

Half a dozen Emergency Services Unit officers in full tactical gear were stacked up in the apartment hallway. Parker, the big guy at the front, gave her a wink and a thumbs-up.

"The Wild Cards are a dangerous crew," Webb said. "One of their guys wounded a cop last year. Stabbed him in the eye with a dinner fork, if you believe it. We're not taking chances here. If Micheal comes quietly, no problem. But if he doesn't, I don't mind carrying a big stick. He's a lot less likely to fight back with a tac team knocking on his door."

"We don't even have an arrest warrant," Erin said.

"And ESU won't come in unless we need them," Webb replied.

"Yeah," Vic said. "If any of us really thought we'd be getting in a serious scrap, Zofia would've found a way to come along."

"Someone has to mind the baby," Webb said.

"They make Kevlar carriers these days," Vic said, then hastily added, "I'm joking! But if Zofia heard you say that, she'd call you a sexist dinosaur."

"I'm endangered," Webb said mildly, "not extinct. And sexism doesn't have a thing to do with it. You're the ones who wanted to be on the same squad."

"Hold on," Vic said. "You mean you don't want both of us on the same call, in case it goes sideways and everyone gets killed? That's not your decision to make!"

"Silly me," Webb said. "There I was thinking I was your Lieutenant, which makes it exactly my decision. We're done talking about this. Knock on the door or I'll have Parker do it with your stubborn skull."

Vic stood to one side of the door and banged on it with his knuckles. "Hey, Shaw!" he shouted. "NYPD! Open up!"

There was a lengthy silence.

"That's what we get for making a social call after midnight," Vic muttered. He knocked again, louder. "It's the cops, buddy! We just want to talk to you!"

"The hell you want?" asked a sleepy, surly voice through the door.

"I just told you!" Vic shot back. "You're Micheal Shaw, aren't you? Open the damn door!"

"I don't see no cops," Shaw said.

Erin unclipped the gold shield from her belt and held it in front of the peephole in the door, making sure to keep her body to the side. You never stood directly in front of a door when you didn't know whether the guy on the other side had a gun or not. Even an inch of solid wood wouldn't stop a bullet.

"Screw you guys," Shaw said. "I didn't do nothing!"

"Didn't you hear us?" Vic shot back. "I said we just want to talk! Do you really want us kicking your door down?"

There was another pause. A door at the end of the hall swung open. A very large, very irritated woman loomed in the doorway, clad in a truly hideous pink bathrobe.

"What's the matter with you?" she shouted, so loud Erin could swear the floorboards trembled. "Keep it down, can't you? We got people trying to sleep here!"

"Go back inside, lady," Parker said. "Right now."

"Am I supposed to be scared of you?" the woman retorted angrily. "Just 'cause you got your big guns and your fancy helmets? Where was you when LaRayne got killed, right in the middle of the street, broad daylight, huh? You got no problem knocking on doors in the middle of the night, but when there's ordinary folks getting killed and bullets flying all over the place, what about then? Y'all ain't nowhere in sight! You ain't nothing!"

"Ma'am, please," Webb said. "LaRayne is the reason we're here. If you could let us do our job, we'll be on our way with no further trouble."

"The police never done a damn thing for me!" the woman announced. "And don't be so damn loud!" Then she slammed her door. The doorframe rattled.

"Sorry about the noise," Parker said in a stage whisper. "We'll be real quiet."

"You guys really got a damn SWAT team out there?" Shaw demanded.

"What if we do?" Vic replied.

"Jesus, what for?"

"Open up and we'll talk about it."

"Fine, fine. Sheesh. I'm doing it. Don't go busting caps in me, man."

No fewer than three locks and a deadbolt clicked. Erin took a step back and eased her Glock out of its holster, just in case. Rolf tensed.

The door swung inward. A muscular young man stood in

the doorway, clad in a white tank top and red boxers. His bulky shoulders showed an impressive array of tattoos. An ace of spades stood out on his right bicep. His hands were open and empty.

"Damn," he said, poking his head into the hallway. "I don't think you brought enough guys. I mean, shit. You want me, you could've just talked to my PO, he could've brought you with him."

"Micheal Shaw?" Webb said.

"That's me," Shaw said. "You in charge?"

"Lieutenant Webb, Major Crimes," Webb said, showing his shield. "May we come in and talk to you?"

"What, all of you? I ain't got that much furniture."

"Lieutenant Lewis, why don't you take your team downstairs," Webb said. "I don't think we'll be needing you tonight."

"Copy that," Lewis said. He made a circle in the air with his forefinger and led the ESU squad away, leaving just Webb, Vic, Erin, and Rolf.

"Is that better?" Webb asked.

"Yeah," Shaw said grudgingly. "What's with the dog?"

"He's a K-9," Erin said. "Don't worry, he's very well trained. He won't damage anything unless I tell him to."

"You a Narc?"

"I'm Detective O'Reilly, Major Crimes."

"I heard of you," Shaw said, giving her an appreciative look. "Hell, I've seen your face. Damn, girl, you're finer than you look on TV. I bet you get this a lot, but you're smokin' hot."

"Thanks," she said dryly.

"But I know you ain't allowed to go out with guys like me," he said. "So I won't ask."

"Thanks," Erin said again.

"C'mon in," he said, stepping back and waving an arm.

"Sorry about the mess. I wasn't expecting company."

The apartment was definitely messy. Dirty dishes filled the sink. Crumpled clothes lay on the floor and draped over the threadbare couch. But under the clutter, Erin saw hints of good housekeeping. The wallpaper had been recently redone and the floor didn't show the ingrained filth she'd come to expect from poorly maintained housing. The furniture was sparse, but seemed to be in fairly good repair.

"What do you want?" Shaw asked once the detectives were inside. "I ain't had no trouble with my PO. I ain't had no violations. And they wouldn't send no damn detectives for that anyhow. You said this was about LaRayne. What about her?"

"Were you and your sister close?" Webb asked.

"What kind of question is that? After Mom died, she was the only family I had. You got a sister?"

"No," Webb said.

"Then you don't understand," Shaw said angrily. "LaRayne was something special. I know what you think of me."

"You really don't," Webb said.

"Hell yes, I do! You came to my door after midnight with a friggin' SWAT team! I got a record. I got a gang. Of course I do! Growing up with no brothers, no dad in the house, what you think I had to do? I bet you grew up in some fancy 'burb, nice house, white fence, mom and dad, huh? Whatever, it don't mean nothing. But LaRayne was a sweet kid. She was my baby sister, you know? When I did my time and got out, she gave me a place to stay. She said she'd take care of me, and she did. My kid sister! I shoulda been the one taking care of her. And now she's gone, my PO says they're gonna kick me out, they don't want a single guy with a record. I gotta find another place by the end of the month. You believe that? I never caused no trouble here for nobody! All we wanted was to get a life going, and now she's gone and you punks come in here and you ask if we was close?

Screw you!"

Shaw was shouting now, his hands clenched into fists. Vic casually took a step, setting himself to one side of the angry young man and getting ready for the fight he saw brewing.

"I apologize," Webb said. "I didn't mean to upset you. I'm just trying to understand what happened."

"What happened was, that jerkoff shot her," Shaw snapped. "That little bitch killed my sister and you assholes let him get away with it!"

"You're pretty angry at Kamal Lobert, aren't you?" Webb said in quiet, encouraging tones. "I can see why."

"Hell yes!" Shaw burst out. "You know what? Some guy just like you, some fat old bullshit cop came in here and sat right on that sofa over there, and he promised me, he gave me his *word*, he was gonna get the guy! He said I could trust him, that he'd get justice for LaRayne. I dunno what we got, but it sure as shit wasn't justice!"

"What would justice look like to you?" Webb asked. His voice was still mild, pleasant, inoffensive. Erin was impressed. Webb was better at getting information out of suspects than any cop she'd ever known. Everybody underestimated Harry Webb because he looked like a tired old detective. Which he was. What they forgot was that being old and tired meant he'd been doing this a long, long time.

"It'd look like his brains all over the street, just like he did to her!" Shaw retorted.

"Sounds good to me," Webb said. "It makes me sick, seeing scum like that get away with it. You were in court when he skated?"

"Yeah," Shaw said bitterly. "The look on his face, the way he *smiled*, I could've killed him right there."

"And nobody would've blamed you," Webb said. "Where'd he go afterward?"

"Beats me. He ran like the little bitch he was."

"I'll bet." Webb nodded sympathetically. "I'd have run too, if I'd done anything to your sister. You're nobody I'd want to mess with. Why do you think I brought the tactical team?"

Shaw smiled for the first time. Webb had stroked his ego and tough guys always liked that. "I feel you," he said. "I wiped the smile off his face, at least."

"You sure did," Webb said. "He had it coming."

"Somebody's gonna pop him real soon," Shaw said. "And it's gonna hurt."

Webb didn't give anything away. From his lack of reaction, he might have been playing championship poker. "Somebody?" he said. "Why not you?"

Shaw's smile turned cunning. "Hey now," he said. "You're trying to trick me into saying something. I ain't making no threats. I'm on parole. I got no weapons, no drugs. LaRayne, she didn't want none of that shit here. I'm a reformed good citizen."

"Of course you are," Webb said, nodding. "But how would you feel if somebody did spread Kamal's brains all over the street?"

"I'd buy the guy who did it a beer," Shaw said. "No law against buying a beer. What, you want me to say I'd feel bad? He's an asshole, he didn't look what he was doing, and he killed my sister like she wasn't nothing. And he didn't even say he was sorry, 'cause he ain't. Not yet."

"That's some nice ink you've got there," Vic said suddenly. "Some of it's prison tats, but that one on your shoulder, that's good professional work. I've been thinking about getting one. Where'd you get it?"

"The ace?" Shaw said, rubbing his shoulder proudly. "Guy called Grinder, at a place a couple blocks from here. The Needle X-Change. That's the letter X, then the word 'Change.' But don't wear that badge if you show up there. He don't like cops."

"We'll look him up," Vic said. He didn't shoot the other detectives a triumphant look, but they all felt the spark. Shaw had just admitted to frequenting the business outside of which Lobert had been killed.

"You wouldn't mind if we took a quick look around, would you?" Webb said. "Since you told us you don't have any contraband."

"Knock yourself out," Shaw snorted. "But you ain't gonna find shit. My PO goes through the place whenever he comes. Hell, when I was in prison at least I had a shiv in my mattress. Here, the sharpest thing you're gonna find is a kitchen knife. Just try not to leave shit all over the place, and don't screw nothing up in LaRayne's room. It's all that's left of her."

Webb nodded to Erin. She and Rolf made a sweep of the apartment, while Webb and Vic kept an eye on Shaw. She found no other people and, as Shaw had promised, no illicit drugs or weapons. The apartment was depressingly ordinary. Shaw, living alone, had let the housekeeping slide, but the only things lying around were clothes and random belongings.

One of the bedrooms had obviously been LaRayne's. It was decorated in a more feminine style and had a poster of an R&B group on the wall. That room, in contrast to the rest of the apartment, was scrupulously tidy. A picture of LaRayne sat on her dresser, surrounded by bits of jewelry, a couple of stuffed animals, and some dried flowers. It was just like one of the little roadside shrines put up by friends and family when someone got run over by a car. The sight brought unexpected tears to Erin's eyes. LaRayne was a round-faced, cheerful-looking young woman with a mane of black, curly hair and a brilliant smile.

What Erin didn't find was a sock full of ball bearings, or a deck of cards missing a jack, or anything else to tie Shaw to Lobert's murder. He'd had motive, means, and opportunity, but that didn't equate to evidence.

When she returned to the living room, she found Webb talking to Shaw about the trial.

"Nah, I don't blame the judge," Shaw was saying. "He was okay. He was this white-haired dude, old as God, but tough. He stepped on that punk's lawyer a couple times. I don't think he was happy about how it came out neither."

"Would this judge be named Ferris, by any chance?" Webb asked.

"Yeah, that's the guy," Shaw said. "You know him?"

"We do," Webb said. "You must've felt so helpless, sitting there watching your sister's killer go free."

"Yeah," Shaw said again. "But I told him he was gonna get his."

"What'd you say?"

"I looked him in the eye and said, 'Punk, you're gonna know what it feels like,'" Shaw said with angry satisfaction. "'You're gonna end up just like her someday.'"

"And you made sure of that," Webb said. "It felt good, didn't it?"

"Telling him off? Hell yes, it did," Shaw said.

"That first swing," Webb said, smiling. "That was a good one."

"Huh?" Shaw's grim smile dissolved into puzzlement. "What swing?"

Vic mimed swinging a blackjack. "Bam," he said. "Right into the back of the skull. I bet you could feel the crunch."

"What the hell are you talking about?" Shaw demanded. "I didn't take no swing at him. Hell, you got cameras in that courtroom, you can check!"

"We're not talking about the courtroom," Webb said. "We're talking about the Needle X-Change."

"I just told you about that place. It ain't got shit to do with nothing!"

"Mr. Shaw," Webb said. "I'm placing you under arrest for the murder of Kamal Lobert. You've been through this before, so you know how it goes, but I'll remind you."

Vic and Erin were ready if it turned into a fight, but Shaw was too surprised to offer any resistance. Webb read him his rights while Vic cuffed him. In deference to his cooperation, Erin fetched him a pair of jeans and his shoes, so he'd be decent when they hauled him down to the station. Then they locked the apartment and marched Shaw out to Vic's car.

Chapter 3

"And that's what happened," Erin said. "I was expecting more fireworks, but he came quietly. I think he was confused."

"You sound disappointed, darling," Morton Carlyle said.

They were sharing the couch in Carlyle's living room, sipping Glen Docherty-Kinlochewe whiskey. The clock on the wall claimed it was a little after three in the morning, but they paid no attention to it. Cops and pub owners were used to late nights. So was Rolf, but the Shepherd also recognized good napping time when he saw it. He was under the coffee table, eyes closed, chin resting on Erin's foot.

"I feel bad about the whole thing," she said. "Shaw's a criminal, sure, but the guy killed his sister!"

"Did he?" Carlyle asked quietly. "The jury decided otherwise, from what you're telling me."

"The jury decided there was reasonable doubt," she said. "That doesn't make the guy innocent."

"Under the law, that's precisely what their decision does," he said. "Most of us live in the gray between black and white, as I fear I've taught you too well."

She smiled ruefully. "Maybe," she said. "Can I ask you something?"

"Anything, darling. I've no secrets from you."

"That guy you..." she hesitated. "That guy in the bar, when you first came to America."

Carlyle's gentle smile stayed on his face, but his eyes went hard and wary. "What about him?"

"You told me he was one of the men who killed your wife," she said.

"My Rosie, aye."

She made herself say the words. "You beat him to death with a barstool. Is... is that the only man you've ever killed?"

"So far as I know," he said. "Though when I served in the Brigades back in Belfast, I built bombs that killed men. That makes me an accomplice in those deaths. But that was war, you ken. It's a mite different. I've never killed another with my own hands."

"How did it feel?" she asked. "Getting your revenge?"

He stared into the whiskey glass and swirled the amber liquid. "Empty," he said at last. "Hollow. You never knew Rose, of course. She was a kind soul, a sweet lass from County Down, a country girl. She'd never had anything to do with the Troubles. That was one of the things that drew me to her, you ken. She was so pure, so innocent. She'd have been horrified at what I'd done and I knew it, even then. You can't avenge a good woman's death through an evil act. I may have escaped human justice, but I've a notion I'll answer to God for it someday."

She put out a hand and took his, squeezing it. "I'm sorry," she said. "I was just wondering. Lots of people do things to get even. So I guess it wasn't satisfying?"

"It was pointless," he said. "And it put me in Evan O'Malley's power, so it ruined the next twenty years of my life.

If not for you, it would have destroyed me. Haven't you heard the phrase, 'An eye for an eye makes the whole world blind?'"

"Yeah," she said. "Who said that?"

"Gandhi," Carlyle said. "Another lad who fought the British, though he managed it with fewer bombs than the IRA."

"We were supposed to give Shaw his revenge," she said. "Within the law. And we failed. I guess I'm feeling crummy because I don't blame him."

"It's certain he did it?" Carlyle asked.

"We're charging him tomorrow morning," she said. "But we need a lot more evidence if we're going to take him to trial. Otherwise we'll end up with two killers walking free."

"And that'd be ironic," he said with a thin smile. "A lad murders another lad who escaped punishment for murder, then escapes in his own turn. Some might call that its own form of justice."

"Not me," Erin said. "It's my job to make the best case I can, and that's what I'm going to do. I can't punish Kamal Lobert; he's dead. Hell, it's not my job to punish anyone. I just catch killers."

"Killers like me?" Carlyle asked with a slight twinkle in his eye.

She smacked him on the shoulder. "No! You signed your deal with the DA. You're square with the house. Quit screwing around. I'm being serious."

"I know, darling," he said. "And I'm certain you'll find your way to the truth. You most always do in the end. But perhaps you'll do it better with the benefit of a wee bit of sleep?"

"That's a good idea," she said. "I'll try to grab some before the sun comes up."

* * *

Three hours' sleep left Erin feeling like she'd been blackjacked herself. Her head ached a little worse than the rest of her, but her whole body regretted the past twenty-four hours. Coffee helped a little. So did her morning jog with Rolf. It was a beautiful late-spring day. The fresh air revived her and the motion loosened her up. By the time she'd showered, changed, and gotten herself to the Eightball, she felt just about human.

Zofia was waiting for her. "Saddle up," the blonde said. "We're going to the courthouse."

"To talk to the DA?" Erin guessed.

"Nope. Judge Ferris. Lieutenant Webb is meeting the DA as we speak. They're offsite at a coffee shop, enjoying a nice, leisurely breakfast meeting. Rank's privileges and all that. Webb wants to know what exactly happened between Shaw and Lobert at the end of the trial, so he tapped us."

"Where's Vic?"

"Down in the morgue, talking to Dr. Levine."

"Did either of you get any sleep last night?"

"Mina got fussy," Zofia said. "Vic sat up with her. She finally settled around six. Vic left me a note saying he'd gone on ahead to try to get some work done. I guess he figured an hour-long catnap wasn't worth taking."

"Your mom has Mina now?"

"Yeah." Zofia smiled. "It's good having Grandma nice and close. Too bad your folks are way upstate."

"I don't have a kid," Erin said.

Zofia was still smiling. "Yet," she said. "C'mon, you're getting married in a couple months, right? And you're Catholic. You're gonna be pumping out babies like shells from a twelve-gauge."

Erin made a face. "Thanks for that image."

Zofia mimed pumping a shotgun. "Cha-chink!" she said.

"I'll drive," Erin said. "On the condition you shut up about pregnancy right now."

"You're grumpy this morning. Sounds like somebody's hormones are acting up."

"Enough with the damn female shit. I'm tired, I'm caffeinated, and I'm armed."

"Copy that. Not another word."

*　　*　　*

"The delightful Miss O'Reilly," Judge Ferris said, beaming. "And her equally lovely companion. Miss Piekarski, isn't it?"

"That's right, your Honor," Zofia said. Words that would have been sexual harassment from another man somehow came across as compliments from Ferris. Maybe it was the fact that at eighty-three years of age, his interest in women was largely hypothetical. But mostly it was his natural charm and dignity. He was a fugitive from a more honorable century, a man whom Erin could imagine fighting a duel to defend a lady's honor.

"The two of you arrested the Central Park Strangler," Ferris said. "Exceptional work, truly exceptional. And instead of resting on your well-earned laurels, I find you gracing my chambers. It is far too early in the day, and you are on duty, or I would certainly offer you some of my personal stock of bootleg moonshine. As it is, would you accept a cup of fresh-ground Colombian blend and a shortbread biscuit or two?"

"That'd be great," Erin said.

Ferris's secretary, Julia Lockhart, brought the coffeepot and a tray of very good shortbread cookies. Ferris insisted on pouring the coffee for them.

"Now that we are more comfortable," he said, settling back in his leather swivel chair. "How may I be of assistance?"

"We had some questions about the Lobert trial," Erin said. "You remember it?"

"I remember it well," Ferris said. "I am old, but my cognitive faculties remain unimpaired. And it has only been a few days, you know. The charges were second-degree homicide, possession of an unlicensed firearm, and misdemeanor heroin possession. The dastardly fellow was acquitted on the major charges. He was found guilty of a lesser offense, but that was small consolation."

"So you think he was guilty?" Erin asked.

"Oh, most definitely," Ferris said. "However, I cannot let my personal opinions color my courtroom conduct. In fact, in those situations where I believe the accused to be guilty, I am particularly scrupulous in protecting their right to a fair trial. And that is what Mr. Lobert received. The state, alas, failed to make a convincing case. While they were able to prove the defendant was present at the time the fatal shots were fired, they could not provide concrete proof that he fired them, nor even that he was in possession of the relevant weapon. The pistol was never retrieved, you see, and while he did have gunpowder residue on him, his lawyer convincingly argued that he might have acquired it simply by standing next to the actual shooter. Witness testimony was not persuasive."

"I see," Erin said. "We talked with Micheal Shaw, the victim's brother, last night. Apparently he had a confrontation with the defendant after the verdict."

"Yes," Ferris said. "I remember it. I fear I was too far away to overhear what was spoken. While my wits remain sharp, my hearing has dulled somewhat of late."

"Did anyone hear it?" Erin asked.

"You would have to ask Mr. Lefkowitz," Ferris said.

"I'm sorry, who?"

"Vernon Lefkowitz. He is one of the court stenographers, a fine fellow. He recorded that particular trial for me, along with quite a few others. A very reliable young man. Even if the transcript does not include the altercation, as it very well might not, since it occurred after court was adjourned, he should recall the argument. You ought to find him somewhere in the building. Julia?"

The secretary appeared in the doorway as if by magic. "Your Honor?"

"Is Mr. Lefkowitz taking notes on a trial at the present moment?"

"I'll check. Just a moment."

After a couple of minutes, and another shortbread cookie for everyone but Rolf, Julia returned.

"He's in the building," she reported. "Probably in Courtroom One. That proceeding is set to start at ten o'clock."

"About half an hour from now," Ferris said, checking his old-style pocket-watch. "You ought to have time for a brief consultation. Good luck, young ladies."

"Who uses a pocket-watch?" Zofia said as they walked quickly down the wide staircase toward the courtrooms. "People don't even wear wristwatches anymore. That thing was on a gold chain, clipped to his vest!"

"The old guy's got style," Erin agreed.

"It's like he came out of a movie," Zofia said. "One by Scorsese, maybe, or Stone. Is he for real?"

"As real as they get," Erin said. "He's a judge clean through to his backbone. He'll never retire, either. The only way they'll get rid of him is by wheeling him out the door feet-first."

The courtroom was empty except for the stenographer and a newspaper reporter who was catching a quick snooze in the back row. The court recorder was setting up a laptop computer. He was a stout, middle-aged, balding man hiding behind wire-rimmed glasses. In addition to the computer, he had a stenographer's pad next to him.

"Mr. Lefkowitz?" Erin said.

"Yes?" He blinked at her. His eyes were very watery.

"Detective O'Reilly," she said, angling her hip to show her gold shield. "Major Crimes. This is Detective Piekarski."

"Oh dear," Lefkowitz said. "Am I in some sort of trouble?"

"Not at the moment," Erin said. "We need to ask you about a trial that happened a few days ago."

"I'm just a stenographer," he said. "I take down what is said. I'm really just a sort of automaton. They could probably dispense with my services altogether, but like baseball umpires, I persist as a human relic. The transcript should tell you whatever you need to know. I assure you, it's comprehensive and accurate."

"That's just the thing," Erin said. "I'm asking about something that happened right after the trial."

"Oh, well, I wouldn't know anything about that," he said.

"It was in the courtroom," she pressed. "This was at the end of the Lobert trial. He'd been acquitted of Firearms and Murder Two, but convicted of misdemeanor heroin possession. Another man, Micheal Shaw, accosted him while he was on his way out. You're trained to listen to conversations and remember them. What did they say to one another?"

"I wouldn't like to get anyone else into trouble, either," Lefkowitz said, looking away and fiddling with his pencil.

"Why would you say that?" Erin asked.

"You're a detective," he said. "In the Major Crimes unit. I assume you're here investigating some sort of major crime. I'm an employee of the court, but I'm not a law-enforcement officer. It isn't my place to speculate as to the actions of others."

"I'm not asking you to speculate. I'm asking you to tell me what you heard."

"Oh yes. Well. Let me think." He straightened his necktie and cleared his throat.

A few moments passed. Lefkowitz remained silent, staring into space, slack-jawed and unfocused. Erin and Zofia exchanged puzzled glances.

"Yes?" Erin prompted.

"You killed my sister, you son of a bitch!" Lefkowitz suddenly exclaimed in a very different tone of voice from his hesitant half-stammer.

Erin and Zofia jumped. Even Rolf twitched in surprise.

"You think you got away with it," the stenographer went on, and Erin realized he was doing a credible impression of Micheal Shaw. "But you'd have been safer in jail. Inside, it's nice and cozy. Out there, on the street, there's me. Keep an eye out, watch over your shoulder, because one of these days I'll be there, and you'll end up just like her!"

"Okay, thanks," Erin said. "I appreciate—"

"You're a real tough guy, hiding behind the cops," Lefkowitz interrupted, shifting to a different voice. "You want to throw down on the street, bitch, you know where to find me."

"He's good," Zofia murmured. "He could do stand-up."

"That's right," Lefkowitz said, changing back to Shaw's voice. "I do."

The stenographer sagged in his chair and his eyes came back in focus, more or less. "That's what they said to one another," he said in his normal voice. "The bailiff separated them and ejected the agitator from the courtroom."

"Did they have any other contact?" Erin asked.

"Not that I'm aware of. Is that all, ma'am? I have to prepare. I have backups and notes and documents to set up. I can't lose any testimony."

"Of course," Erin said. "Thanks for your time, sir. Have a good day."

Chapter 4

"He's our guy," Webb said. "I don't see any way around it."

Erin, Zofia, and Rolf had returned to the Eightball, where they found Vic and Webb in the Major Crimes office. They'd given their report and added the courthouse testimony to the whiteboard. The board was far from full, but the information on it looked pretty conclusive.

"We still don't have proof," Erin said, but it sounded weak even as she said it.

"The motive is rock solid," Webb said. "Payback is a time-honored tradition. Shaw has a history of violence and a connection to a rough street gang. He openly threatened to kill our victim. He knows the area; for crying out loud, he got one of his tattoos at the crime scene! This fits like a glove, and I'm not talking about the OJ Simpson glove."

"This is how you can tell a former LAPD cop," Vic said. "More than twenty years, and he won't let that one rest."

"Interesting metaphor, sir," Erin said. "Because that was a trial that ended in an acquittal, too. Even though a lot of people figure he did it."

"It doesn't matter whether or not we think Lobert killed Shaw's sister," Webb said. "What matters is that Shaw believes it. There's the motive. The means were well within his reach and as far as opportunity, the murder happened less than six blocks from his apartment, in a neighborhood he knows well. His alibi, if you want to call it that, is he was in bed and asleep."

"The murder happened in the middle of the night," Erin pointed out. "That's not an unreasonable alibi."

"It's unverifiable," Webb said. "He was sleeping alone."

"Poor lonely bastard," Vic said. "You know, I'm so good at sleeping, I can do it with my eyes closed."

"And there he goes again," Zofia muttered. Nobody else reacted.

"We don't have the murder weapon," Erin said. "We don't have a confession. And we don't have any physical evidence tying him to the scene."

"You're a real spoilsport this morning, you know that?" Vic said. "This is an easy closure, the easiest one we've had in months, and you want to piss all over it. What's the matter? Are you feeling okay?"

"What did the autopsy show?" Erin asked Vic.

He shrugged. "The son of a bitch got his brains, such as they were, beaten in. Levine found fibers in the wound, black-dyed cotton and polyester. She concluded the weapon was a cheap black sock full of ball bearings. Which we already figured."

"I've asked CSU to canvass Shaw's apartment," Webb said. "They're going to analyze any socks they find. If we get one with blood or hair on it, or even an identical fiber match, that's the ball game. I've also asked them to note any single socks."

"Good call," Vic said. "If he ditched the sock, maybe he kept the other half of the pair."

"Lots of people have single socks," Erin said.

"O'Reilly?" Webb said. "I can't believe I'm saying this, but I agree with Neshenko. What's eating you? Are you just playing Devil's advocate?"

"The way Shaw talked," Erin said. "He was pissed at Lobert, but he didn't seem to know the guy was dead. I thought he seemed surprised. And it wasn't what I'd have expected someone to say if he'd just killed a man. He should've been cagier."

"We'll drill down on him in interrogation," Webb said. "With a good lawyer, he might be able to bargain it down to Murder Two, or even Manslaughter. That might be good enough for him to cop a plea."

"Assuming he's guilty."

"If it's not him, who the hell killed the guy?" Vic demanded.

"A rival gang member, maybe?" Erin suggested. "Or a mugger who got spooked when he realized he'd killed the guy, so he ran off without going through his pockets. Or how about some random guy Lobert picked a fight with? He wasn't exactly a quiet, peace-loving citizen."

"I agree that we don't have enough to take to trial yet," Webb said. "But we have plenty to charge him. That buys us time to build the case. The DA is behind us a hundred percent. The City's really cracking down on gang violence. There'll be proof if we look hard enough."

"Meaning we'll find it whether it's there or not?"

Erin's words hung in the sudden silence. Webb gave her a long, slow look. Vic coughed into his fist. Zofia looked very uncomfortable.

"You've been working in this office a couple of years now," Webb said. "In that time, has any detective here said or done anything that would justify what you just suggested?"

"No, sir," Erin said quietly. "Sorry. I shouldn't have said that."

"What I *meant*," Webb said, "is that when someone is guilty, they always leave something. There's trace evidence, an eyewitness, some bit of rope we can use to tie them to the crime. Am I making myself sufficiently clear?"

"Crystal, sir," she said. "I just think we should be open to other possibilities."

"Noted," Webb said. "But in the meantime, we have some paperwork to process."

"I have an idea, sir," Vic said.

Webb visibly braced himself. "By all means, share it with us," he said through clenched teeth.

"How about we rewrite the laws so when a perp commits a crime, part of the punishment is that he has to fill out his own arrest reports?"

"You really think that would work?"

"No. I just think they'd deserve it."

"We're in the police business, not the justice business. If you wanted to punish the bad guys, you should've become a prosecutor."

Vic's face wrinkled. "A *lawyer*? I hate friggin' lawyers!"

"But we need them," Webb said. "Without good prosecutors, bad guys walk."

"They do that anyway," Vic grumbled. "That's what got us in this mess in the first place."

"Stop blaming the victim," Webb said. "And the victim's lawyer. Kamal Lobert didn't ask to get his head bashed in. And please try to remember, half the lawyers are on our side."

"Oh, that doesn't bother me," Vic said more cheerfully. "I've got no problem hating people on my own side. I spend more time with them, so it's actually easier."

* * *

The arrest report and the ubiquitous DD-5 forms took time to fill out. Then there was evidence to examine, Levine's autopsy report to peruse, and all the other bureaucratic confetti that surrounded every homicide in the big city. Erin sailed through it on autopilot, checking boxes and scrawling signatures. She was thinking about Micheal Shaw. He was an angry young man, definitely capable of murdering the man he believed had killed his sister. But she kept coming back to the surprise in his eyes when they'd accused him of murder.

She'd looked in the faces of plenty of murderers who'd been surprised when the cuffs came out. Arrogant killers who thought they were smarter than they were; what surprised them was that they'd been caught. Shaw had been different. Erin would have bet twenty bucks he hadn't known until that moment that Lobert was dead. And if that was the case, either he'd only intended to give the man a thrashing and leave him alive, or they had the wrong man downstairs in Holding.

But she didn't have a better theory. The possibilities she'd thrown at the other detectives had just been brainstorming. She didn't really believe any of them. Muggers didn't leave hundreds of dollars in their victims' pockets. A blackjack wasn't a typical gang weapon. Gangsters killed one another with knives and guns, or the occasional baseball bat or length of pipe. A sock with ball bearings was very unusual. Her dad had told her to look for "odd socks" at crime scenes, by which he meant things that didn't belong. But he hadn't been talking about actual socks.

"Black socks," she murmured. Who wore black socks? Businessmen, waiters, anybody who wore black shoes. Gangsters didn't. They went in for sneakers, mostly. Guys wore white crew socks with sneakers.

Of course, the killer might have chosen a black sock purely to blend into the darkness. It was a lot harder to see a black weapon coming at your head at night. Maybe it didn't mean a damn thing. She sagged down in her chair, resting her cheek on her left hand and scrolling lackadaisically through the CSU report on the crime scene. The cigarette butt they'd retrieved from the alley was a match for the other cigs found on Lobert's body and they'd matched a partial print to the dead man. That meant the DNA on the cigarette would be a dead end. Besides that, they had almost no evidence. The sidewalk concrete didn't take footprints, the tattoo parlor didn't have a security camera out front, and in spite of Patrol units scouring the block, not a single eyewitness had come forward. Grinder, the tattoo artist, might be lying about not seeing or hearing anything, but they couldn't prove he was.

It really wasn't hard to commit an unsolvable murder. All you had to have was good luck and good timing. If you got rid of the weapon right afterward and ditched all the clothes you'd been wearing, and if you didn't get blood on yourself, even the best forensic technician would have a hell of a time proving you'd been there at all. They needed a solid motive to pin down a suspect, which was why Shaw was their one and only. But Erin still wasn't sure Shaw was their guy.

Her phone buzzed, jolting her out of her paperwork-induced stupor. As she fumbled in her pocket, she realized she'd drooled a little on her hand. She really was getting more like Rolf all the time.

The name SHELLEY showed on the screen. Erin blinked at it. Her sister-in-law didn't usually call her at work. Her heart skipped a beat. Had something happened to her brother or her niece and nephew?

"Hello?" she said.

"Hi, Erin," Michelle O'Reilly said. The breezy good humor in her voice immediately dispelled Erin's half-formed fears. "I was just wondering if you wanted to grab a quick bite before we hit the boutique."

"Oh, shit," Erin blurted. The late night and lack of sleep had blurred her schedule in her brain. She'd completely forgotten her plan to meet with Michelle over her lunch break to go wedding-dress shopping. It was the sort of errand she preferred not to think about and had therefore forgotten.

"What?" Michelle asked. "Is something wrong?"

"Forget about it. No problem." Erin looked at the clock and saw it was quarter to twelve. "Where are you now?"

"I'm heading south. We've got that appointment at Grace Loves Lace, but if they don't work out I figured we'd have time to swing by Vivienne Atelier Bridal, or Lovely Bride New York if you'd rather. I can go straight to the shop, or we can eat first, whichever works better. I'm wide open."

"I'll meet you at the dress shop," Erin said, wincing at the cutesy names of the stores. "The first one, I mean. I'm on my way."

*   *   *

It wasn't that Erin didn't want to get married; she really, really wanted to. Just looking at the emerald Claddagh ring on her finger gave her a warm, tingly feeling a tough street cop shouldn't have. What she hated was the planning. The details were endless: venue, clothing, flowers, catering, gift registry, marriage license, clergyman, wedding party, honeymoon, and more and more. The actual date was still four months away, but time was slipping away from them. Thank God for Shelley.

A bride needed a reliable matron of honor the way a military officer needed a good sergeant. Michelle had thrown herself into the planning with delight, acting as a buffer between Erin and her mom while providing endless ideas about the color palette, the decorations, Erin's hairstyle, and a bunch of other things Erin knew were important but had trouble caring much about.

The only real problem with having Shelley as matron of honor was that James Corcoran would be Carlyle's best man, and Corky had once very nearly seduced Shelley. That lapse of judgment had killed several people, wounded several others including Erin herself, and almost destroyed Shelley and Sean Junior's marriage. Sean and Corky had thus far managed to avoid one another, but they were bound to run into each other at the rehearsal and the wedding itself. And Erin shuddered to think how Junior would react to Corky and Michelle walking down the aisle arm in arm.

A couple of Irish guys with a grudge over a woman, in an emotionally-charged atmosphere, with access to an open bar, Erin thought sourly. It wasn't so much a question of what could go wrong as it was a question of whether anything could possibly go *right*.

She'd talked to both men about it, and both had promised to be on their best behavior. But Corky's best behavior didn't necessarily count for much, despite his recent efforts to reform.

That was the difference between Erin and Michelle. It boiled down to a question of priorities. Shelley was planning all the nuts and bolts of the wedding, worrying about getting all the ducks in a row. She was thinking of beauty and love and happily-ever-after. Erin was more concerned with making sure the members of the wedding party didn't murder one another at the reception.

The woman at the bridal shop was delighted to meet Rolf. She cooed over him and kept calling him a "big, beautiful boy," until the Shepherd gave Erin a look that was almost embarrassed. Michelle's arrival saved what was left of his dignity. He was content to retreat to a corner of the fitting area and observe the odd human obsession with clothing from a safe distance.

Michelle came armed with pages and pages of designs. Erin had never been overly concerned with dresses and found herself a little lost in the discussion of waistlines and fabrics.

"I think with your body type, Empire or natural waist is the way to go," Michelle said. "You've got fantastic legs, but we want something that'll accentuate your bust."

Erin was five-foot-six and in very good physical condition, but she felt slightly intimidated to be talking with Shelley about flattering waistlines. Michelle was five-ten and possessed the kind of statuesque beauty found in runway models. Even after two kids, her belly was flat and nothing sagged. Her bone structure was legendary. Erin sometimes wondered how her brother, who she'd never found all that handsome, had managed to land a woman like Shelley.

"You know it doesn't matter what you put on me," she said. "If you're standing next to me, everyone's going to be looking at you."

"Not on your day," Michelle said. "Believe me, no one in that church will be able to take their eyes off you. We're going to make you gorgeous. Well, even more gorgeous."

"Absolutely," the sales girl agreed. "You've got amazing shoulders. I think spaghetti straps are the way to go. Let's try this one over here..."

"I feel like a Barbie doll," Erin muttered. Her usual mode of shopping was to look for something comfortable in her size in a color she liked. She'd worn two fancy dresses in as many years. But in spite of her grumbling, there was a sneaky little part of her that liked being prettied up. She hoped Vic never found out about it.

"I've been thinking about the wedding party," Michelle said as the clerk moved around Erin with tape measure in hand.

"What about it?" Erin asked.

"We're going with green for the dresses and vests. Your otherwise sensible fiancé wanted shamrock, for obvious reasons, but that's way too bright and garish. I'm thinking more of an emerald shade. Blue would go better with your eyes, but I understand how the Irish can be. Anyway, you won't be wearing it. Have you given any thought to your jewelry? You'll want a necklace and matching earrings. Emeralds, of course. If you don't have the perfect thing, you can always rent it. But that's not what we need to talk about."

"Thank God," Erin said.

"The best man is... well, we all know who he is," Michelle said, and Erin was startled to see the woman blushing slightly. "And then there's Ian Thompson and Sean. We'd better put Ian between the other two."

"I'm still surprised Carlyle wants Junior on his side of the aisle," Erin said.

"Sean did save his life," Michelle said. "But it's a little awkward. I hope Ian can keep his head and stop them fighting."

"If there's one man in the Five Boroughs who can keep his head in a combat situation, it's Ian," Erin said. "It'll be a little weird, you're right. But they'll be good. Corky really has changed. He won't say or do anything out of line, not on his best friend's wedding day."

"I suppose," Michelle said. "But there's the question of your side. Besides me, there's Zofia. That's it."

"Is that a problem?" Erin could hear the defensiveness in her own voice.

"It's an imbalance," Michelle said. "There would have been three on each side, but..."

"We'll leave a space," Erin said firmly. "We're not replacing Kira Jones with somebody else. This isn't up for debate."

"If you're sure," Michelle said doubtfully. "It'll look a little strange in the pictures."

"It'll look like we left a place for my friend," Erin retorted. "My friend who won't be there because she got murdered."

Michelle flinched. "I'm sorry," she said.

"Forget about it." Erin immediately felt bad. "But this is important."

"It's your call," Michelle said, a little too briskly. "Now, Anna's very excited about being a flower girl, but Patrick's a little scared of being ringbearer. It's a long walk down the aisle and he's pretty self-conscious. I think if he could have someone walk with him, he'd feel a lot better. But Sean and I will be up front."

"How about Rolf?" Erin suggested. "Patrick can put a hand on his back and they can go together."

Michelle clapped her hands delightedly. "That's perfect!" she exclaimed. "It'll be absolutely adorable! And we can get one of those doggie tuxedo costumes for him..."

Erin glanced at Rolf. It was hard to know how much the dog understood, but she could've sworn she saw an expression of long-suffering patience on his face. She didn't think he'd enjoy wearing the canine equivalent of black tie, but that was a discussion for another day. With someone like Michelle, you had to pick your battles.

*   *   *

After all the comparing and measuring and fitting, they stopped at a nearby deli for sandwiches. Erin got a Reuben and a bag of potato chips, while Michelle ordered some weird vegetarian wrap full of bean sprouts and God only knew what else.

"I've never understood how you keep your figure, eating stuff like that," Michelle said.

"Lots of cardio," Erin said. "And a really high-stress lifestyle. Chasing perps and constantly dumping adrenaline into the blood keeps my metabolism high."

"After the kids start coming, you may have trouble," Michelle predicted. "You won't have time for exercise, and kicking the pregnancy weight takes some serious effort. I did a lot of yoga."

"Sheesh," Erin growled. "You're the second person to be talking about kids. Is someone dumping hormones in the water supply? Is there some sort of baby fever going around?"

"No!" Michelle exclaimed. "I just thought... I mean, I assumed..."

"We'll see," Erin said. "Carlyle wants them and I guess I do, too. But I've gotten pretty used to not being a mom. It's hard to see how I can do what I do while juggling a kid. Zofia and Vic do okay, I guess, but it's a struggle."

"Everything's a struggle," Michelle said. She was staring at the tabletop between them, suddenly very interested in the salt and pepper shakers. "Sorry if I'm being awful about the wedding."

"Shelley!" Erin exclaimed, genuinely shocked. "You're not being awful. You're terrific! I don't know what I'd do without you. I'd probably have to elope, and then Mom would kill me. I'm the one who should be sorry. I'm no fun at all when I do this sort of thing. I was always more of a tomboy."

"And I'm a girly-girl," Michelle said with a thin smile. She still didn't look up. "Sean and I have been seeing someone."

"What do you mean?"

"A couples counselor. She says..." Michelle trailed off and fiddled with the tail end of her wrap. "She says I had an emotional affair. Even though we didn't, you know, *do* the actual…"

"There aren't many women Corky's brought back to his place that can say that," Erin said, trying to lighten the mood. "You kept your virtue intact."

"No, I didn't," Michelle said in a low voice. "That's the point. It really hurt Sean, what I did. And we've been hiding it from the kids. He's been hiding it from me. He's been trying so hard to pretend it didn't happen, but it did, and it affects him. People *died*, Erin, and it's my fault!"

"No!" Erin snapped. "Look at me!"

Michelle reluctantly raised her eyes.

"Mickey Connor wasn't your fault," Erin insisted. "Some of it was my fault, some of it was Carlyle's, most of it was his own. But there was also that jackass who planted the bomb in Mickey's car and set him off in the first place, and we never even found out who it was! There's plenty of blame to spread around. If you want to pin it on a woman who screwed around with the wrong guy, she's sitting across from you right now. I knew Carlyle was trouble and I fell for him anyway. At least you were smart enough to stomp on the brakes before Corky actually got you in bed with him!"

"That's true," Michelle said. "But I did betray my husband. That's what I'm trying to deal with. I wish Cork—Mr. Corcoran wasn't going to be at your wedding, but that's a selfish wish. Anyway, I don't blame him. If anything, it was flattering. He's a charming man, attractive as anything."

"He is that," Erin said, remembering her own almost-fling with Corky.

"And my vows were mine to keep, not his," Michelle continued. "I should have told Sean I wasn't happy, and given him a chance to make things right, instead of looking somewhere else. It wasn't fair of me to keep that from him.

We've been struggling, Erin. I'm trying so hard to be good to him, but I'm starting to think we're never going to be okay. He... I'm starting to wonder if he still... if he still... I'm really scared I'm going to lose him."

Erin took Michelle's hand between her own. "That's not going to happen, sis," she said. "I've known Junior a lot longer than you have. He's my big brother, remember? He still loves you. It's all over his face whenever he looks at you."

"That only makes it worse," Michelle said, blinking several times and sniffling. "It's worse getting away with something than getting punished, sometimes. Because I'm punishing myself. That's why I'm trying so hard to make your wedding go perfectly. I want to do something right, and I want you two to be happy."

"Oh, Shelley," Erin said, giving her hand a squeeze. "It's going to be okay. You'll see. And don't feel bad because Junior's not punishing you. He's too nice a guy to do that. I think what it comes down to is, nobody really gets away with anything. All our checks get cashed sooner or later."

"Is that Erin the Catholic or Erin the cop talking?" Michelle asked with a small but genuine smile.

"Both," Erin said. "Junior doesn't really want you to be sorry anyway."

"He doesn't?"

"He wants you to be better. If you keep beating yourself up every time you're around him, you'll keep bringing Corky into your life. And believe me, you don't want that man sneaking into your bedroom."

Michelle gave a startled laugh. "Thanks," she said.

"You know, I woke up in his apartment once with a new tattoo and no memory of how I got there."

"God," Michelle said.

"So cut everyone a little bit of slack. Can you do that?"

"I can try."

"Now I'd better get back to the Eightball," Erin said. "I have to sort out a guy who definitely didn't get away with his sins."

"What happened to him?"

"You don't want to know."

"Come on, Erin! Tell me."

"Someone cracked his head open with a blackjack."

"Why?"

Erin stood up. "Because we didn't do our job right the first time," she said. "If the Homicide boys had built the case right, and the prosecutor had pounded in the nails hard enough, that miserable son of a bitch would be warming a cell at Riker's right now instead of cooling on a slab in the Eightball's basement. That's street justice for you. And that's why you and Junior are lucky."

Chapter 5

"My client has no comment at this time."

The kid sitting next to Micheal Shaw couldn't have been more than a year or two out of law school. His briefcase was so new that Erin could smell the leather from across the interrogation-room table. His suit was fresh off the rack, his shoes shined to a mirror finish. He was working as a public defender to bulk up his skinny resume. He was the best Shaw could afford.

But for all that, Micah Goldman had a law degree and knew how to use it. He was calm, competent, and professional. He'd probably be working for one of New York's big legal firms inside two years, Erin thought. One year if he knew the right people.

Webb sighed and rubbed the bridge of his nose. "Mr. Goldman," he said. "Your client explicitly threatened Kamal Lobert within hearing of a court stenographer. He openly expressed his hatred of the victim to several NYPD detectives, including Detective O'Reilly and myself. He'll be arraigned within the next twenty-four hours. He's being charged with first-degree murder, which carries a minimum sentence of twenty to twenty-five years. With his criminal record, he's looking at life. He's only lucky the state isn't handing down death sentences anymore."

"That's bullshit!" Shaw exclaimed.

Goldman held up a hand. "Please, Mr. Shaw," he said. "It's my job to look after your interests and see that your rights are protected. Please let me do it. If you have anything to say, I'm going to ask you to discuss it with me before speaking to these detectives."

"I didn't kill that little rat bastard!" Shaw insisted.

Goldman winced slightly and Erin could see him working on his courtroom defense. *Ladies and gentlemen of the jury, when my client referred to the deceased as a "rat bastard," he was not admitting to a desire to harm him, but was merely making a colloquial observation as to the deceased's lackluster personal qualities.*

"The circumstances are extenuating," Webb said. "I'm sure the judge can be persuaded to take them into consideration. The DA will almost certainly be willing to drop the Murder One charge down to second-degree, or even manslaughter, in exchange for a plea deal. If all Mr. Shaw wanted to do was give Lobert a beating, not kill him, I'm nearly certain manslaughter will be the worst charge he faces. That's five years, and I'm betting he'd be out in three with good behavior. That's the best deal he's likely to get, but if this goes to trial, the deal is off the table."

"I'll need to consult with my client," Goldman said. "We'll need privacy for our discussion."

"Of course," Webb said.

After a pair of officers had escorted the lawyer and the prisoner away, Webb shifted in the uncomfortable metal chair and sighed again.

"You think he'll take the deal, sir?" Erin asked.

"It's the smart play," Webb said. "Guys like Shaw expect to spend a fair part of their lives behind bars. He's already served a long enough sentence that he knows he can do the time. If you had a choice of getting locked up for three years or twenty, which would you do?"

"That'd depend on whether I was innocent or not," she said.

"He's not innocent. He's a gang member and career criminal."

"He's a paroled criminal who's been fulfilling the conditions of his parole," she shot back.

"Beating a man's head in is a pretty significant violation," Webb retorted. "And he might take the deal even if he didn't do it."

"Why?"

"Because he knows he's a crummy defendant," he explained. "He's a tattooed thug with a violent record. He knows he won't get a fair shake at trial, even if he's got a hotshot youngster for a lawyer. Even if our case isn't as strong as it could be, he knows his chances are worse than even. And he might not mind taking credit for killing Lobert. It'll win him some serious street cred with his gang. That might be worth a few months behind bars."

"I'd never go to prison for something I didn't do," Erin insisted.

"You wouldn't *want* to," Webb replied.

"But *we* should care whether he really did it," she said. "What if he pleads guilty even if he's innocent?"

Webb spread his hands. "What do you want me to say, O'Reilly? That the world's perfectly fair and everybody gets what they deserve? That may be the ideal world, but it's not the one we live in. Yes, I'm all in favor of finding the killer. In my opinion, Micheal Shaw is probably that killer. Am I sure? Not completely. You've been a detective too long to expect a hundred percent certainty all the time. But the particular hell of it is, we may never know for sure. And you have to be able to live with that."

Erin nodded and said nothing.

Webb's face softened. "Do you sympathize with him?" he asked quietly. "Do you think the murder was justified?"

"I don't know," she said. "Hell, I don't even know for sure that Lobert killed LaRayne. What if he didn't? What if the jury got it right and let an innocent man go? And then what if Shaw killed him, thinking he was guilty? How messed up is that?"

"That's the problem with street justice," Webb agreed. "Our legal system sometimes gets it wrong, in spite of all the checks and balances, all the lawyers and procedures. But what's the alternative? If it's one angry man with a loaded sock, what are the chances he won't make a mistake, compared with the full legal apparatus of New York City? That's why people can't take the law into their own hands. I don't care how many Charles Bronson movies you've seen, there's a reason vigilantes are criminals. Besides, personal revenge isn't justice."

"I've spent a lot of time with people who think revenge is justice," she said.

"Where are most of those people now?"

"In jail."

"That point may be worth considering."

There was a knock at the interrogation-room door, followed by one of the uniformed officers, prisoner and lawyer in tow. Goldman had a pretty good poker face, but Erin thought he looked tense, even worried.

"Have you considered your options, Mr. Shaw?" Webb asked.

Shaw didn't even bother to sit down. "Yeah," he said. "I have. And here's what you can do with your deal. You can ram it right up your ass. I'm not gonna throw away three years of my life just to save trouble for your fucking court. I didn't kill that punk Lobert. I wasn't anywhere near him when he went down. And I ain't taking the fall for it. Do I wish I'd killed him? Hell yes. I hated that son of a bitch. But there's just one problem. I didn't do it! And I don't care how good you think your case is, it ain't good enough, because it's nothing but bullshit! So I'll take my chances, I'll see you in court, and fuck the both of you!"

Webb's expression didn't change. Neither did Erin's. They'd had worse things said to them by worse people.

"I'm sorry we couldn't come to an agreement," Webb said calmly. "I'll see you at your arraignment. Mr. Goldman."

"Detectives," Goldman said, shaking hands with Webb and Erin. "I'll look forward to meeting you in court and proving my client's innocence."

Erin wasn't paying any attention to the lawyer. She was watching Shaw. His face was angry and defiant. But was it honest? She'd met plenty of good liars. Carlyle was technically honest. He could tell you the truth, straight to your face, and make you believe something he hadn't even said. And she *trusted* Carlyle.

She wasn't sure what to believe.

* * *

"Maybe Webb is right," Erin said.

The glass of whiskey didn't disagree. Neither did the Irishman beside her. Carlyle just listened. Pub owners tended to be good listeners.

"I've been dealing with too much complicated crap," she said. "Not everything is a conspiracy. Sometimes murder is just a guy who gets really mad at another guy and decides to kill him."

"Quite so," Carlyle agreed.

The Barley Corner was humming with its usual dinnertime hubbub. The clientele was different than it had been when Erin had started coming here. Most of the old-time regulars had been locked up when Erin and her colleagues had cleaned out the

O'Malleys. Now the pub catered to ordinary New Yorkers and a fair number of tourists who'd read about the gangster bar and wanted to see it for themselves.

"But Shaw insists he's innocent," Erin said.

"Many a guilty lad maintains his innocence," Carlyle observed. "But I'm thinking that's not what's truly troubling you."

"You're right," she said. "I'm supposed to trust the system. If he's innocent, then he ought to win his trial and walk. But the other guy walked, and everybody seems to think he did it, the judge included. I wish I'd been investigating Lobert's case. Then I'd have a better idea whether he was guilty or not, and maybe I'd be feeling better about the courts."

"That reminds me," Carlyle said. "Have you been keeping up with the news?"

"I've been trying not to," she said. "Ever since that serial killer was feeding off the media, I've kind of lost my taste for it."

"You're a wise woman, as I've long known," he said. "But surely you remember a Boston lad by the name of Wendell Jeremy Stone, the Third?"

"The name's familiar," she said without much interest. The shepherd's pie on the bar in front of her was much more appealing than whatever sordid story Carlyle had come across. She shoveled a bite into her mouth.

"It ought to be," Carlyle said. "Seeing as how you threw him in jail some months ago."

Her head snapped up. She swallowed the mouthful of food, managing not to choke on it. "That's right," she said. "He tried to rape that girl in the hotel and killed her instead. What about him?"

"His lawyers appealed his verdict," Carlyle said. "They argued he'd been improperly detained across state lines by New York police officers outside their jurisdiction."

"I remember," she said grimly. "I was one of those officers."

"So I recall. You hitched a ride back to New York aboard a truck driven by one of Corky's associates. How is our friend Wayne McClernand these days?"

"Awaiting trial," she said. "Just like a bunch of Corky's buddies. Why was Stone in the news?"

"The judge overturned the verdict," Carlyle said.

"He what?!"

Erin's shout caused heads to turn all over the room. She was off her barstool and on her feet without consciously standing up. Rolf was on his paws in an instant, alert and ready for action.

"He said the hot-pursuit doctrine didn't apply in that particular case," Carlyle said. "Since you weren't technically pursuing Mr. Stone until you were already aboard the train. It's a wee bit complicated."

"No, it isn't," she growled more quietly. She didn't sit down, leaning forward and gripping the edge of the bar. "Vic and I went after him because that son of a bitch murdered a girl! We caught him and we brought him back. It was totally legal. I've done some shit that was borderline, I'd be the first to admit it, but that arrest was clean. He confessed!"

"His lawyers argued he was improperly pressured into his confession," Carlyle said. "But the judge didn't rule on that, since he decided the arrest itself was invalid, which nullified everything that came after."

"Which judge?" she grated out.

"One I don't know," Carlyle said. "Hennessy, I think the name was. Fairly new to the bench."

Erin didn't know him either. "God *damn* it!" she burst out. The Barley Corner's bar was solid hardwood, but the blow of her fist still made her plate and glass jump. Silverware rattled. More heads turned her way.

Carlyle smiled at the onlookers and nodded politely to them. When no further entertainment was immediately forthcoming, the other diners turned back to their meals and the soccer game on the big-screen TV.

"We had him," Erin said. "He was guilty! Everybody knows it! He said so himself! Now what? He walks?"

"He already did," Carlyle said. "From what I hear, he left the courtroom about an hour ago."

"And now he's on his way back to Boston," she said bitterly. "To spend what's left of his money after buying his way out of prison and paying his goddamn attorneys. I think I understand how Micheal Shaw feels. And it wasn't even my sister Stone killed. I can't do a damn thing about it, either."

"My sympathies, darling," he said. "I wouldn't have brought it up, but you've a right to know."

"I'm not mad at you," she said. "Thanks for the heads-up. I would've heard sooner or later. I'd rather get bad news from you than anyone else."

"To get all the difficult topics out of the way," he said, "how was your shopping expedition? I hope it wasn't too excruciating."

"It was fine," she said. "I've been told I'm going to be the most beautiful bride in New York."

"I knew that already," he said with a twinkle in his eye. "I'm counting the days myself."

"What for, you old smoothie?" she asked, feeling some of the anger loosen in her. "I'm already living with you. It's not like you're going to be getting anything on your wedding night you haven't already had."

His smile, and the look in his eyes, warmed her right through and melted the rest of her anger away. "Darling, I'll only stop wanting you when my heart stops beating. I love you, and the closer we grow, the truer it is. Don't you know that?"

"I guess I do," she said. "But it's nice to hear you say it. You do know how to make me feel beautiful, you silver-tongued swindler, you."

"I'd be happy to use more than my tongue," he replied, still smiling. "Once we're finished with supper, of course."

"We can take the rest of it upstairs," she said. The frustrations of the day were falling away and she could use a distraction. To her own surprise, she realized she was looking forward to the wedding, too. He was right. Having him for a boyfriend was lovely. Having him for a husband would be even better.

* * *

They were in the bedroom for about an hour, then the shower. Erin would have liked to share the shower, but Carlyle's bathroom had a combination bathtub-shower that didn't safely fit two, so they had to take turns. Ever the gentleman, he let her go first. She was sitting on the edge of the bed, a towel wrapped around her, when her phone rang. The noise was almost drowned out by the sound of Carlyle's shower, but Erin saw Webb's name on the screen and groaned.

"Oh no," she said to the little black box, not touching it. "Not now. I'm off duty. This can wait for tomorrow. You kept me up all last night."

The phone continued ringing. She picked it up off the nightstand and considered throwing it against the wall. "O'Reilly," she said into it instead, trying not to sound irritated. At least he hadn't called while she'd been busy with Carlyle.

"You were right," Webb said. "Or if you're wrong, it's one hell of a coincidence."

"Sir? What do you mean? Shaw is innocent?"

"If he's not, something very strange is going on," he said. "Get to Grand Central Terminal as soon as you can."

"The train station?" Erin was utterly perplexed. "What happened?"

"We have another victim," Webb said. "You remember our old friend Wendell Stone?"

"Yeah," she said. "Carlyle just told me he beat the rap. The bastard got away with it!"

"Not for long," Webb said. "He made it as far as Grand Central, but that's as far as he's going. He ended up on the New Haven Line just as a train was coming in."

"Is he dead?"

"That's what usually happens when you're run over by a train," Webb replied dryly.

"How is this connected to Lobert's death?"

"Because Stone's head was bashed in *before* he hit the tracks. With a semi-rigid blunt instrument, just like Lobert's."

Erin shed the towel and went to the closet for a fresh set of clothes. "I'll be right there," she said.

Chapter 6

"What the hell are we dealing with here?" Vic wondered aloud. "A spree killer who only knocks off assholes? A civic-minded murderer?"

"We don't know for sure it's the same guy," Webb said. "Dr. Levine may be able to make a fiber match between Stone's wound and Lobert's, but otherwise there's no way to tell."

"At least he didn't miss his train to Boston," Vic said. "Or maybe I oughta say, his train didn't miss him. Anyway, now we know the killer's crazy."

"How do you figure?" Erin asked.

"He had a loco motive."

Nobody laughed.

"Get it?" Vic said. "Loco...motive? Locomotive?"

"We get it," Webb said.

"You're not laughing. Was it my delivery? I gotta work on that."

They stared down at the broken body on the tracks. One thing was certain; Wendell J. Stone III was most definitely dead. Erin had seen the aftermath of quite a few vehicular fatalities in the course of her NYPD career. This was one of the messier ones.

Levine was down on the tracks with the body. Erin was just as glad to stay up on the platform.

"Dr. Levine?" she called.

"I'm busy," Levine said.

"How can you tell he was hit on the head before he fell?"

"The cranium is otherwise largely intact," Levine said. "There is a single depressed-skull fracture on the right temple, consistent with being struck by a semi-rigid object. I hypothesize he was either rendered unconscious or stunned, probably as a result of receiving a blow from behind by a right-handed assailant. He then fell forward from the platform, landing directly in the path of the locomotive with his body perpendicular to the direction of the train's motion. The locomotive's wheels struck him at mid-thigh and throat, traumatically amputating the head and both legs. Death was obviously instantaneous."

"I'll say," Vic said.

"Yuck," Zofia said.

"Do you really think it's appropriate to bring your daughter to this sort of thing?" Webb asked.

Zofia gave her chest-rig a playful jiggle. Mina gurgled happily and grabbed one of her mom's fingers.

"It's fine," the blonde said. "She's too young to know what's going on. She just knows she's with Mommy and Daddy. Isn't that right, little *kochanie?* Who's Mommy's best little girl?"

Webb shook his head and turned his attention back to the late Wendell Stone. "With all the stuff kids see on their phones and TV screens, maybe it doesn't matter. I suppose it's academic whether the blow to the head killed him. It's murder either way."

"This doesn't make sense," Erin said. "He wasn't all alone out here, was he?"

"The platform had other people on it," Webb said. "But Stone's lawyers weren't with him. They were clearing up some of the legal stuff back at the courthouse. He didn't want to wait. I think he wanted to get out of New York as fast as he could."

"Sounds like he was smart," Vic said. "He just wasn't fast enough."

"Dispatch took a dozen 911 calls from bystanders," Webb continued. "Transit cops were on scene in less than two minutes. They took statements from everybody they could, including the engineer who was driving the train."

"Let me guess," Vic said. "Nobody saw nothin'."

"No one was able to identify an assailant," Webb said. "In fact, nobody saw the attack. It was quick and efficient. One blow to the head, then a quick fade into the crowd. The witnesses missed everything before our victim fell off the platform. The people who saw him fall were watching him. They figured it was a suicide."

"The station has cameras," Erin said.

"It does," Webb agreed. "And we'll check them. But they don't have coverage of this particular spot. The best we can do is get a few hundred possibilities and try running facial recognition on them."

"This is gonna lead to one of us sitting in front of a security monitor for the next six hours," Vic predicted.

"Excellent assessment, Neshenko," Webb said. "Thank you for volunteering. Look for Sergeant Rendell. He'll get you access to the footage."

"Shit," Vic said, unsurprised and unenthusiastic.

"Oh, and one other thing," Webb said.

Vic paused. "Yeah?"

"Where were you this evening, before I called you in?"

"I was home with Zofia and Mina, enjoying some well-deserved downtime after working a double shift for the great city of New York. Now I'm back here, hoping I get paid overtime. Thanks for asking."

"And you?" Webb asked, turning to Erin.

"I was at the Barley Corner," she said. "With my fiancé, and I'm afraid I agree with Vic. I wish I was still there."

"Can anyone corroborate that? Besides your respective significant others?"

"Hold on," Erin said angrily. "You're not saying—"

Webb held up a hand. "Cool it, O'Reilly."

She had no intention of cooling it. "I didn't even know Stone had been let out!" she snapped. "Not until Carlyle told me. I didn't know he was at Grand Central, and I sure as shit didn't crack him on the head and shove him in front of a train! And if you don't believe me, you can ask anyone who was working at the Corner or eating there. I was having supper at the bar and then Carlyle and I went upstairs to our apartment. Two dozen people must've seen us. I don't have names, but you can ask Danny Sullivan at the bar or Caitlyn Tierney, the waitress."

"Good," Webb said. "I wanted to make sure you had an airtight alibi. It might not have looked good to our beloved Internal Affairs Division otherwise. Of course I don't think you bumped Stone off. But my opinion isn't the only one that matters here."

"Not that the bastard didn't deserve what he got," Vic said.

They all looked at him. Even Mina and Rolf.

"What?" he said. "Everybody's thinking it. And Zofia and I ran into our downstairs neighbor on our way over. Beulah Vandervoort. She's sixty-five, and besides having an obnoxious little yappy dog, she's a solid citizen. So there's my friggin' alibi. Sir."

"We need to pull Stone's old case file," Webb said. "Find out who wanted him dead, and whether there's a connection with Lobert."

"Of course there's a connection," Erin said. "Both guys got away with murder."

"I know that," Webb said. "And there's enough similarity in the MO of the killings that it seems likely they were done by the same perp."

"Shaw was in custody when Stone died," Erin pointed out.

"Speaking of airtight alibis," Vic said. "Maybe you and I should've gotten arrested, Erin. Then we'd be above suspicion."

"We need to start considering the possibility of an outside contractor," Webb said.

"A hitman?" Erin said.

"Exactly."

"I kinda like that theory," Vic said. "A guy who's privatized justice. Screwed by the courts? Just give him a call and he'll provide payback. Have blackjack, will travel."

"That reminds me," Webb said. He walked back to the edge of the platform. "Dr. Levine! Is the deceased holding anything in either of his hands?"

"No," Levine said.

"Oh." Webb was disappointed.

"Expecting another playing card?" Erin asked.

"I was," he said.

"Doc!" Erin called. "Does he have anything in his pockets?"

"I'm still doing my preliminary examination," Levine said. "The contents of his pockets will be catalogued by the Crime Scene Unit when the body is collected."

"Would you please check now?" Erin asked. "We're particularly concerned with whether there's a playing card on his person."

"I don't like to do things out of sequence," Levine said. "That's how steps get skipped. We have procedural checklists for a reason."

"I could come down there and look," Vic said.

"Not without my permission," Levine replied.

"Okay. May I have your permission?"

"No."

"Then would you look? Pretty please?"

Erin could feel the irritation radiating off Levine even from ten feet away, but the Medical Examiner quickly frisked the corpse's pockets. Stone had been wearing a very nice suit, the better to impress the judge. It wasn't so nice now. Levine reached into the left front pocket of the jacket and brought out a card between two gloved fingers. She held it up.

"Jack of clubs," Webb said.

"Another black jack," Vic said. "Cute. You think he'll move over to the red suits next, or start on the kings?"

"Maybe he'll crack open a new deck," Erin said.

"You're both acting like you're expecting more bodies," Webb said.

"Aren't you?" Erin replied.

*　　*　　*

Erin called Carlyle on her way back to the Eightball, letting him know it was looking like another late night. "Good thing we got our date in early," she added.

"I'm already treasuring the memory," he replied. "How bad is the situation?"

"Pretty bad," she said. "This is the second body in two days. There might be more we don't know about. If this is just one guy, he's being efficient. Assuming it's a guy. Last time it was a woman."

"Anything I can do?"

"You know a shady defense attorney."

"You're referring to Mr. Walsh, who represents Evan O'Malley and most of his lieutenants?"

"That's the guy. I wish we'd been able to throw him in jail along with his dirtbag clients."

"I believe that's what they do in totalitarian regimes, darling. Here, if the lawyer hasn't committed crimes, you're required to allow him his freedom. And I'm thinking you're going to ask me to ask him a favor, so we'd best keep this as civil as possible."

"Can you talk to him?"

"Cautiously. He's defense counsel for a number of lads against whom I'll be testifying as a key witness. For the sake of all concerned, it's best if we proceed with a certain amount of circumspection. What is it you're needing from him?"

"I think he'll be interested in this. He's gotten bad guys off. Someone's nailing the guys who walk, either on technicalities or acquittals. Some of Walsh's own clients might be in danger if this keeps up. I need to know about the back channels the lawyers use."

"Back channels?" Carlyle repeated.

"Their fixers. The people they go to when they need something done to tilt the trial. Frame jobs, locating problematic witnesses, that sort of thing. You can't tell me Walsh has never gotten a witness to disappear in order to get a client off."

"Erin, he's hardly going to tell me that," Carlyle said patiently. "I'm the enemy, you ken. If he's intending to commit any dirty tricks in the upcoming trials, he'll not be spilling them to the likes of us."

"I don't need his whole bag of tricks," she said. "I just need to know if there's somebody the lawyers go to if they want to take a particular person off the board. Someone who'll kill for cash, uses a blackjack, and likes to leave a calling card on the body."

"I'll see what I can discover," he said. "And I'll have Corky ask around as well. But don't be expecting miracles. Just to be clear, the lad you're seeking is targeting criminals. What makes you think Walsh would know him?"

"Because we're looking for a hitman," she said. "One with connections. I know it's a shot in the dark, but you don't have the underworld contact you used to."

"That's on account of most of them getting killed or incarcerated by your lads."

"Are you wanting an apology?"

"Merely making an observation."

"Just ask, please." She took a breath. "And warn him. Otherwise his clients are liable to get killed."

"As you wish, darling."

Back at Major Crimes, Erin, Webb, and Zofia got busy pulling case files and starting a file on the Stone killing. Vic had stayed at Grand Central to review the station's security footage. Mina and Rolf fell asleep, the girl in her portable playpen, Rolf just outside it, curled protectively around one corner of the pen.

"Stone killed a girl named Sarah Devers," Erin said. "He thought she was a hooker and when she resisted his advances, he drugged her and tried to rape her. But she OD'd and died. He did try to resuscitate her, which is the only good thing I can say about that sack of shit. He didn't deliberately murder her. When CPR didn't magically bring her back like it does on TV, instead of calling 911 he ditched her body. Devers ended up in a hotel fishtank."

"Vic told me that story," Zofia said. "It sounds horrible."

"This is Major Crimes," Webb said. "If it's not horrible, we don't hear about it. Devers wasn't a local girl. Where was she from, again?"

Erin paged through the file. "Athens, Georgia," she said. "Sarah had a mom down there. The mom got her into modeling at an early age. Thought the world of her. She was pretty devastated, as I recall."

"Of course she was," Webb said. He shook his head. "I hardly see my daughters these days, but if anything happened to them..."

"You should call them," Zofia said. "Get out to visit. Be part of their lives."

"That isn't so easy," he said. "Besides, I feel like they do better when I'm not around."

"Bullshit!" Zofia snapped.

Erin and Webb both stared at her.

"Respectfully, sir, it's my opinion that what you just said can be compared to what comes out of a cow's backside," Zofia said, turning red. "Sorry. I forgot who I was talking to for a moment."

"Your candor would be refreshing," Webb said. "If I didn't already get more than the normal amount from your boyfriend. Instead of apologizing, why don't you explain yourself?"

"My dad's gone," Zofia said. She spoke slowly at first, but sped up as she got rolling. "Heart attack, a little more than two years now. He wasn't a real sensitive guy. In fact, he was an emotional dumpster fire. He drank too much, he swore a lot, and he could be a real ass a lot of the time. But he was there when I was growing up. I'm over thirty now, and I didn't lose him before I got out on my own, but I still miss him like hell. If you think your girls don't miss their dad, you're not anywhere near as good at psychology as I thought you were. And it'd be better if they didn't have to miss you while you're still breathing. Sir."

Zofia finished. She glared at Webb, silently daring him to chew her out.

"Point taken, Detective," Webb said. "I suppose being a new parent yourself has given you some perspective on this. I'll take it under advisement. Now, if we could return to the current homicide, let's consider the inverse perspective. This isn't a girl who lost her parent; this is a parent who lost her daughter. Try putting yourself in Ms. Devers's shoes. If some evil bastard tried to rape your little girl, then murdered her and got away with it, would you be willing to hire someone to kill him?"

"No," Zofia said at once.

Webb raised his eyebrows. "Really?"

"Absolutely not, sir," she said. "I wouldn't pay anyone else. I'd do it with my own hands. I'd want to hear him scream. I'd want to drag the life out of him right through his goddamn throat. And I wouldn't do it from behind. I'd want him to see it coming and know why."

He nodded. "Yes, but while I think we can assume Ms. Devers isn't quite as fiercely combative as a Street Narcotics cop, I think we can agree she's probably emotionally capable of homicide."

"She's also in Georgia," Erin said.

"You assume," Webb said. "I think we'd better double-check what we know about her before we jump to any conclusions."

"I really don't like this," Erin said.

"What don't you like?" Webb asked.

"Investigating the families of victims as suspects."

"They're the ones who have motive."

"They're also the ones who've already suffered the most. Sarah Devers has been dead over a year now. Maybe her mom's finally starting to heal a little. I don't want to rip the scab off unless we have a damn good reason."

"She'll know about Stone getting let out," Webb said. "If she hasn't already heard, she has a right to know. Since you seem to be aware of the emotional ramifications of speaking with Ms. Devers, I think you ought to be the one to do it. A phone number for her should be in the file."

"Yes, sir," Erin sighed.

"It's only seven-thirty. She should still be awake."

"Yes, sir."

"We have to do difficult things in the line of duty, O'Reilly. It's the Job."

"Yes, sir."

"Piekarski?" Webb said, pivoting to the other woman.

"Sir?"

"You can atone for your insubordination by looking into Micheal Shaw and Ms. Devers's finances. You're specifically looking for any unusual cashflow out of their accounts."

"Money that might be used to pay for a hitman, sir?" Zofia asked.

"Precisely."

"I'm on it."

"I'll be working with Neshenko to see whether we can get an image of our killer," Webb said. "The resolution will be garbage, of course. But even if facial recognition doesn't pop, it may at least give us some idea who we're looking for."

"I can't believe he just walked up to a guy in a crowd and offed him," Zofia said. "And then got away clean."

"It's easier in a crowd," Erin said. "If the platform had been deserted, Stone wouldn't have let the guy sneak up on him. The only thing that keeps you safe in a crowd is your anonymity. If somebody's following you, they can get awfully close."

"Thanks for that," Zofia said sourly. "I'll enjoy the paranoia next time I'm walking down the street."

Chapter 7

"Ms. Devers? I'm Erin O'Reilly, with the New York Police Department. You may remember we spoke last year."

The voice on the other end of the line had a soft Southern drawl. "Yes, Ms. O'Reilly, I remember our conversation perfectly. You were the one who told me about the loss of my poor Sarah. It was a terrible blow."

"I'm sorry to call you again," Erin said. "I wish I didn't have to remind you."

"Every detail of that day is carved into my memory. I think of my dear little girl every day, morning and night."

"I'm sorry," Erin said again. "Did you come up to New York for the trial?"

"There was no trial," Ms. Devers said. "That awful man pled guilty. He had no choice, thanks to the good work of your department. You ran him to ground and cornered him like the vermin he is, may God forgive my vengeful heart."

Erin winced. "Have you been to New York in the past year?" she asked.

"Of course. I had to bring my poor Sarah back to Athens. I couldn't bear the thought of her all alone in the cold ground of a place so far from home. I visit her resting place every Sunday and ensure fresh flowers are always there. My Sarah did love flowers."

"Have you been here recently?"

"No. Ms. O'Reilly, why are you asking me these questions? Has something occurred?"

Stone's death had been too recent to make the evening news. And it might not have made the national news at all. If Ms. Devers hadn't been involved, she probably had no idea it had happened yet.

"Have you ever spoken with Wendell Stone?" Erin asked, avoiding the bereaved mother's questions.

"Not directly. I do not trust my imperfect soul to talk with that... *man*." Ms. Devers put a vicious twist on her final word. "I did visit your courthouse for his sentencing, to give a statement about what he did to my family. I wrote a short speech, for I was uncertain whether I would retain my composure and my faculties. I shed some tears, but thank God I was able to finish. I can forward you a copy of my little speech, if you are interested."

"I'd like to see that," Erin said. "If it isn't too much trouble. I can give you an e-mail or a fax number." She did both and Ms. Devers wrote them down.

"It was kind of you to call me," the other woman said. "It is so very easy to assume my daughter has been forgotten by everyone else. I know you are a busy woman, with many cares and trials. But you are a good woman as well."

"Thank you," Erin said. "Did you see Mr. Stone at the sentencing?"

"Yes. I could see he was a very wicked man, though he pretended to feel remorse. I tried to master the hate in my heart. I have prayed, oh I have prayed for God to take the hate from me, but it is so deeply buried in me. The Devil works through our imperfect nature. How is Mr. Stone, may I ask? Does he suffer in his confinement? Has he found true remorse and repentance? Has he heard the word of our Lord and Savior and forsaken his wicked ways?"

"I don't know about that," Erin said truthfully. "Mr. Stone is dead."

There were about ten seconds of complete silence.

"Then I fear his soul burns in eternal perdition," Ms. Devers finally said. "As a good Christian woman, I should not celebrate the damnation of another human soul, but I cannot deny a bitter satisfaction. Such is the fate of the ungodly. How did he perish?"

"Someone hit him on the head and pushed him in front of a train," Erin said, opting for brutal honesty. It could be the best way to shock an admission out of an interviewee.

"A suitably violent and terrible end," Ms. Devers said. Then she paused. "A train, you said?"

"On the Hudson Line," Erin confirmed. "At Grand Central Station, earlier this evening."

"I do not understand. Mr. Stone was incarcerated, was he not?"

"Yeah. He was."

"Then what was he doing at a train station?"

Erin gritted her teeth and took a deep breath. "His conviction was overturned by the court," she said.

"What? But why? He was guilty! He *said* he was guilty!"

"Yes, ma'am, he was. It was a technicality, a procedural thing. The judge said the NYPD hadn't followed proper protocol when we arrested him."

"But..." Ms. Devers began, but trailed off into silence.

"I'm sorry," Erin said for the third time in the conversation.

"Did you and your people follow the rules?" Ms. Devers asked.

"I beg your pardon?"

"It is a very simple question. Did you break your precious rules to catch the man who murdered my sweet little girl?"

"I don't think so," Erin said slowly. "The judge disagreed."

"Why?"

"I don't know. I haven't spoken with the judge."

"When you do, as I am certain you will, I would like you to do me a small favor."

"What is it?"

"Look him in the eye and ask whether he is a father. Ask him whether he has ever loved a child more than life itself and had that child snatched away from him. Then ask him what he will tell God, on that day when he is called before the throne of Heaven and is asked to account for his sins. Ask him why he set my girl's murderer free."

Erin had no intention of saying any of those things to a New York judge. "I'll do my best to get to the bottom of what happened," she promised. The best thing to do when asked to do something you couldn't was to pretend you'd been asked to do something else instead, and to agree to do that other thing.

"Did he suffer terribly?" Ms. Devers asked. "Mr. Stone, I mean, not the judge, though I confess I have some hopes in that direction as well."

"He got run over by a train," Erin said. "It was horrible, but it was over pretty quickly."

"That is a pity. But I take consolation knowing his torment is only beginning. Good day, Ms. O'Reilly."

Before Erin could say anything else, Ms. Devers hung up.

"Learn anything?" Zofia asked. She was at her computer, wading through bank records.

"Religion can only take you halfway," Erin said. "That woman has a lot of hate in her heart."

"Can you blame her?"

"Hell no. But she seemed like she didn't know Stone was dead. And here's what's bothering me."

Zofia swiveled her chair and leaned her elbows on her desk. "Do tell."

"Stone's hearing was this afternoon," Erin said. "Only the judge knew how it was going to come out. I don't think anybody knew Stone was planning on taking the train to Boston, even if they'd known he was going to walk out of that courtroom a free man."

"It does seem pretty spontaneous," Zofia agreed.

"The killer had to be in or near the courtroom," Erin said. "They would've had to follow him to the station, looking for their chance. This feels almost like a crime of passion."

"Except for the calling card," Zofia said. "And the blackjack."

"Yeah," Erin said. "The card makes it premeditated."

"What the hell is going on?" Zofia wondered. "Was he just a target of opportunity, or what?"

"Hitmen don't kill targets of opportunity," Erin said. "They go after specific people."

"Why Stone and Lobert, out of all the defendants in New York? There have to be dozens of bad guys who should be in jail but aren't."

"The world doesn't run on 'should,'" Erin said absently.

"Maybe our killer decided it ought to," Zofia replied.

"Say that again," Erin said more sharply.

"Maybe our killer decided the world ought to run on 'should,'" Zofia said.

Erin snapped her fingers. "You're absolutely right," she said. "This isn't about revenge. This is about justice."

"Same thing," Zofia said.

"Only on the street," Erin said. "I'm not surprised you didn't find anything linking Stone and Lobert, or Shaw and Devers. I don't think you will. That's not what's going on here."

"Then what is going on?"

"Street justice."

"That's what I thought."

The ancient fax machine in the corner of the office whirred to life. Erin stood up and walked over to see Ms. Devers's victim statement arriving from Georgia.

"What does it say?" Zofia asked.

"'My daughter was a beautiful girl,'" Erin read aloud. "'She was a kindhearted, sweet young woman who saw beauty everywhere in the world. She believed in the best in other people and was open, friendly, and innocent. She was my only child and I loved her with all my heart. When she was taken from me, my life was shattered. Not a day goes by without tears coming to my eyes at the memory of Sarah's smile and the light in her eyes. Mr. Stone snuffed out that light. He took my sweet child from me. I wish I could have given my life in her place. There is nothing I would not give to have her back with me. I wish for no revenge. Vengeance is mine, saith the Lord. But the court has asked me to give a statement of how this tragedy has impacted my life, and here is the truth. My life has been broken forever, and nothing can amend or repair it.'"

"Jesus," Zofia said. "That's sad."

"She said she didn't want revenge," Erin said.

"Do you believe her?"

"I believe that's what she wanted to say. I'm not sure it's what she believed."

"Is she a suspect?"

Erin shrugged. "I guess."

"She sounds pretty religious," Zofia said.

"Religious fanatics make some of the best killers," Erin said. "Haven't you ever heard of the Crusades? Or 9/11?"

"I guess. What's our next move?"

"I'm going to talk to the judge," Erin said. "I want to find out why Hennessy let Stone walk."

"I'll come too," Zofia said eagerly. "Anything to get away from this damn desk."

Rolf also volunteered by means of a raised forepaw and cocked head.

*   *   *

"Why Hennessy?" Zofia asked as Erin piloted the Charger through the Manhattan streets toward Hennessy's apartment. "He wasn't the judge presiding over the Lobert trial."

"Ferris doesn't have anything to do with this," Erin said. "He hates criminals, but he's as straight as they come. He'd never break the law hunting bad guys down. Besides, he's eighty-three and he has a pacemaker. If he tried to cold-cock a perp, he'd probably have a heart attack on the spot. But I don't know Hennessy. He's new to the bench. And it wouldn't be the first time I've heard of a judge letting a perp out so someone could whack him on the outside."

"You mean that guy who was working for the Mafia? Hennessy's his replacement."

"I know."

"Meet the new boss, same as the old boss?"

"Something like that," Erin said.

"You're not going to pick a fight with him, are you?" Zofia asked worriedly. "You can get in a lot of trouble mixing it up with judges, and we're already bothering him after hours."

"I arrested one judge," Erin said. "*One!* And I didn't do it alone."

"I know. Vic was there."

"So was Lieutenant McDowell," Erin said. "The Cast-Iron Bitch herself. Internal Affairs had my back. She isn't here this time. I'll behave."

"Good," Zofia said. "I like being a detective. I'd hate to get demoted to meter maid."

"Don't worry," Erin said. "It wouldn't be so bad. They don't make you wear those little skirts anymore."

Hennessy's apartment was in an eye-wateringly expensive Tribeca high-rise, all shiny steel and mirror glass. The doorman looked like a Third World dictator in his spotless uniform, gold braid, and snooty mustache. He gave the detectives a very disdainful look, and the gold shields they showed him didn't change his expression a bit.

"I'm quite sure we haven't had a criminal complaint at this address, ma'am," he said to Erin in a tone suggesting a criminal wouldn't dare break in for fear of bringing down the property values.

"Of course not, sir," she said. "We're here to meet with one of your residents. Judge Hennessy. It's official NYPD business."

"Indeed," he said doubtfully, but he grudgingly opened the door. Neither Erin nor Zofia tipped him. Rolf matched him stare for stare as the K-9 stalked inside.

Hennessy was on the 13th floor, which meant it was labeled as the 14th. Erin didn't find it weird. Cops had their superstitions, so architects were entitled to their own. Twelve flights were a lot of stairs, so they took the elevator. A young, freckle-faced man in a much less fancy uniform than the doorman's punched the button for Fourteen. Erin tipped him a dollar for doing it and wasn't sure why.

The detectives walked to Hennessy's door on hallway carpet thicker and richer than the stuff in Carlyle's bedroom. Zofia knelt and ran her fingers through it.

"If this guy is up to something, let me in on it," she said. "Looks like it's paying pretty well."

"Wasn't your old Street Narcotics squad famous for *not* taking payoffs?" Erin asked.

"Yeah," Zofia said regretfully. "And I never did. So now I'm living on one floor of a converted brownstone where we found a dead guy in the bathroom."

Erin rang the bell. The door was opened a moment later by a fortysomething woman clad in a truly stunning turquoise dress whose plunging neckline showed the upper portion of a fantastic body and an even more fantastic diamond necklace.

"Yes?" the woman said, giving Erin, Zofia, and Rolf a puzzled once-over. "I think you may be lost, dears."

"Ms. Hennessy?" Erin guessed.

"Wolfram, dear," the woman corrected her. "Rebecca Wolfram."

"I'm sorry," Erin said. "We're looking for Judge Hennessy."

"Oh, yes. Of course." The woman turned her head. "Alan, darling. A pair of young women and their... service animal are here to see you."

A man a little older than Rebecca stepped into the doorway. He was taller than average, his dark hair going silver at the temples. He had a strong jawline and intense brown eyes. He was knotting a bow tie at his throat by feel, never an easy task, and doing it skillfully. He wore a tuxedo, which Erin figured either meant he was about to go to some formal event, or he was supplementing his judicial income by moonlighting as a maître d' to afford his Tribeca rent.

"Good evening, ladies," he said. "I don't believe we've met."

"Erin O'Reilly, Major Crimes," Erin said, dropping a hand to the gold shield at her belt. "This is Zofia Piekarski."

Recognition lit up his face. "Ah, yes!" he said. "I thought you looked a little familiar. I've seen you on the news. I'm sorry, but

Rebecca and I were just on our way out. We have tickets to the Met."

"At Citi Field?" Zofia said.

Hennessy gave her a blank look.

"I think he's talking about the Metropolitan Opera," Erin said out of the side of her mouth. "Not the New York Mets."

Rebecca laughed. "Oh, that was a good one!" she exclaimed. "Can you imagine us traipsing around a baseball stadium dressed like this, Alan?"

Zofia went pink. "Oh," she muttered. "Yeah, that makes more sense."

"If you can spare a few minutes, your Honor, I'd be grateful," Erin said.

Hennessy glanced at his watch. "We have a little while," he said. "Rebecca, why don't you go on down to the car. I'll join you in a moment."

"Certainly, darling." Rebecca pursed a perfect pair of glossy lips and blew him a kiss. Then she swished out into the hallway past the detectives. Rolf gave her a cool, disdainful look the doorman might have envied.

"Come in," Hennessy said, holding the door. "I'd offer you a drink, but you seem to be on duty and we don't have time to fire up the coffee pot."

The apartment was furnished in a modern style that Erin found impressive but impersonal. Everything looked expensive. She was afraid to sit on anything, so she stayed standing.

"I really am on a schedule," Hennessy said. "So let's get down to brass tacks. I assume this is about the Stone decision."

"That's correct, your Honor," Erin said.

"I didn't just recognize you from the news," Hennessy said. "I know your name. You were one of Stone's arresting officers. Are you here to complain about my decision?"

"You let a self-professed murderer walk free," Erin said, meeting his bluntness with her own.

"Incorrect," Hennessy said. "By violating procedural and jurisdictional rules, *you* let him walk free. Had you followed proper extradition procedure, Stone's appeal would have been on much shakier ground."

Erin clenched her jaw, feeling her teeth grind. "I believe I followed the rules, sir," she said.

"I know," Hennessy said and smiled. He had a very pleasant smile, warm and engaging. It even looked genuine. It made Erin want to punch him in the face.

"Then I don't understand," she said.

"I'm not your enemy, Detective," he said. "If I truly believed you were deliberately ignoring NYPD policy and state and Federal laws, I would have referred the matter to your department's Internal Affairs division. I believe you made an unintentional and forgivable error in the heat of the moment. Nonetheless, Mr. Stone's lawyers made a legitimate argument and I was forced to rule in their client's favor."

"Less than two hours before he was murdered," Erin said.

"I am a judge, Detective O'Reilly," he said. "Not a psychic. Are you suggesting I should have unjustly kept a man behind bars for his own theoretical protection?"

"It's an interesting coincidence," she said.

"All coincidences are interesting," Hennessy replied. "That's what makes them coincidences."

"This is a nice place you have here," Zofia said.

"Thank you," the Judge replied.

"How much does the rent set you back?"

"That isn't a very polite question."

"Have you ever noticed something, Erin?" Zofia said. "The rich and the poor have something in common. Neither one likes to talk about money. And I think it's for the same reason."

"What reason is that?" Hennessy asked, an amused smile crossing his face.

"Shame."

"You're saying the poor are ashamed of being poor and the rich are ashamed of being rich?"

Zofia nodded. "Aren't they?"

"Maybe we are, at that," Hennessy said. "You're very forthright and outspoken, young lady."

"If you think I am, you ought to meet my boyfriend," Zofia said, with a look that silently added, *and if you weren't a judge and I weren't a cop you'd be picking your teeth out of the carpet for calling me "young lady," you condescending bastard.*

Hennessy tapped his chin with his forefinger. "If I'm following the thread of this conversation," he said, "it's being suggested that I have more money than I should, and that I discharged a prisoner under suspicious circumstances, adding up to a thinly-veiled accusation of bribery and corruption. Is that an accurate summation?"

"I'm surprised and disturbed to hear you suggest such a thing, your Honor," Erin said, keeping a straight face.

"This is especially telling given the fate of my predecessor," Hennessy said. "I'd be inclined to resent your insinuations, Detectives, if not for that unfortunate circumstance. The actions of the man who previously filled my position explain and excuse your suspicions. However, they are nonetheless completely unfounded. Now, if you will excuse me, while it may not be over until the fat lady sings, the opera starts at nine o'clock and I really do need to be there for the sake of my marital happiness."

"Just two more quick questions, your Honor," Erin said.

He raised his eyebrows politely and waited.

"Where did all this money come from? Judges don't get paid this much."

"Rebecca comes from a wealthy family," Hennessy said. "And I myself had a rather lucrative private legal practice prior to ascending the bench. Those billable hours really do add up. It's interesting, isn't it? Our society emphasizes the acquisition of wealth and lauds it as a virtue, but once you obtain it, you are considered some sort of scoundrel. Did you know that the original inalienable rights were life, liberty, and property? They changed it to the pursuit of happiness... not the attainment of it, but the pursuit. Your final question?"

"Can you think of anybody who was in that courtroom who'd want to kill Wendell Stone?"

"The man is—excuse me, was—a disgrace to humanity. I expect everyone in that room, with the very possible exceptions of his lawyers, would be glad of his death. However, I don't think any of them, lawyers included, are likely to have actually done the deed. Will that be all, Detectives?"

"Thank you for your cooperation," Erin said. She didn't mean it, but sometimes you had to tell polite lies.

Chapter 8

"I don't like him," Zofia said.

"You don't like him for the Stone murder, or you don't like him personally?" Erin asked. She pushed the button for the lobby and the elevator started down. They'd waited for Hennessy to take the first elevator and had called another to avoid a long and awkward ride to the lobby.

"Personally."

"Yeah, those polite, sophisticated civil servants sure are hard to put up with," Erin said with a poker face.

Zofia grimaced. "You know what I mean. The guy's a rich lawyer, for God's sake. Show me one of those that's a good guy, just one!"

"He's not in the private sector anymore," Erin said. "Maybe he decided to do some good for a change."

"I can't believe you're defending him! You're from Queens. You've got a thicker blue-collar accent than I do! How about a little goddamn class loyalty?"

"Zofia, he said so himself," Erin said patiently. "Being rich isn't a crime."

"But crime makes you rich," Zofia shot back.

"Okay, I'll bite," Erin said. "What do you think he's guilty of?"

"He was a defense attorney," Zofia said. "Remember Kingston Schultz? He was a defense attorney, too."

"I don't like lawyers very much either," Erin said. "But they're a part of the system. We need them. Are you mad because he let Stone off the hook? So am I! He basically accused me of being a sloppy cop and blamed me for his decision. But this isn't a popularity contest. We're trying to find out who murdered Stone."

"And you think it was someone in the courtroom," Zofia said. "Why not the judge?"

"You think Hennessy turned Stone loose, shrugged out of his robes, followed him to the train station, and bashed his head in?"

"It's a theory," Zofia said a little sulkily.

The elevator reached the ground floor and opened its doors. The detectives started across the lobby toward the exit. The lobby even *smelled* expensive, Erin thought. The scent of high-quality leather wafted off the furniture.

"A millionaire who sometimes wears long black clothes and moonlights as a vigilante?" Erin said. "Oh my God! You think he's Batman!"

"No, I don't," Zofia said. "Batman is cool. I wouldn't want to punch Batman."

"I guess it's possible," Erin said, nodding to the doorman as he opened the outside door for them. "That Hennessy might be our guy, I mean. Not the Batman thing. Maybe he feels guilty after getting all those crooks off for all those years. But I think we need to look at everybody who attended both hearings."

"How? It's not like they have a registration book. Outside of the courtroom staff, there won't be a record of who was in the room."

"There's the courthouse security cameras," Erin said. "We'll want to take a look at those anyway, to see if anyone was tailing Stone when he left. And speaking of cameras..."

She took out her phone and called her commander.

"Webb," he said.

"O'Reilly here. Did you guys get an ID off the security feed?"

"No. Too many people passed through, and the facial recognition software isn't as good as the technophobes would have us believe. Not yet, at any rate. We'll keep trying. Any luck on your end?"

"I think the mom down in Georgia is a bust. We just talked to Judge Hennessy and we're not sure about him."

"Where?"

"At his place."

"You went to a judge's home after hours," Webb said flatly. "To interrogate him about complicity in a homicide."

"It wasn't an interrogation, sir," Erin said. "It was an informal interview. He was very polite and understanding."

She could practically picture Webb pulling out an emotional-support cigarette. "O'Reilly, you're experienced enough that I don't need to spell out for you how bad an idea that could be."

"Sir, I think the killer was in court when Stone got released," she said.

"So you put the finger on the judge?"

"He's a person of interest. If it wasn't for his decision, Stone wouldn't have been at the train station."

"You understand this could look like the NYPD is personally harassing a judge who handed down a decision that was unfavorable to the Department, and to you individually?"

"It wasn't like that!"

"Aren't you the one who likes to say the truth doesn't matter as much as the perception people have?"

Erin closed her eyes. "Yes, sir," she muttered.

"So let's hope this doesn't make the news," Webb said briskly. "In the meantime, I like your idea about the courtroom. See if you can compile a list of potential people. Court closed at five, so get down there tomorrow morning."

"Copy that, sir. What should Zofia and I do now?"

"You're done for the night. Go home. See your loved ones. Sleep a little. Pretend to be normal human beings. Speaking for myself, I'm planning to call my kids. My biological kids, you understand, not the ones issued to me by the NYPD for my sins. I'll let you know if anything happens overnight."

"Goodnight, sir."

"I appreciate the wish, but I never expect a good night. See you tomorrow."

* * *

"She's right, you know," Erin told Rolf as she pulled into the parking garage across from the Barley Corner. They'd dropped Zofia off at the Eightball on their way home.

Rolf cocked his head at her in the rearview mirror. He hadn't followed the thread of her thoughts.

"Zofia," Erin clarified. "I don't like Hennessy either. God only knows why I felt the need to defend him."

Rolf had no opinion on Hennessy one way or the other.

"But that doesn't make him guilty," she added. "Hell, I don't like Lyons and Spinelli down at the One-Sixteen, but as far as I know they've never killed anyone. And *nobody* likes Sergeant Brown in Vice, but the only thing he's guilty of is terminal cynicism, and that's pretty typical for a veteran cop."

She slid the Charger into its parking space and climbed out. She reached for the back door.

"I heard you wanted to talk to me," a man said from somewhere behind her.

Erin's nervous system kicked from zero to overdrive. Her adrenal glands made a full dump. She spun and snatched out her Glock before she'd even consciously registered trouble. She didn't see a target. The garage was lit by sickly yellow overhead lights which left shadowy alcoves behind the concrete stanchions. A bad guy could be hiding any number of places.

A matchhead flared in one of the deepest shadows, illuminating a face for a second. A pair of hands cupped the match, then shook it out, leaving the glowing red ember at the end of a cigarette.

Erin relaxed just a little. The stranger had used both hands to light the cig, which meant he wasn't holding a weapon, and nobody sensible would light up a smoke to start a gunfight. But he'd still sneaked up on her, which was bad, or had been waiting for her, which was worse. The garage had security, handpicked by Carlyle; former Marines. This guy had either sneaked past them or come up with their permission.

"Identify yourself," she said, keeping her pistol trained on him.

"I'm sorry," he said. "I didn't mean to startle you. John McGraw, at your service."

He stepped out of the shadows. In the light, he didn't look threatening, at least not at first glance. About average height, lightly built, plainly dressed. His black leather jacket was understated, lacking the chains and studs favored by punks. His black hair was neatly trimmed and combed. Erin's street-trained eyes caught a small scar over his left eyebrow and, more importantly, a faint crosshatch of scars on the knuckles of both hands. He wore an onyx ring in a silver setting on his right ring finger. His hands were empty, but the way he held them, wrists loose, suggested a man who knew how to fight and was ready to throw down.

"Never heard of you," Erin said. Keeping her gun on him with one hand, she opened the Charger's back compartment with the other. *"Fuss!"* she told Rolf, who obediently took up position beside her.

"I'll take that as a compliment," McGraw said, taking the cigarette out of his mouth and blowing a stream of smoke. "And I apologize again. I prefer to meet on my own terms, so when I heard Cars Carlyle and Corky Corcoran were asking around, I did a little asking of my own. We know some of the same people. I went through back channels. Imagine my surprise when I learned Junkyard O'Reilly was interested in me. I can't imagine why."

"Who *are* you?" Erin demanded.

McGraw raised an eyebrow. "John McGraw," he repeated. "On the street, they call me Black Jack McGraw. I understand you're a fan of my work."

Remembering the conversation she'd had with Carlyle, Erin said "You're muscle for hire."

"I prefer to think of myself as a freelance problem solver," McGraw said.

"Problem solver," Erin repeated, deadpan. She'd lowered her gun but hadn't holstered it.

"I think it was Al Capone who said you could get farther with a soft word and a gun than just with a soft word," McGraw said with a light chuckle. "I don't use a gun, but I understand the sentiment." He had a hint of working-class Brooklyn accent. Erin couldn't figure him. He came across as polite and even friendly, but he'd approached her like a street thug. He had a Mob nickname. He wasn't an O'Malley or she would have heard of him. Where had he come from?

"How'd you get in here?" she asked.

"Trade secrets," he said. "But you might mention to whoever's in charge of Facilities that the lock on the basement service door could stand to be replaced."

"I'll pass that along," she said. "What do you want, Mr. McGraw?"

"Jack, please," he said. "And should I call you Junkyard? Or Ms. O'Reilly? The future Mrs. Carlyle, maybe?"

"Detective O'Reilly will do," she said. "What do you want, Jack?"

"You're the one who wants to meet me," he said. "Are you looking to engage my services?"

"What services do you provide?" she countered.

"Proactive dispute resolution," he said. "And home improvement."

"With a blackjack?" she guessed.

"I have a toolbox," he said. "The tool I use depends on the job in question."

"I wasn't speaking metaphorically," Erin said.

"Neither was I," McGraw said calmly. "I have an actual toolbox. Clawhammer, pliers, hacksaw. You'd be amazed what results can be achieved with ordinary hand tools. Nothing illegal, of course. I don't even own a handgun. But you're right, I know the value of a bag of ball bearings."

"Do you know Kamal Lobert?" she asked.

"The young man who was recently killed in Hell's Kitchen? I read about him in the *Times*."

"How about Wendell Stone?"

"The golden boy of Boston society? The man who suffered an unfortunate accident immediately upon his release from prison? It really hasn't been his year, has it?"

"Did you ever meet either of these men?"

"I ran into the late Mr. Stone at a dinner in Boston two or... yes, it was three years ago."

"What were you doing in Boston?"

"My job. Have you ever been to Boston?"

"No," Erin said.

"You should go," McGraw said. "It's a lovely city. Maybe as part of your honeymoon this coming fall?"

"Where were you between three and six o'clock this afternoon?" Erin asked, refusing to be drawn into a discussion of her upcoming wedding.

He took a drag on his dying cigarette, dropped it to the concrete, and stubbed it out with the toe of a black sneaker. "I'm not precisely prepared to say," he said.

"Why not?"

"Let's say I'd like to keep my options open at this time. I don't like being pinned down."

"Were you in or around Grand Central Station?"

"Might've been," McGraw said. "I can't really recall. I get around a lot."

He reached into a pocket. Erin felt herself tense, but his hand came out with a pack of Camels. He held it out toward her.

"No, thanks," she said. "I don't smoke."

"That's smart," he said, shaking a fresh cigarette out of the pack and returning it to his pocket. "I keep trying to quit, but can never quite kick the habit."

"Maybe you should try a less stressful occupation," Erin suggested.

"Like yours?" he replied with a wry smile. "I think I'll stick with what I know, thanks all the same. It's not so bad, being a private contractor. I choose my own clients and make my own hours. I do what I'm good at."

"Did you kill Wendell Stone?" she asked, deciding to stop beating around the bush.

"From what I understand, a locomotive killed him," McGraw said coolly. He opened a matchbook and flicked it, igniting one of the matches with a finger-snapping motion. He shot her a quick, genuine grin, obviously proud of the sleight-of-hand. He lit the cigarette, shook out the match, and tossed it aside.

"Did you hit him on the head?" she pressed.

"Would you believe me if I said no?" he answered.

"I'm more likely to believe it if you say it," she said.

"Why do you care? Wendell Jeremy Stone the Third was a bottom-feeder. He was an entitled, unpleasant man who thought his money and influence could get him out of trouble, and from a legal perspective, he was right. Stone was a pretentious jerk. Kamal Lobert was street trash. Both of them deserved exactly what they got, so why worry who gave it to them? I've heard all about you, Junkyard O'Reilly. You and your squad have piled up more lowlife bodies than I ever could. You might argue we're all on the same side, doing the same righteous work."

"We're nothing alike," Erin said. Her jaw was tight. She had a sudden urge to grab McGraw by his collar and choke some sense into him, to do anything to shake that calm, superior, maddening smile off his face.

"This from the woman who killed Dmitri Ivanov, Hans Rüdel, and Mickey Connor," McGraw said. He held up a hand. "Don't get me wrong. Those were human trash-bags who had it coming. Ivanov was a white slaver, Rüdel was a neo-Nazi terrorist, and Connor was a sadistic rapist and pretty much a serial killer. I'm not judging you. I'm just saying what a fine job you're doing keeping the streets clean. It sounds like someone else is doing the same work, just outside the law. Maybe you should stand aside and let him do it."

"Is it you?" she demanded.

"Reputation is a funny thing," McGraw said with a mischievous twinkle in his eye. "It's never about what you do.

It's about what people *think* you do. You of all people should know that. If a guy can take credit for something he didn't do, it's like finding a twenty-dollar bill on the street. He didn't earn it, but it buys just as much."

"That's one way to look at it," she said.

"Money is money," he said. "Speaking of which, let me know if you ever need help fixing any of life's little problems. Goodnight, Detective O'Reilly. You don't need to see me to the door. I'll let myself out."

McGraw flicked the half-smoked cigarette out of his hand. It spun through the air toward Erin, who reflexively stepped back, her eyes following the glowing trail. When she looked back, McGraw had disappeared around the back of the concrete column.

It wouldn't have been hard to chase him. Rolf could run him down with no trouble at all. But what was the point? He hadn't admitted to anything. Erin had no evidence he'd committed any crime at all. She could haul him downtown, but he'd be back on the street in an hour or two.

"Besides, it was a good trick," she admitted to Rolf. "The guy's a street magician on top of his other talents." She'd have to remember that one, though she didn't smoke herself. Toss something glowing at somebody and they'd look at it. You could buy a second or two that way, and they might be important seconds. At any rate, she didn't intend to be caught by it again.

Carlyle was at his usual place at the bar. His smile of greeting faltered when he saw the look on her face.

"Who's Black Jack McGraw?" she demanded.

"Just the lad I was hoping to tell you about," he said, confused. "I've been making inquiries, just as you asked, and came up with his name."

"Yeah," she said. "He heard."

"What's happened?"

"I just had a little conversation with him in the garage. By the way, he says you should replace the lock on the service door. Who the hell is this guy, and why haven't I heard of him before now?"

"Why don't we have a seat and a drink," he suggested, "and I'll tell you what I know."

A smooth shot of Glen D helped soothe Erin's nerves, still jangling from the encounter. Carlyle sipped his own whiskey while he talked.

"John McGraw comes from your old environs," he said. "He grew up right on the line between Brooklyn and Queens. He's a handyman, a fixer. He runs a legitimate business helping other lads with their wee problems. Electricity, plumbing, drywall, appliance repair, he does a bit of everything. If you've a problem south of the East River, word on the street has it, Black Jack can mend it."

"A jack of all trades, you mean?" Erin said with a thin smile.

Carlyle returned it. "Aye, so to speak. Corky knows him, as one might expect."

"Corky knows everybody."

"Just so. If you're wanting the details, he's the lad you'll be needing to speak to. But as I understand it, Mr. McGraw will solve all manner of problems, not merely the mechanical. Suppose you're in debt to a Shylock, or your child's being bullied, or you've a supervisor at work who's making you miserable. He'll deal with that sort of thing as well."

"A child being bullied?" she repeated. "You mean he kills kids?"

"Not kills them," Carlyle said. "At least, not to my knowledge. But according to Corky, he shattered a fourteen-year-old's kneecap. Left the lad with a permanent limp."

"Jesus," Erin said, thinking of McGraw's pleasant, cheerful face. "This guy's a frigging psycho."

"That's oversimplifying matters," Carlyle said. "The kneecap was payment for the teenager kicking another lad's puppy to death."

Erin couldn't help glancing down at Rolf, who looked back with his big brown eyes. Erin felt judged.

"You still can't go kneecapping kids," she said, but heard the lack of conviction in her own voice. If someone kicked Rolf's head in, her conscience whispered, she might not stop with the knees.

"In any case, he's precisely the sort of lad you were seeking," Carlyle said. "I'm sorry he accosted you. I'll have words with Corky on the subject. Apparently he asked questions a bit too loudly and they reached unfriendly ears."

"McGraw didn't admit to the attacks," she said. "But he went out of his way not to deny them, either. He pretty much told me he wants people to think he did it."

"A reputation as a vicious lad can take you far on the street," Carlyle said. "Did you arrest him?"

"No. He did a quick fade, and besides, I didn't have anything I could pin on him. Where does this guy hang out?"

"In Queens, most of the time. I believe he has a criminal record, so your system ought to know as much as I on the subject. Did he threaten you?"

"No. Just startled me. You shouldn't sneak up on a cop. And I'm surprised he managed it."

"As am I. You're a difficult woman to creep up on."

"I think I'd better look into this guy. It's just..."

"What, darling?"

Erin stared into the bottom of her empty shot glass. "I feel like he *wants* me to."

Chapter 9

"John McGraw, alias Black Jack," Webb said, reading off his computer screen. "Age thirty-two, height five-eleven, weight one eighty-three. Hair black, eyes brown. Legal occupation, handyman. Resident of Queens. Here's his mugshot."

Erin peered over his shoulder. "Yeah, that's the guy," she said. "Is he *smiling?*"

"Looks like it," Webb said. "Not much, more what you'd call a Mona Lisa mysterious smile than a big grin. Looks to me like he's laughing at some private joke."

"Not many guys smile in their mugshots," Vic said. He was looking over Webb's other shoulder. "That Corcoran punk did, as I recall."

"Corky smiles pretty much all the time," Erin said.

"McGraw has a jacket," Webb said. "But not a very thick one. He's been busted for Aggravated Assault, Assault with a Deadly Weapon, and First-Degree Assault causing serious physical injury. Murder would be a new one on him."

"Not for lack of trying," Vic said, examining the charges that had been brought against Black Jack. "It says here he clocked a guy on the head with a claw hammer. Put the poor bastard in a coma."

"He told me he's a problem solver," Erin said. "The way he said it was like he thought he was doing a public service."

"Maybe he thinks he is," Webb said. "I don't see any specific ties to organized crime. And his victims are all small-time crooks, juvenile delinquents, and guys like that. I think that's why he only has one conviction, even though he's been arrested eight times and charged five. These aren't the sort of people who like to testify in court."

"What's the conviction for?" Vic asked.

"He wrecked a fourteen-year-old's leg," Webb said. "Hammer again. The kid's mom testified against him. He got three years, served fourteen months. The kid needed surgery and may not ever get full use of the leg."

"He did *what?*" Vic growled. "Crippled a kid?"

"The way I heard it, the kid kicked another kid's puppy to death," Erin said.

"So?" Vic retorted.

"What do you mean, so?" Erin snapped. "You think that's okay?"

"Wait a second," Vic said. "You're defending this son of a bitch? He smashed a kid's leg with a friggin' hammer!"

"He won't kick any more puppies," Erin replied. "Who owned the dog?"

Webb brought up the case file. "Neighboring family," he said. "You're right, O'Reilly. The other boy's mother spoke in court as a character witness. She said the wounded kid was a bully and McGraw was a really upstanding guy. Kindhearted, polite, wouldn't normally hurt a fly."

"I'll bet," Vic muttered. "Did she hire him to beat the crap out of the other kid?"

"If so, it wasn't mentioned in the courtroom," Webb said. "This McGraw is an interesting character. True freelance muscle is pretty rare. These guys almost always work for crime bosses. How exactly did he hear about you?"

"Corky Corcoran was asking around," Erin said. "At Carlyle's request, because I asked him about guys whose MO might be a match. Corky was careless and word got back to McGraw. He said he wanted to meet on his own terms."

"Corcoran was careless?" Vic said. "I'm shocked to hear it. Absolutely shocked. But if McGraw didn't confess and didn't claim to be innocent, what the hell did he want?"

"He talked about reputation," she said thoughtfully. "I think he wanted to take credit for Stone and Lobert, without taking the fall."

"His street rep goes up but he doesn't have to do time," Vic said, nodding. "He gets to have his cake and eat it too."

"He wants us to think he's guilty, whether he is or not," Webb said. "He's confident we can't prove it. That either means he's innocent of the killings or he's very confident he didn't leave evidence linking him to them."

"He's definitely confident," Erin said. "Cocky, even."

"You should've dragged his ass downtown," Vic said.

"That's what he wanted me to do," she said. "It'd be like free advertising for him."

"Know what I hate more than street punks?" Vic asked.

"I can't even begin to guess," Webb said.

"Arrogant street punks."

Webb rubbed his face. "This is getting very strange," he said. "Revenge isn't your typical service industry."

"He also does plumbing, electrical, and drywall," Erin said.

Vic snickered. "Plumbing can be dangerous," he said. "You know, Zofia and I—"

"Yes, we know about the dead guy in your bathroom," Webb interrupted.

"You know the problem with plumbing jokes?" Vic said.

Erin braced herself.

"They're too draining," Vic said.

"Did McGraw give you an alibi?" Webb asked, ignoring Vic.

"No," Erin said. "He was very careful not to. But he also didn't admit to a single thing, not in so many words."

"This would be a lot easier if you'd made a recording of the conversation," Webb said.

"Unfortunately, sir, since I'm not infiltrating the Irish Mob anymore, I've gotten out of the habit of wearing a wire in my underwire," Erin retorted. "I didn't know this was going to happen. Maybe that's why McGraw surprised me."

"McGraw could've done Stone but not Lobert," Vic suggested. "We could have two hitmen on the loose."

"It's got to be the same attacker in both cases," Webb said. "According to CSU, the jacks were from the same deck."

"They can tell that?" Erin asked. "I mean, I know they're both Bicycle brand, but the exact same deck? How do they know?"

"Magic," Webb said.

"Really?" Vic said.

"Are you familiar with Clarke's Law, Neshenko?"

"Is that something about busting pedophiles?"

"No," Webb said with exaggerated patience. "Clarke's Law states that any sufficiently advanced technology is indistinguishable from magic. I'd argue any sufficiently esoteric branch of science is the same way, including forensics. That's part of the problem, too."

"How so?" Erin asked.

"Juries don't understand forensics either," Webb explained. "They don't understand DNA, they don't understand transference, and they don't understand chemistry. Know what they do understand?"

"Eyewitness testimony?" Erin guessed.

"Exactly," Webb sighed. "The most unreliable evidence you can get."

"No wonder we get so many botched verdicts," Vic said. "But black jacks are a little obvious, don't you think? For Black Jack McGraw? Has he ever done that before? Left a calling card?"

"Not as far as we know," Webb said. "Piekarski and I will look into McGraw. I'd particularly like to know if we can match his face to the security footage from the train station. Neshenko, you go to the courthouse with O'Reilly to work the legal-system angle."

*   *   *

"They won't get a facial match from the cameras," Erin predicted, putting the Charger in gear.

"You don't think McGraw is our guy?" Vic replied.

"I don't know," she said. "But if he was there, I guarantee he avoided putting his face on camera. This guy's a damn ghost. He was standing less than ten feet away and I had no idea he was even there until he spoke up. It was creepy. If he doesn't want to leave footprints, I don't think he will."

"I hate competent criminals," Vic said. "But at least I get to pound some pavement with you. I'm sick of staring at shitty black-and-white security feeds."

"And Webb's probably sick of you sitting beside him and bitching," Erin said.

"You think that's why he swapped Zofia and me around?"

"It's a theory."

"I'm not *that* annoying."

Erin said nothing.

"Okay, fine," Vic said. "What if I am? You haven't gotten rid of me."

"Yet," she said.

"I think you like me," he said. "Deep down. I mean, real deep. So deep you probably don't even realize it."

"That's what you think, is it?"

"It is. But enough about me. What do you think about all this?"

"All what?"

"These bad guys getting popped. It's illegal, sure, and we need to find the guy who's doing it, but is it really such a bad thing?"

"Vic, what if Lobert wasn't the guy who shot LaRayne Shaw?" Erin replied. "What if he really was innocent?"

"You really believe that?"

"I'm supposed to believe it. The jury voted to acquit him."

"Because they didn't have enough proof," Vic scoffed. "It never would've gone to trial if he hadn't been guilty."

"By that argument, why have trials at all?" Erin shot back. "Why not just throw them in prison when we arrest them?"

"I kinda like that idea," he said.

"Vic, we're cops. We don't get to make those decisions. We're not a jury and we're sure as hell not judges or executioners. That's what cops do in fascist countries."

"I know, I know. But it really burns me up when we nail the bad guys and they get away. I mean, we practically gift-wrap the SOBs for the DA and what happens? Stone was guilty as sin and everybody knows it."

"Of course he was."

"Your pal Thompson would've just blown his head off and called it a day."

"Ian's not a murderer," Erin said hotly.

"That's exactly what he is," Vic replied. "He killed that one Colombian cartel punk, he shot that Finneran chick in your own damn apartment, and he wasted two of Mickey Connor's guys. He's a gun-toting vigilante, just like the Punisher in the comics. And that's not even counting everybody he offed when he was a Marine. If you're willing to give him a pass, why not this other dude?"

"It's different," Erin said.

"How?"

"The DA didn't press charges on Ian," she said. "If he holds off on this guy, whoever he is, then we'll see."

"I still don't like Thompson," Vic insisted.

"He saved my life," Erin reminded him. "And my niece and nephew, and probably my sister-in-law. Every single time he's killed a man, it's been to save someone else."

"Then why don't we give him the keys to the goddamn city? Even bad guys do the right thing sometimes. It's like what they say about a broken clock. It's right two times a day."

"You're okay with Stone getting whacked," she said. "So which one of us is being hypocritical?"

Vic snorted in frustration. "Fine! We'll lock this bastard up. But I still think Thompson oughta be behind bars too."

"He's a firefighter now," she said. "He's saving lives, not taking them."

Vic was silent a minute, frowning.

"What's the matter?" Erin asked.

"When a building burns, what's the one thing a firefighter always saves?"

"What?"

"The foundation."

"Do you have a book of these? *A Hundred and One Terrible Jokes?*"

"Don't underestimate the power of the Internet," Vic said. "And on the subject of your precious ex-Marine fireman, you know what they say about dogs and chickens?"

"Is this another joke?"

Vic had stopped smiling. "No. After a dog gets one taste of a live chicken, you can't let him back in the henhouse. Doesn't matter if he was a good dog before. He'll be a chicken-killer for the rest of his life, so you'd better either put him down or get used to picking up loose feathers."

Erin glared at Vic.

*   *   *

"Ah, the lovely Miss O'Reilly once again," Judge Ferris said. "And the redoubtable Mr. Neshenko."

"Uh... thanks," Vic said.

"'Redoubtable' means you're a badass," Erin murmured out of the side of her mouth.

"I knew that," Vic said a little too quickly. "Thanks for seeing us, your Honor."

"I'm delighted," Ferris said. "To what do I owe the pleasure? I assume you are still investigating the death of the late, unlamented Mr. Lobert?"

"And Wendell Stone," Erin said.

"Ah yes," Ferris said. "I cannot imagine you were pleased with my colleague's decision regarding his case."

"It worked out in the end," Vic said.

"For everyone but Mr. Stone himself," Ferris said placidly. "I have my own opinions, naturally. But I cannot comment on a fellow judge's decision. I know you understand."

"Of course," Erin said. "But there's a pattern forming here."

"Somebody's killing the people you guys are letting go," Vic said bluntly.

"Young man," Ferris said, staring down his nose at the Russian. "I passed New York's bar exam fifty-seven years ago, long before you were born. I went to work for the District Attorney and became a prosecutor. From that position I advanced to the bench, where I have sat for over thirty years. I have given my entire life to public service. Over the decades I have sent hundreds of felons to serve lengthy prison terms. Many of those miscreants have died behind bars. Only the absence of capital punishment in this state has prevented my imposing a more extreme sanction upon the worst malefactors. If a jury finds a defendant not guilty in my courtroom, I do not 'let the defendant go.' I release a man or woman whom the law has presumed, and continues to presume, innocent."

"Whatever," Vic muttered.

"It doesn't matter whether Lobert or Stone was guilty or not," Erin said. "Not to us, not right now. What matters is that someone is using the courthouse as a hunting ground. We have a spree killer taking out guys who've slipped through the legal system."

"So it would seem," Ferris said. "I trust your efforts with respect to LaRayne Shaw's brother have not borne fruit?"

"Micheal didn't kill Wendell Stone," Erin said. "He was in a holding cell when Stone was attacked."

"He could have an accomplice," Ferris said. "Another family member, perhaps?"

"Micheal Shaw had no reason to go after Stone," Erin said. "We 'd like to know who else was in court when Lobert was acquitted. Then compare the list with Stone's hearing."

"Your perpetrator need not have been physically present in the courtroom," Ferris pointed out. "The verdicts are a matter of public record as soon as they are issued. The reporters who buzz around these hallowed halls like so many mosquitoes see to that."

"The killer tailed Stone to Grand Central Station," Erin said. "Either they were in the courthouse or nearby."

"Do you suspect a professional contractor?" Ferris asked, leaning forward. "I encountered such a man myself not so long ago."

"Yeah," Vic said. "We remember. He nearly got you a couple times."

"He did 'get' my dear friend and protégé," Ferris said in icy tones. "Assassins are a blight upon our society; vicious animals employed by cowards. If you suspect such a parasite, I will assist in every way possible."

"Have you seen this man?" Erin asked, sliding a printout of Jack McGraw's mugshot across the Judge's desk.

Ferris studied it for a long moment. "I do not recollect his face," he finally said. "Who is he?"

"If you haven't seen him, it doesn't matter," she said. "Do you and Judge Hennessy share any staff?"

"We have our own clerks," Ferris said. "There is no overlap."

"Who else might have been in both courtrooms?"

Ferris tilted his chair back and began counting on his fingers. "There is the Court Liaison Officer, the Probation Officer, the Court Reporter, and the Bailiff. I do not know whether the prosecutor was the same in both cases. Then, of course, it is possible the defendants employed one or more of the same defense attorneys, though it seems unlikely. Mr. Stone was quite wealthy and could afford to employ a team of excellent private practitioners, while Mr. Lobert was thrown upon the mercies of a public defender. And speaking of the public, any New Yorker who wished to attend would have been free to do so. Any number of individuals may have been present on both occasions. Let me remind you, as well, your suspect may not have been there in the flesh."

"We have to start somewhere," Erin said. "Would your secretary have information on the Lobert case?"

"Julia will be delighted to be of service," Ferris said. "She should be able to obtain Judge Hennessy's relevant documents as well."

"What do you know about Hennessy?" Erin asked.

"He is a judge in good standing," Ferris said, his voice growing slightly colder again. "I trust you harbor no personal animosity against him for ruling in favor of the late Mr. Stone?"

"This is just business, your Honor," Erin said, earning a muffled snort from Vic. "It's not personal."

"It is unusual for a former defense attorney to become a judge," Ferris said, "but hardly unheard-of. Many more of us make our way to the bench by the route I traveled, through the District Attorney's office."

"Don't you worry he'll be partial to the criminals?" Erin asked.

"A defendant might worry just as much about my partiality toward the prosecution," Ferris replied. "I do attempt to preserve objectivity, but we all must come from somewhere, and all judges practiced criminal law on one side or the other. I, for one, applaud Judge Hennessy's decision to forsake the private sector and devote himself to public service. It is a considerable sacrifice."

"Even if he lets guilty perps walk?" Vic asked.

"I believe I already said I would not express an opinion on a fellow judge's decisions," Ferris said mildly. "I am not overly fond of having to repeat myself."

"Sorry, your Honor," Erin said. "Thank you for your time."

Ferris waved a hand dismissively. "The time simply flies in your presence, Miss O'Reilly. Do talk to Julia on your way out. She will offer her full cooperation. I wish you the best of luck in your endeavors. And let me say how much I am looking forward to attending your nuptials. Thank you for your invitation."

"We'll be glad to have you," she said.

Chapter 10

"It's not any of the spectators," Vic said, a long hour and a half later.

"No," Erin agreed. They'd been studying at the footage from the courtroom cameras. After an unfortunate incident involving a Mafia chieftain, a disgruntled young mobster, and a length of piano wire, the courthouse had revamped its security and the camera feeds' resolution was excellent. The detectives had a great view of everyone who'd been in both courtrooms when the verdicts had been announced.

"None of the same people in the audience," Vic said. "The bailiff's the same guy, and so is the stenographer, and I think that officer against the wall there is the same one who was guarding the door during the Lobert trial. I gotta say, though, the steno doesn't look like he could beat a man's head in, and neither does the bailiff. That boy's been hitting the donuts way too hard, you ask me."

"He is a little pudgy," Erin said. "But fat guys can be strong. And a blackjack can take you out without too much muscle behind it."

"Maybe," Vic said. "If I had to put my money on one of those three, it'd be the guard. He looks like a bad mofo. Do you know him?"

"No," Erin said. "But we can get an ID. Here's what we're going to do. We're going to run backgrounds on him, the bailiff, and the stenographer. We're looking for ties to gangs, particularly the Trip Sixes or the Crazy Knives. We need to check their financials for money coming in or out that we can't explain. And we want to see if any of them have had any recent personal tragedies."

"Like a family member getting offed by a crook?" Vic asked. "That's what usually sets vigilantes off. See, the Punisher loses his whole family in Central Park in a gang shootout. Batman's parents get murdered outside the opera. And—"

"Vic?"

"Yeah?"

"This isn't a comic book."

"I know that. If it was, I'd have a cool costume that'd show off my muscles. And you'd wear skintight spandex and a real low-cut top."

Erin gave him a look.

"And a cape," he added. "You'd definitely have a cape."

She maintained the look. Rolf joined in.

"Backgrounds and financials," Vic said. "Copy that."

*   *   *

"We have our killer on film," Webb announced as Erin, Vic, and Rolf walked into Major Crimes.

"Who is he?" Vic asked.

"We don't know," Zofia said.

"But—" Vic began.

"Maybe it's one of the guys from the courtroom cameras," Erin suggested. "We can compare footage."

"Maybe," Webb said. "But it won't do us any good. Our guy isn't facing the camera. He's wearing a hat and a trench coat. We're pretty sure it's a man, but that's about all we know for certain. Have a look."

They clustered around Webb's monitor. On it was a grainy black-and-white image of what was probably a man, seen from the back, clad in a long coat and fedora.

"You know," Vic said. "From this angle he kinda looks like you, sir. Trench coat, hat like yours, kinda wide in the body."

"Very funny," Webb said.

"Where were you when Stone was whacked?"

"Neshenko?"

"Sir?"

"We're looking for someone outside this room."

"Yes, sir."

"Other people wear trench coats and fedoras."

"Yes, sir."

"And I'm not just talking about old Humphrey Bogart movies."

"No, sir."

"And it's borderline insubordinate to ask your commanding officer for an alibi."

"Copy that, sir."

"He's about average height," Erin said, studying the image. "Hard to tell his build in the coat, but I think Vic's right. He isn't skinny."

"Could be any of the guys from the courthouse," Vic said. "Or none of them."

"What did you turn up at court?" Webb asked.

"Three men were in both rooms," Erin said. "The bailiff, Orlando Ortiz; one of the courthouse cops, Moe Perkins; and the recorder, Vernon Lefkowitz."

"Any criminal records?" Webb asked.

"We checked on the way back," Erin said. "Nothing."

"Which makes sense," Vic said. "Given that they were working in a courthouse. If these guys had felonies on them, I don't think they would've gotten hired."

"That's a good point," Webb sighed. "Time to start digging. You know what to look for?"

"Erin told me," Vic said. "I think she's angling for your job, boss."

"She's welcome to it," Webb said. "Retirement can't come a minute too soon."

"That reminds me," Erin said. "How'd things go with your kids last night?"

Webb's face cracked into a faint but unmistakable smile. "They're good," he said. "Erica just turned nineteen. I can't quite believe it. She's going to UCLA, just like I did, but I hope to God she chooses a different career than mine."

"What's she studying?" Erin asked.

"She wants to be pre-law."

"That's just what we need," Vic growled. "More friggin' lawyers."

"She'd like to be a public defender," Webb said with slow, deliberate malice.

"That's teenagers for you," Zofia said. "She's probably rebelling against her dad being a cop."

"Most likely," Webb agreed. "She wants to help minorities in LA navigate the legal system, especially Hispanic immigrants. It's good work that needs doing and she has my full support."

"Of course she does," Erin said, keeping her tone neutral. Webb sounded a little prickly on the subject.

"Dani's seventeen," Webb went on. "She has a boyfriend and I don't like him."

"Have you even met him?" Vic asked.

"I don't need to meet him," Webb said. "She didn't even admit to having one."

"Then how do you know?" Erin asked.

"I'm a detective," he said. "People tell me things by what they're not telling me. When my teenager lies to me, or leaves stuff out, I can fill in the blanks. Dani's seeing a guy and she's afraid I won't like him, which means I won't. He's probably either a drug dealer, a wannabe actor, or a slacker living in his mom's basement. In that case he's way too old for her."

"Which of those would be the worst?" Erin asked.

"Actor or basement-dweller," Webb said. "Drug dealers are criminals, but at least they have a trade."

"But you're glad you called the girls, aren't you?" Zofia asked.

"Of course I am," Webb said. "I don't see them very often. It's been almost a year since I got out there."

"What about their mom?" Zofia asked.

"What about her?" Webb replied.

"How's she doing?"

"She's fine."

"Do you keep in touch with her?"

"I'd like to focus on our case," Webb said briskly. "You have work to do."

* * *

"What's the story with the Lieutenant's ex?" Zofia asked a couple hours later, when Webb stepped outside for a smoke break.

"I have no idea," Erin said.

"Me neither," Vic said. "Hell, I don't even know her name."

"We met his second wife, Cathy Simmons, when she came out here," Erin said. "She was going into real estate, or at least she was until her paranoid boyfriend got murdered."

"If a guy gets murdered, maybe he isn't paranoid," Zofia said.

"He had guns all over his home," Erin recalled. "Not that they did him any good."

"Real estate is dangerous," Vic said. "Like that guy we found in our bathroom."

"Yes, dear," Zofia said. "We know. I was there."

"But we don't know a thing about his first wife," Erin said. "I don't think he's ever mentioned her."

"Maybe it hurts too much," Zofia said.

"Or maybe he's forgotten her name," Vic said.

"Speaking of names, I might have a hit on Orlando Ortiz," Zofia said, abruptly changing the subject. Erin was a little confused by the sudden shift until she realized Webb had come back in.

"What about Ortiz?" Webb asked.

"He's related to a guy from the *Cuchillos Locos*," Zofia said.

"No kidding," Erin said. "Brother?"

"Cousin."

"Where's his cousin now?"

"Bellevue Hospital. He got shot in the same shootout that killed LaRayne Shaw."

"That's interesting," Webb said. "I'd call it quite the coincidence if I believed in coincidence."

"Hold on," Vic said. "That shooting was months ago. This schmuck is still in the hospital?"

"He took two in the abdomen," Zofia said. "According to what I've got here, he's paralyzed from the waist down and has a colostomy bag."

"That sucks," Vic said. "Give me a good clean headshot any day."

"Kamal Lobert ran with the Trip Sixes," Webb said. "We've been thinking his killing was revenge for LaRayne Shaw. Maybe Ortiz wanted payback for his cousin getting crippled instead."

"But what about Stone?" Erin asked. "Ortiz wouldn't have any reason to care about our second victim."

"It's possible he discovered a taste for it," Webb said. "Good work, Piekarski. Keep digging on Ortiz. What about the other two? Anything?"

"I've got nothing on Lefkowitz," Erin said. "This guy's an absolute nobody. No wife, no family, zero social media footprint. He lives in an apartment on the Lower East Side, by himself as far as I know. No trouble with the law. If he didn't have a Social Security number, he might as well be a robot."

"I bet he has cats," Vic said. "Three or four of them."

"And Perkins?" Webb asked.

"He used to be NYPD," Vic said. "He transferred to the courthouse gig last year."

"What does his service jacket say?"

"He's decorated," Vic said. "He ran into a house fire and brought two kids out, one in each arm. He got burned in the fire bad enough for partial disability."

"So we have a hero, a nobody, and the relative of a disabled gang member," Webb said. "If I was a betting man, I know where I'd lay my money."

"I'm not so sure," Erin said. "If Perkins thinks he's some sort of hero, he might be bored working courthouse security. If he misses the action, he could be making his own."

"That's an excellent point," Webb said. "Any financial irregularities on any of these guys?"

"Perkins doesn't have much money," Vic said. "Unless it's stuffed in a mattress somewhere off-grid. I thought my bank balance was low until I saw his. He's carrying credit card debt, too."

"And no other relatives who've been killed or injured in violent crimes?"

"Not that I know of," Erin said. The others nodded agreement.

"Nothing on Lefkowitz's financials," Erin said. "His bank balance goes up a little every month. He doesn't seem to spend much."

"Ortiz's finances are mess," Zofia said.

"He owes money to the wrong people?" Webb asked.

"Not exactly. I meant they're a *mess*. He's a shitty bookkeeper. He bounces checks, he's been audited by the IRS for screwing up his taxes. None of it looks criminal. It just looks sloppy to me."

"Being bad at math isn't a crime," Webb said. "But his association with his cousin is still suspicious. This gives us five persons of interest: Shaw, Perkins, Ortiz, Lefkowitz, and McGraw. Ortiz and Shaw have the clearest motive. They may even have been working together. We still have Shaw in Holding. I'll grill him again. Neshenko, keep going on Perkins. If he's having money troubles, he's vulnerable to corruption. O'Reilly, I want you to go to the hospital and talk to Ortiz's cousin. Give him a good shake and see what comes loose."

"Won't that tip Ortiz off that we're looking into him?" Erin asked.

"There's no way to avoid that," Webb said. "Sometimes you can get good results by playing it straight. Pedro Ortiz was wounded in the shooting Lobert was on trial for. Just talk to the guy and see what you can find out."

"Copy that, sir," Erin said.

* * *

Erin spent more time than she wanted in Bellevue Hospital, but she usually hung around the ER or ICU. Long-term patients didn't tend to be of great interest to the NYPD. This wing of the building held unpleasant associations for her. This was where her mentor and friend Phil Stachowski had spent weeks trying to rebuild his shattered faculties after a bullet to the brain had nearly killed him. Now Phil was home with his family and doing as well as could be expected, but he was wheelchair-bound and would never be quite the same man. This part of the hospital was a reminder to Erin that death wasn't the only terrible thing that could happen on the Job.

Pedro Ortiz's room was surprisingly peaceful. No insistently beeping machines were plugged into him. No doctors or nurses hovered. There wasn't even a guard on the door. It would be terribly easy, paranoia whispered, for rival gang members to walk in and kill him. They wouldn't even need a weapon. It was harder to smother a guy with a pillow than the movies made it look, but a half-paralyzed man missing a chunk of his guts wasn't exactly a difficult target.

If you looked past the gang tattoos on his face and neck, Pedro looked like any other patient. He was a young man, no more than twenty-three, and good-looking under all the ink. The hospital staff were keeping him clean-shaven and combed. His bed was cranked partway upright so he could watch TV without wrecking his neck. The set was tuned to a Spanish-language channel and was playing some sort of daytime soap opera.

"Excuse me," Erin said, knocking on the open door.

He glanced at her without much interest. Then he took in her face, and the German Shepherd at her side, and his eyes focused. He picked up the remote and muted the TV.

"Hello, *señora*," he said. He had a soft voice with a moderate Hispanic accent. "I don't think I know you."

"My name's Erin O'Reilly," she said. "This is Rolf."

"Is he one of those dogs they bring to hospitals to cheer people up?" Pedro asked. "A therapy dog?"

"Sorry, no," she said. "He's a K-9. I'm a detective with the NYPD."

A complicated combination of wariness and disappointment blended in his face. "That's too bad," he said. "I like dogs, but I don't like narcs."

"Rolf isn't a drug dog," she said. "He sniffs out explosives and people."

Pedro spread his hands. "You can search the room if you want," he said. "But you won't find anything that goes boom. I wish I had one of the nurses hiding under the bed, especially Maria, the little one with the black hair and the cute smile, but it's just me in here."

Erin smiled. This was going better than she'd expected. "Don't worry," she said. "You're not in any trouble. I was just hoping to talk to you for a little while."

"About what?" The wariness was still there, hiding behind the smile.

"I know you're a member of the *Cuchillos Locos*," she said. "But I don't really care. I'm not on the Gang Task Force. I work Major Crimes."

"I don't think I've committed any major crimes, *señora*," Pedro said. "And if you're talking about anything that's happened in the past four months, I have a very good alibi."

"You're a victim, not a perp," she said. "You were shot a couple of times."

He shrugged. "I forgot to duck. It happens."

"Who shot you?"

"I couldn't say."

"You don't want to say, or you don't know?"

"Whichever you like."

"Was it Kamal Lobert?"

"I don't know any Kamal Lobert."

Erin sighed. "Kiddo, you don't have to play dumb. I know the code of the street and I know you ain't no rat. But Lobert wasn't in your gang and he wasn't your friend. I'd think you'd want to get him in whatever trouble you could."

"It doesn't matter," Pedro said. "Where I come from, you don't ever talk to the police. Not even a good-looking *chica* like you. And you're very fine, *señora*. A lot of guys, they like the big curves, but I always went for the athletic ones. You've got the best legs I've seen in a long time."

"You got shot twice," she said, ignoring the compliment. "Once in the belly, once in the spine. Speaking of legs, your medical file says you're not going to regain the use of yours. I understand you'd be a little upset about that."

"What would you know about it?" he shot back. "You don't have any idea what it's like to lie here like this."

"You might be surprised," she said. "I've caught a couple of rounds."

"Oh yeah? Where'd you get shot?"

"Here." Erin indicated the scar on the side of her scalp.

"No kidding?" Pedro was surprised and impressed. "Someone shot you? In the *head*?"

"Yeah."

"And you survived?"

"No," she deadpanned. "I'm a zombie."

He laughed. "You're something else, *señora*."

"Wouldn't you like to get back at the guy who did it to you?" she asked.

"How can I?" he replied. "I'm stuck here."

"Lobert is dead," she said bluntly.

Pedro didn't flinch, didn't blink.

"Anything to say about it?" she asked. "How do you feel?"

"That's a stupid question," he said. "You think I'm going to cry because some Trip Six *hijo de puta* got whacked?"

"So you do know him," she said.

"I never said that."

"You know he was in the Trip Sixes and you know he got murdered."

"I hear things," Pedro said.

"You get visits from your gangbanger buddies?" Erin asked.

He said nothing.

"I can check," she said. "Visitors have to log in."

"Why are you hassling us, *señora*? Is it against the law to visit a man in the hospital now?"

Erin had already checked the log on her way in. She knew he'd gotten recent visits from his mother, two sisters, and several guys with Hispanic names, along with his cousin Orlando.

"Lobert was a piece of shit," she said. "He killed an innocent girl. Then he beat the rap. I'm not mad somebody took him out. I'm just trying to figure out what happened so more civilians don't get hurt. You have a couple of sisters, don't you?"

"What about them?"

"You want them getting caught in the crossfire?"

"Nobody's going to fuck with my family," Pedro said with sudden fierceness. "They try, it don't matter if my legs don't work. I'll crawl out of this bed and come find them."

"A man has to look out for his family," she agreed. "You've got a good, tight family. I can tell."

"Yeah," Pedro said. His eyes softened slightly. "My mother, she comes to see me a lot."

"It's good you have people looking out for you," she said. "Good people who have your back."

"That's the way it's supposed to be," Pedro said.

"You have a brother?"

"No."

"Cousins?"

"A couple."

"I think I met one of them," she said. "I was down at the courthouse for work and I ran into a guy with the same last name as you."

"Ortiz?" Pedro chuckled. "Some parts of town, you can't throw a rock out the window without hitting a guy named Ortiz. I can't be related to all of them."

"Orlando, that was his name," Erin said, snapping her fingers. "It's funny, a guy working at the courthouse while his cousin's a banger."

"Hey, it's a free country, *señora*. Orlando can work wherever he wants."

"Has he been to see you?"

This was a test, mostly to see whether Pedro would tell an obvious lie. It was wise in an interview to sprinkle in a few questions you already knew the answers to, so you could get a sense of the subject's honesty.

"What about it?" Pedro said. "Look, don't go making trouble for Orlando. He's a good guy. My life, it's got nothing to do with him. He doesn't have nothing to do with the street."

"Why'd he become a bailiff?" she asked.

"It's a job, you know? Why'd you become a cop?"

"My dad wore a shield," she said.

"Really?" Pedro was interested now. "Family business, huh? How do you like it?"

"It's the best job in the world," she said with complete sincerity. "How'd you become a gang member?"

"Where I come from, you have to be in one," he said. "Otherwise you're all alone on the street, and the street eats you if you're alone. A lot of cops, they're the same way. Your gang's just bigger than mine."

Erin had to smile at that. "We're the biggest," she said. "And you'd like to be on good terms with us, wouldn't you? I can make serious trouble for the Crazy Knives, you know."

"And we can make trouble for you," he answered, not smiling.

"Did you seriously just threaten the NYPD?" Erin said, the smile still plastered on her own face but falling away from her eyes. "Because you really, really don't want to do that."

"We don't want trouble," Pedro said. "And neither do you."

"Then talk to me. How did Lobert die?"

"I don't know! The only reason I know he's dead is it was on TV. That's all I do now, is watch TV all day. I can't walk, I can't even take a piss by myself. You asked, was he the guy who shot me? I don't know, okay? That's the truth. Everybody was shooting. Bullets flying all over the place. I think I saw him, yeah, but it could've been him or five other guys. None of them were even looking at me. Just ducking behind cars and shit, holding their guns sideways, popping off rounds all over the place. The shot that hit me wasn't some crazy good sniper. It was just bad luck or fate or whatever you want to call it. The shooter might've been him, it might've been one of the others, it might've been two different guys. I don't know! You ever been in a gunfight?"

"Yeah," Erin said quietly. "A few."

"Then you know what it's like. All I know is I got hit in the back, then I got hit again when I was lying in the street. Then, next thing I knew, I was here and some *gringo* was stitching me up like I was a torn-up old shirt. And that's all I know. So can I get back to my telenovela now? The main girl's long-lost twin sister just showed up and it's getting good. I'm missing the best part right now."

"Sure," Erin said. "Here's one of my cards. If you hear anything—"

He held up a hand. "No, thanks," he said. "Keep it. You're the first pretty lady I've turned down a phone number from, but you know what would happen if someone found that in here? A cop business card? I might as well cut my own throat and be done with it."

"Okay, forget about it," she said. "I'm sorry for your troubles, Mr. Ortiz. You get better and try to be good, okay?"

"I don't have much choice," Pedro said. "I can't get into much trouble in here."

Chapter 11

Erin called Webb on her way back to her Charger. She'd parked in one of the police spaces on East 28th Street, just around the corner from 1st Avenue. Parking, as always in Manhattan, was worse than driving. She understood why so many New Yorkers didn't bother with cars.

"What's the word?" the Lieutenant asked.

"Pedro Ortiz was more polite than I expected," she said. "He seemed pretty harmless, as gang members go. I left him watching Mexican soap operas. He claims he doesn't know who shot him, so he wasn't particularly mad at Lobert."

"Do you believe him?"

Erin had been asking herself the same question. "The Crazy Knives might've taken revenge on his behalf," she said. "But if they did, I don't think he told them to. And he got upset when I mentioned Orlando's name. He insisted his cousin doesn't have anything to do with any gang activities."

"Was it genuine indignation, or staged?"

"It felt real to me." Erin glanced up the street to check for oncoming traffic and started across. A beat-up old sedan was coming, but she had plenty of time before it got to her. "I have the feeling Orlando isn't part of the Life and Pedro wants to keep it that way."

"Oh well," Webb sighed. "It was a thought. Circle back to the Eightball and we'll talk about the next step. Neshenko wants to talk to Perkins."

"Copy that. I'm on my way."

Tires squealed and an engine roared.

Nineteen out of twenty pedestrians would have frozen in place and turned to see what was making the noise. They would have gone down like bowling pins. Erin, part of the other five percent, reflexively bolted for the nearest curb without even looking. Rolf easily matched her stride for stride.

Erin saw the oncoming car out of the corner of her eye, still accelerating. She caught a confused glimpse of a face behind the wheel, eyes invisible behind black sunglasses. It looked vaguely familiar, but there was no time to be sure. The car swerved, but it arced toward her instead of away.

She launched herself between a pair of parked cars, diving headlong like one of the New York Yankees sliding into home. Her toes cleared the front fender of the onrushing sedan with a coat of paint and a prayer to spare. Her phone tumbled through the air and skittered across the sidewalk, fetching up against the wall of the building across from the hospital. She landed and skidded on concrete, ripping the skin on her palms and tearing the hell out of the knees of her slacks.

Erin shunted the pain aside for later consideration. She dropped Rolf's leash and rolled to her right, putting a parked Chevy between her and the other car. She snatched out her Glock, came up on her skinned knees, and aimed the pistol over the hood of the Chevy, keeping the engine block between her and incoming fire.

She didn't have a target. No bullets came her way. The sedan was speeding off, laying rubber and fishtailing as the driver stomped on the gas. Erin didn't dare send rounds down a Manhattan street with civilians in her background, so she held her fire. She saw part of the license plate before it was too distant to make out.

Rolf stood stiff-legged and alert beside her, nostrils flaring. He had no idea what was going on, but he could see his partner had drawn her weapon and he could smell the excitement coming off her in waves. He watched her hopefully, waiting for the "bite" command.

He'd have to go on waiting. Erin shoved her pistol back into its holster. The stinging pain in her palm got her attention then, a prelude to the pains in her other hand, knees, and elbows. Blood streaked her from contact with the rough concrete of the sidewalk.

"Shit," she said, walking over to her phone and scooping it up. The phone's protective case had done its job. It had taken the fall better than she had.

"O'Reilly? O'Reilly? Talk to me!"

Webb's voice, increasingly agitated, emanated from the little black box.

"Here I am, sir," Erin said. "I'm okay."

"What just happened?"

"Someone tried to run me over."

"Manhattan drivers," Webb said in disgust. "They're worse than the folks in LA, and that's saying something."

"No," she said. "He actually tried to hit me. Brown Saab sedan. I got a partial plate. G-E-X. I didn't catch the numbers. He's headed east on East 28th toward FDR."

"Are you hurt?"

"Just a little road rash."

"I'll call it in. Maybe we'll have a unit in the right place to nail him." Webb hung up.

Erin looked down at Rolf, who wagged his tail. He still thought there was an outside possibility of biting, but it was looking less likely by the moment.

"What the hell was that all about?" she asked.

Rolf had no answers. He extended his snout, sniffed her leg, and gently licked her skinned knee.

*　*　*

"Don't," Erin said to Vic, pointing a finger as he opened his mouth. "Just don't."

"I was just wondering what the other guy looks like," he said, taking in her battered appearance.

"Are you okay?" Zofia asked.

"I'm fine," Erin said, but she went to the first-aid cabinet and got out the antiseptic and a handful of Band-Aids.

"I heard from Dispatch," Webb said. "Patrol units found the car just off FDR Drive, by the Bellevue Sobriety Garden."

"Let's hope the driver wasn't drunk," Vic said and snorted. "That'd be ironic."

"Any sign of the driver?" Erin asked.

"Long gone," Webb said. "They couldn't find any witnesses. Did you get a good look at him?"

Erin shrugged. "Male," she said. "White. Sunglasses."

"You're a crummy eyewitness," Vic said.

"I was a little busy at the time, trying not to get killed."

"Excuses, excuses. Hey, since a guy tried to run you down with a car, but missed, does that mean you have an autoimmune condition?"

Everyone looked at him.

"You know," he said. "Auto-immune... as in, you're immune to cars..."

"Tell you what Mr. Funny-bone," she said. "You go stand in the middle of the street. I'll borrow a car and try to run you down. Then we'll see how many details you pick up while you're diving for cover. I don't have eyes in my ass."

"CSU could probably pull DNA off the car," Zofia said.

"And we can match it to a perp in three or four months," Webb said sourly. "If we're lucky. You think it's worth pursuing, O'Reilly?"

"What about the car?" she asked.

"Reported stolen last night."

"Forget about it," she said. "Either it was some dumbass kid joyriding, or..."

"Or what?" Webb asked.

"Or it was a clumsy hit attempt on me," she said.

"That's kind of a big deal," Zofia said. "We should figure out who did it."

Erin shrugged again. "Lots of people try to kill me," she said. "Most of them do a better job than this asshole."

"Not much better," Vic said. "You're still alive, so none of these jerks really know what they're doing. If you had a really competent guy after you, wouldn't you be dead?"

"You're a real ray of sunshine," Erin said. "My point is, this didn't feel professional. Pros don't take a run at you in the middle of the street. They pull up alongside at a stoplight and blow your brains out. They use guns and bombs and sometimes knives."

"I don't like it," Webb said.

"You think I do?" Erin retorted. "But let's keep this in perspective."

"From my perspective, it's attempted murder of a police officer," Webb said. "That's a major felony. CSU is dusting the car for prints as we speak. If they get hair fibers, they'll get in the queue for DNA testing. And yes, it'll take forever, but we might still get a result before I retire. It won't stop you getting murdered, but it might help us catch the guy who did it."

"That's comforting," she said. "It's so nice to know you care."

"What makes you think this is about you?" Webb replied. "I care about my closure rate."

Erin finished bandaging her hands. "I'm going downstairs," she said. "To change into my spare clothes."

"Then we can go brace Moe Perkins," Vic said. "Maybe if we're lucky your mystery hit-and-run guy will make another try for you on the way and we can kick his ass. I haven't been in a high-speed chase in a while."

"Did you miss the part where he dumped the car?" Erin said. "What's he going to do, run me down with a bike? Or maybe a Segway?"

Vic chortled. "Now that I'd love to see. Then we could call him the Segway Slayer. I bet that's never happened before."

"Maybe not," Zofia said. "But the owner of the Segway company died when he drove his scooter off a cliff."

Vic stared at her. "You're shitting me."

"Jimi Heselden," Zofia said. "Back in 2010."

"She's right," Webb said. "I read about it when it happened. He was walking his dog, riding his Segway. He backed up to get out of the way of another dog walker and backed right off a cliff. Down he went. Not the best publicity, I have to say."

"This crazy friggin' world," Vic said. "I swear to God, you can't make this shit up."

"Did Micheal Shaw give you anything?" Erin asked, turning back to Webb.

"He insists he didn't kill Lobert," Webb said. "And he couldn't have killed Stone. He's glad Lobert's dead and told me he wished he'd done it. He says he hopes whoever's out there whacking punks keeps right on doing it. Too many punk-ass bitches in this city. That's a direct quote."

"The DA would love cross-examining this guy," Vic said.

"We can hold him," Webb said. "But if we don't get more evidence, it'll only result in the charges getting dropped in a week or two. He can't post bail on a murder charge; he's barely solvent. So we'd end up costing the city a lot of money for no good reason. We're turning him loose."

"Damn it," Vic growled. "This guy's a scumbag. He oughta be locked up."

"What do you base that assertion on?" Webb asked.

"His record, his attitude, and the way he smelled."

"You think body odor is a good enough reason to incarcerate someone?"

"He does," Vic said, cocking a thumb at Rolf.

"Leave my K-9 out of this," Erin said. "I'm getting changed, then I'm going to the courthouse. You coming?"

"Sure," Vic said. "Sounds like we'll have a holding cell empty and waiting, in case Moe Perkins turns out to be our guy."

*　*　*

Erin had run into lots of dangerous guys on the street. You could usually tell if a man was going to be trouble. You noticed build, posture, tattoos, and scars. But mostly you saw the look in his eyes and the way he paid attention to his environment. Truly dangerous men never lost track of where they were and who was around them. They were aware of all the exits and all the available weapons. And they had a look in their eyes that said they'd killed men and could do it again. Ian Thompson had that look. So did Vic. So did Jack McGraw. Erin had even seen it in her own eyes, staring back at her in the mirror.

Moe Perkins was a dangerous man in the Ian Thompson mold. He was quiet, competent, and perceptive. His hands and cheeks had the distinctive stretched, puckered skin of healed-over burns. His eyes were medium brown, thoughtful and calm, but they never stopped moving. He wore a pistol on his belt and his right hand was rarely more than a few inches from it.

Erin was distinctly aware that neither she nor Vic was carrying a firearm. They'd had to surrender their guns when they entered the courthouse. She wasn't overly worried, not with Rolf and Vic backing her up, but it was a balance of power she didn't appreciate.

They were meeting Perkins in a break room in the courthouse. He'd been guarded but polite, offering them coffee from the machine. Vic had refused, Erin had accepted. It wasn't the worst coffee she'd ever drunk, but it was probably in the bottom ten percent.

Now Perkins just stood with his back against the wall, waiting. He didn't even ask what they wanted. An experienced cop knew that in interviews or interrogations, the way you learned was by listening, not by talking.

"You used to be NYPD," Erin said.

"You still are," he replied.

"You were a decorated officer," she said.

"Still am."

"Why'd you quit the Force and come here?"

"Considering a change of career?" he asked with a hint of a smile.

"How do you like it?" she asked.

"Can't complain."

"How's the pay?"

"Same as everyone's."

"Meaning what?"

There was that hint of a smile again. "Could stand to be a little higher."

"You're having some financial difficulties," she said. "That doesn't seem right to me."

"Why?"

"You saved those kids from that fire. You put it all on the line. What they give us, it's not even enough to live in Manhattan these days."

Perkins shrugged. "Didn't join the Force to get rich. Could be pulling some six-figure private security gig."

Damn, Erin thought. She'd dangled one piece of bait and gotten nothing. Time to try another angle.

"The way I figure it, you're either like Vic here or you're like me," she said.

That got a reaction. Perkins looked curious and amused.

"How's that?" he asked.

"I'm an idealist," she said. "Vic's a street thug. No offense, Vic."

"Why would that offend me?" Vic replied.

"I try to make the world a better place," she explained. "Vic likes to make bad guys pay. So which are you?"

"Bit of both, I guess," Perkins said.

"Only you don't get to do either these days, do you," she said. "How often do you have to pull that sidearm of yours?"

"Well, there was one time last year, this gangster got garroted right in the middle of court," Perkins said. His amusement was more obvious now. "Everybody was hauling out their artillery. We didn't know what the hell was going on. Mob war, terrorism, God only knows. But I guess you'd know all about that, wouldn't you, Detective O'Reilly?"

"Hey, I was there too," Vic said. "Geez, it's like people don't even see me. And I'm not exactly incon-friggin'-spicuous."

"This gig would drive me nuts," Erin said. "I'd be climbing the walls inside a month. Seriously, Mo. Why'd you trade in your shield?"

Perkins stopped smiling. "Why do you want to know?" he asked.

Erin decided she wasn't going to get around this guy by being coy. He was too much of a cop, too canny to walk into an unintentional admission of guilt. She met his gaze steadily.

"Because we're trying to figure out what happened to Wendell Stone after he walked out of court," she said.

"That asshole?" Perkins replied. "From what I saw on the news, he went to the train station, got shoved in front of a train, and died like the little bitch he was. The reporter said it might be an accident, but I know it wasn't."

"How do you know that?" Erin asked, carefully keeping her voice calm.

"It was too perfect," he said. "It was karma, that's what it was. Sweet, sweet karma. He could weasel his way out of mankind's justice, but the universe was watching and it stepped in and kicked his ass for us. I gotta say, I stopped going to church when I was fourteen, but after that I think maybe I'm gonna start going again. You telling me you don't see the hand of God in this?"

"God doesn't deliver His justice with a blackjack," she said dryly.

"He uses the tools that're available," Perkins said. Then he blinked. "Stone got cold-cocked? Who did it?"

Erin kept looking at him. "We're going to figure that out," she said.

Perkins actually laughed. It sounded startled, but genuine. "Wow!" he exclaimed. "Seriously? I always used to think some shit like this was gonna happen to me. You know, one of those wrong place, wrong time bullshit setups like in those old movies. Those ones where the ordinary guy has some schmuck die in his arms, and now everyone thinks he's a spy or something? I love that Hitchcock shit. Sorry to disappoint you, Detective, but you're gonna have to look somewhere else. Sheesh, I wish I had the stones to beat the crap out of that entitled asshole, but you're right. I benched myself when I handed in my shield. I carry a gun, but I'm basically a civilian these days."

"And you still haven't answered my question," Erin said.

Perkins sobered up. "It's kind of personal," he said.

"Family problems?" Vic guessed. "Wife didn't like the bad hours and the danger? Trouble in the bedroom?"

"I've been divorced for the past five years," Perkins said, giving him a withering look. "Not that you didn't know that. You gold shields do your homework. You're just trying to get a rise out of me."

"Get spooked?" Vic pressed. "Did that fire get a little too hot for you, so you decided to get out of the kitchen?"

"Yeah," Perkins said. "But not like you think. You ever get a bad burn?"

"One time I bit into a toasted marshmallow that was a little too hot," Vic said evenly.

"The better you can help us understand, the more likely we are to leave you the hell alone," Erin said, trying to head off the metaphorical dick-measuring.

"I'm not sorry I went into that fire," Perkins said. "I don't give a damn about the burns, or the skin grafts. It hurt, sure, but whatever. That's the Job. What kept me up nights wasn't the pain. Don't you get it? I carried two kids out of that building, but there were four in that apartment."

"Oh," Vic said. He cleared his throat. "Shit. Sorry, buddy. I didn't know. I swear."

"That was in the file, too," Perkins said. "If you'd bothered to read to the end. I could only carry two. They were just too heavy. I tried to go back in, but the gas line went just as I was in the doorway. It was like a friggin' blast furnace. That's when I got these burns. I was off duty for three months, temporary disability, and lucky at that. Afterward, I tried, but I just couldn't do it anymore. I kept thinking about those kids, and I kept thinking I'd picked which ones lived and which ones died. I can't do that again. People talk about playing God like it's fun, but let me tell you, it friggin' *sucks*. It's bad enough I still carry a gun. If that makes me a coward, then I guess I'm a goddamn coward. You bastard."

Vic was looking very hard at his own feet. It wasn't often Erin saw him so sheepish.

"Do you have any idea who might've gone after Stone?" she asked Perkins. "Or Kamal Lobert?"

"Who?"

"Gang member. On trial for Murder Two. He was accused of hitting a bystander during a gunfight. Acquitted."

"Oh, yeah," Perkins said. "I remember him. Trip Sixes, right?"

"That's right."

"Hold it. Someone capped him, too? Was it the same guy who took Stone out?"

"You used to be a cop," she said. "You know we can't reveal details like that."

Perkins whistled. "Someone's doing the Lord's work, all right. Praise Jesus, hallelujah. I don't know who."

"Would you tell us if you did?" Vic asked, recovering a little.

It was Perkins's turn to be taken aback. "I don't..." he began.

"Yeah?" Erin prompted.

"I don't know," he said. "That's the truth."

Chapter 12

"I guess we'd better hit that Lefkowitz mope, as long as we're here," Vic said.

"You don't think he could be our guy?" Erin asked.

He shrugged. "Anything's possible. But a court recorder? The guy's basically an automatic typewriter. These other punks are gang members, former cops, legitimate tough guys. This'd be like finding out the Pillsbury Doughboy was a serial killer."

"Never trust anybody with a laugh like that," Erin said, straight-faced. "I never trusted that pudgy little bastard."

"You got a point," he said. "Let's talk to him."

"The Pillsbury Doughboy?"

"No, smartass. The stenographer."

They found Lefkowitz at his desk, banging away at his computer keyboard. He didn't rate an office of his own and was crammed into a cubicle in a room with half a dozen other stenos. He had a notepad next to him on the desk and was staring at it, not even looking at his screen or keyboard. His fingers were flying over the keys.

"Mr. Lefkowitz?" Erin said.

He didn't respond, continuing to type.

She cleared her throat and tried again. "Mr. Lefkowitz!"

He came to the end of a paragraph and stopped. He peered up at her with watery eyes, made enormous by the thick lenses of his spectacles. "I'm sorry," he said. "I don't like to stop in the middle. May I help you?"

"I'm Erin O'Reilly. We met once before, if you remember. Thanks for your help with my research."

"I hope it was useful," he said. "Did you find what you needed?"

"We're getting there," she said. "If you can step away from your work for a few minutes, we have some more questions."

Lefkowitz looked back at his notepad. "I need to convert my shorthand to a full transcript by the end of the day," he said. "But I want to be helpful. I can spare a little time."

They went to a vacant conference room. There was no coffee machine here, which Erin considered a blessing given the quality of the coffee she'd already sampled. Erin and Lefkowitz sat at the table. Rolf settled under it and Vic stood by the door, arms crossed.

"How long have you been working here, Mr. Lefkowitz?" Erin asked.

"Sixteen years," he said. Then he paused. "Five months, fourteen days, and approximately three hours."

"Thank you," she said.

"Or two hours, not counting the first-day orientation," Lefkowitz added. "But I suppose I did get paid for that time, so that counts."

"Um... yes, I suppose so," Erin said. "That's very... specific. How do you like the job?"

"I like to be precise," he said. "It's interesting work. And I'm performing a valuable service for the city."

"I guess you know a lot about how the legal system operates," she said.

"I didn't attend law school," Lefkowitz said. "I have a journalism degree from New York State University."

"Did you ever work as a journalist?"

"I wasn't able to find a job in the field," he said. "I did data entry for seven years for an accounting firm."

"Which one?"

"Neil McNaughton, in Brooklyn. I have an excellent reference."

"Seven years is a long time to do data entry," she said. "That'd drive me crazy."

"It was pleasant work," Lefkowitz said. "I found it calming."

"Do you get agitated or anxious easily?" she asked.

He took off his glasses, pulled a handkerchief from his pocket, and wiped the lenses. "I don't like conflict," he said. "I'm not a confrontational person. I'd rather work quietly and be left alone."

"Are you married, Mr. Lefkowitz?"

"No."

"Do you live with anyone?"

"No."

"Any pets?" Vic asked.

"I have a cat."

Vic shot Erin a look that said *I told you so*. She resisted the urge to stick her tongue out at him.

"Have you ever been the victim of a crime?" she asked.

"My credit card was compromised, eighteen months ago," he said. "I suffered damages totaling one hundred eighty-five dollars and thirteen cents before successfully canceling the card."

"What about violent crime?"

"I've never been personally victimized," he said.

"How about family members?"

"I understand my great-grandparents were physically assaulted in a pogrom before they emigrated to the United States."

"Anyone while you've been alive?"

"No. I have, however, seen a great many photographs and heard courtroom testimony regarding quite a few violent offenses."

"How do you feel about that?"

"It's unpleasant and unfortunate," he said. "I don't enjoy it. I try to concentrate on my work."

"What about criminals? Are you glad to see them get what's coming to them?"

"That's what the system is for," Lefkowitz said.

"Not always," she said. "Sometimes they get away with it."

"That's up to the jury," he said, fiddling with his glasses. "I'm not empowered to sit on a jury. I don't have the power to make those decisions. All I do is record what is said."

"It must be infuriating sometimes," Erin said. "Being so powerless. Don't you ever think about doing something about all the injustice you see?"

"I'm a very small man, Ms. O'Reilly," Lefkowitz said. "And it's a very large, very unfair world. What can I do? Now, I really have to get back to typing up my notes."

* * *

"Well, that was a waste of time," Vic said after Lefkowitz had gone back to his desk.

"Maybe," Erin said thoughtfully.

"What're you thinking?" he asked.

"I'm thinking he didn't ask why we were asking all those personal questions," she said. "He never asked if we suspected him of something. And he talked about feeling powerless. You've been a detective long enough to know, Vic. We don't expect people to tell the truth, but they sometimes tell us things between the lines. I think maybe we want to look a little closer at him."

"We'll never get a warrant to search his house," Vic said. "Not on that."

"You think I'm wrong?"

"You'd have to express an opinion for me to have an opinion on it. So far all you've said is you want to look."

"Okay, I'm a little suspicious of him. Do you think I should be?"

"Doesn't matter what I think. It matters what a judge thinks. And even Ferris is gonna get twitchy if we start filing for warrants on his own goddamn stenographer. So we better be sure before we move on something like that, and if we need evidence before we can be sure, that's one of those catch-22 things, isn't it?"

"Have you actually read *Catch-22*?" she asked.

"I tried once," he said. "But I got bored. For a war book, it didn't have nearly enough gunfights. Too much hanging around the airfield being bored and miserable. It was too much like being in an actual war. You really have a feeling about this schmuck? Because my feeling is he's a sad, dumpy little man with a shitty job and an even shittier life. And a cat, just like I expected."

"And you don't think a man like that that might want to work out his frustrations as a vigilante?" she replied.

Vic paused. "You know, that's actually a pretty good point," he admitted. "Maybe we ought to be looking at a guy who *doesn't* seem like a tough guy. They can't all be musclebound guys in spandex. Man, I don't even want to imagine Lefkowitz in spandex. Wearing that stuff is a privilege, not a right. You or I could rock the skintight look, but not him. Where's this schlub live?"

"Brooklyn," Erin said.

"Figures," he said. "Nothing good ever comes outta Brooklyn."

"Vic?"

"Yeah?"

"You're from Brooklyn."

"I rest my friggin' case. Should we go down there and poke around?"

"Yeah," Erin said. "I think we're about tapped out here. I'd like to see where Lefkowitz lives."

"It'll be a miserable shithole," he predicted.

"Yeah," she said again. "I think maybe it will."

*   *   *

Lefkowitz's apartment was old and a little run down, but hardly a shithole. Some of Erin's friends, growing up, had lived in worse places. It was a nondescript brick three-story building just across the river from Manhattan, flanked by a parking lot on one side and a tire dealership on the other. Erin saw a little graffiti, none of it tied to any major gang she recognized.

"What do you think?" she asked Vic.

He shrugged. "Pretty typical. What're we looking for?"

"Evidence."

Vic rolled his eyes. "That's like asking somebody what they do for a job and they answer, 'work.' Which unit's his?"

"211."

He snickered. "Too bad Webb isn't here."

"How come?"

"In the LAPD, a 211 is a code for a robbery in progress."

"Unless you've suddenly become an expert on California police jargon, I'm guessing you know that from..."

"...crime movies," he finished, grinning. "Of course."

"How come you watch so many of those? I mean, I like *Heat* as much as the next person, but you're living it. Do you ever want to watch something like, I don't know, *Pretty Woman?*"

"Nah," he said. "Too unrealistic. I've met hookers and they're not exactly Julia Roberts, if you know what I mean."

"Whereas your average Hollywood gunfight is perfectly realistic," she shot back. "Anyway, as I recall, you dated a Russian hooker for a couple of days. She was pretty hot."

"For the last time, I didn't know she was a hooker! Now can we solve this goddamn case, or do you want to pick apart my love life some more? You *knew* Carlyle was a mobster when you hooked up with him and you did it anyway."

"Are you ever going to like him?"

"No."

"He saved my life."

"Is that supposed to make me like him more or less?"

"He got our squad that espresso machine for the break room."

"I hate espresso."

"You hate everything."

"*Almost* everything."

"Zofia's been a good influence on you."

"Really? How?"

Erin smiled. "A year ago you wouldn't have qualified that. You just would've agreed with me and gone on hating the whole world."

He considered this. "Yeah," he said. "I guess so. Damn. I'm going soft."

"You're a regular teddy bear."

"I still hate lawyers."

"Of course you do. So do I."

"When lawyers die, they bury them ten feet deep instead of six. Know why?"

Erin didn't ask. She wouldn't give him the satisfaction.

"Because deep down, they're good people," Vic said.

Rolf gave Erin a look of long-suffering patience. They were in a chase, he was sure of it, and instead of running down the bad guys, the humans were doing that thing where they stood around yapping at one another. It was like being in a dog park full of beagles and chihuahuas. Rolf only barked when he had a really good reason. He had an excellent bark. It echoed in his deep chest. When Rolf barked, humans and dogs alike listened. Sometimes the bad guys would stop running just from the sound, which was one reason he preferred to move silently.

The two-legs finally finished their back-and-forth and walked to the building. Rolf snuffled at the corner as they passed it, identifying half a dozen dogs who'd recently left their mark on the bricks. The humans still weren't in a hurry, so he cocked a leg and added his own signature.

At the front door, he caught a whiff of the human they'd been talking to earlier. Rolf's nostrils flared and he inhaled with greater interest. They weren't following the man; they were going back the way he'd come. But Rolf, like his human counterparts, didn't believe in coincidence. He liked patterns and routines. He appreciated a world where things made sense. If Erin had asked him, he would have known their presence had something to do with Lefkowitz's smell.

This apartment definitely didn't rate a doorman. The lobby door didn't even have a buzzer. It opened when Vic pushed on it, admitting them to a hallway that smelled faintly of old, musty carpet.

"No security," he observed. "Any old punk could walk right in. Surprised they don't have squatters in the hallway."

Erin led the way up a flight of concrete stairs to the second floor. The doorframes and doors were old and worn, but reasonably solid. She could hear the faint sounds of a TV through one of the doors.

She paused outside unit 209 and looked more closely at it. Vic nearly piled into her.

"What gives?" he asked. "This isn't our boy's place. You want the one next door."

"Look at it," she said.

He peered at the door. "What about it?" he asked after a moment. "It's in better shape than any of the others. No signs of forced entry, no scratches around the lock. It's friggin' pristine."

"Exactly," she said. "This door's been replaced, along with the frame, fairly recently."

"So?"

"It's out of place."

"Not really. Something wears out or breaks, the landlord replaces it. That's what he's supposed to do."

"Vic, how many new pieces of woodwork have you seen in this building?"

He shrugged. "Only this one, I guess. I wasn't really looking."

"Yeah," Erin said. "I was looking and I swear this is the only new door we've passed."

"So the old one rotted out or broke. What's your point?"

"Intellectual curiosity."

"I think I heard of that once. I could've looked it up, but I got lazy."

Erin let it be for the moment and moved on to Lefkowitz's apartment. This door looked like all the others except 209. It was a little worn, a little chipped, but solid. It had a doorknocker and a peephole. She rapped the knocker sharply three times.

"Open up in there!" she called. "This is the NYPD!"

"What're you doing, Erin?" Vic asked. "The guy lives alone and he's at work. Who's gonna answer? The cat? They can't open doors, and it's a damn good thing they can't, or they would've taken over the world by now."

"We have his word he lives alone," she corrected him. "Someone could still be in there." She knocked again.

A deadbolt clicked back and a door opened, but it wasn't unit 211. It was 212, across the hall. A gray-haired woman poked her head into the hallway. She wore an old housecoat and, Erin saw with mild amusement, a pair of pink fuzzy slippers shaped like cats.

"Are you really the cops?" the woman demanded in the broadest Brooklyn accent Erin had heard in a while.

Erin dropped a hand to her waist, showing the gold shield at her belt. "Detective O'Reilly, ma'am," she said. "This is my partner, Detective Neshenko. NYPD Major Crimes. And you are...?"

"Susan Rawdon," the woman said. "My friends would call me Sue, if I still had any. Your partner's a big fellow, ain't he?"

"I eat right and work out a lot, ma'am," Vic said, blending lie and truth smoothly and shamelessly.

"If you're looking for Vern, he's at work," Susan said. "He works at the courthouse."

Thank God for nosy old female neighbors, Erin thought. "Do you know Mr. Lefkowitz well?" she asked.

"We don't hardly talk," Susan said. "I think I talk to my son more, and Benny, he don't hardly call no more. Not since he married that blonde *biologist* and moved to San Diego." She said the woman's occupation in exactly the same tone she would've used to say "porn star" or "pickpocket."

"But you do know some things about him," Erin pressed.

"I guess," Susan said. "But Amy was the only one in the building he really talked to, and she ain't here no more."

Erin exchanged glances with Vic. "Who's Amy?" they asked in near-perfect unison.

"Well, I don't like to gossip," Susan said, telling one of the all-time classic lies. "But if you wanna come in, we can talk."

"That'd be great, ma'am," Erin said.

"Your dog," Susan said. "He's trained, right? He don't pee on the carpet or nothing?"

"He's a police K-9," Erin said. Then, exaggerating only a little, "He's the best-trained dog in New York."

"And he's got no problem with cats?"

"None."

"Okay," Susan said. "I'm a cat person myself, but I guess it's all right. Come on in."

To say Susan Rawdon was a cat person was an understatement. She had paintings of cats on the walls, a set of collectible China plates with pictures of cats on them, and a pair of stuffed cats on her mantel. Not plush toys; actual cats that had received a taxidermist's attention. Erin didn't want to stare at them but found it hard to look away. They were uncanny, nearly lifelike but not quite. She'd seen the old horror movie *Pet Sematary* a long time ago, with some high school friends, and these cats reminded her of Churchill the zombie kitty. She was a little afraid they'd start moving.

"Sit down," Susan said, gesturing to the two-seat couch across from the mantel. It was floral pattern and smelled vaguely of old cigarettes. Erin and Vic gingerly sat and tried not to meet the glassy stare of Susan's former pets.

"I don't get many visitors," Susan continued, taking a pack of cigs out of a pocket and lighting one. "Not since Benny moved out and Charles passed."

"You said Benny was your son?" Erin asked.

"That's right," Susan said. "But you wouldn't know it. He couldn't wait to get out of here. He don't call, he don't write, he don't even use e-mail. And he could. I got a computer, had it for years. Charles was my husband. I always told him smoking would be the death of him, but he didn't listen. It was his heart, that's what the doctor said."

"Tell us about Amy," Erin said, deciding to head Susan off before she got too wrapped up in her own family history.

"Amy lived next door to Vern," Susan said, blowing a cloud of smoke toward the detectives. "Sweet girl, I always thought. She worked at the library. She had a nice smile, but a gap in her teeth and big eyeglasses. Brown hair. She coulda done something with her hair, and maybe got her teeth fixed and some contact lenses, or zap her eyes with that new laser treatment they do, and she woulda been pretty."

"Was she in 209?" Erin guessed.

"Yeah," Susan said. "She moved in a couple years ago. Me, I been here twenty years. I'll probably die here. They'll have to carry me out. I ain't gonna live nowhere else. I'm too old to move again. Seventy-three, and some days, I gotta tell you, I feel ninety. It's the damp. It gets into my joints. I got the arthritis real bad. The doctor, he gives me pills, but I swear they don't do nothing for me. They're some of those placebo things, you wanna know what I think."

"Amy?" Erin prompted gently.

"Amy Newman, that was her name," Susan said triumphantly. "Two years ago, that's when she came. I talked to her some, too. She liked talking to people, making friends. She'd just got a divorce and was going out on her own, you see, and she was feeling lonely. She specially liked people who didn't have many friends. She used to come over here and talk with me in the evenings, sometimes. She'd bring shortbread cookies, store-bought but good ones. In one of those red metal boxes, from Scotland or somewhere. Yeah, it was Scotland. I think they're the ones who invented shortbread."

"And she made friends with Mr. Lefkowitz—Vern, I mean?"

"Yeah, it was real sweet. He was way too old for her, of course. She was thirty-five, thirty-six, he's more like fifty."

"Yeah," Vic deadpanned, shooting Erin a look. Carlyle was almost exactly that much older than she was. "That's a big age gap. But you think there was a romance going on?"

"Vern thought so," Susan said. "I never saw him smile so much like he did when he saw her. His whole face would light up. He was real shy, of course, so he'd never ask her out, especially on account of her history."

"What history is that?" Erin asked. "Are you talking about her divorce?"

"Yeah. Her husband was a real piece of work. They'd lived in Pittsburgh. He was some kinda metalworker or something, and well, I don't wanna speak badly of nobody, but he was a jerk. He used to hit her and yell at her all the time. He didn't give her no money or nothing, but he wouldn't let her work neither. She just had to keep the house nice for him. Then one day she had enough and she left him."

"Good for her," Vic said.

"That's what I say," Susan said. "And if life was a Hallmark movie, that woulda been the end of it. But he came after her."

Erin felt a chill. She'd expected something like this, but wasn't enjoying being right. "What happened to Amy?" she asked.

"Her gorilla of a husband kicked the door in and beat her to death with a tire iron," Susan said. "Just beat her to a pulp. Horrible thing. From what I heard, she didn't hardly have a head once he got done with her. Poor Vern, it broke his heart."

"I'll bet," Erin said. "What did he do?"

"He got all closed in on himself," Susan said. "Didn't talk to nobody no more, didn't do nothing but go to work, poor man. Like he was sleepwalking or something."

"What about the husband?" Vic asked. "Did we get him?"

"The cops found him at a bar a couple days later," Susan said. "Dead drunk. They arrested him. It was in the papers."

"Let me guess," Erin said. "Acquitted?"

"Good guess," Susan said. "That just happened a couple months ago. People like to talk about reasonable doubt, but I don't think there was any doubt. The lawyers botched the case, that's what I think, and they can't try him again because of that double-jeopardy nonsense. Not that I'm bad-mouthing *Jeopardy*. I love that show, I don't ever miss it if I can help it."

"Do you remember the husband's name?" Erin asked.

"Earl, I think," Susan said. "I don't recollect his last name."

"Newman?" Vic guessed.

"Nah, Amy went back to her maiden name when she got free of him," Susan said.

Erin stood up. "Thanks for your time, Ms. Rawdon," she said. "We have to go now."

"Did Earl do something else?" Susan asked hopefully. "If he did, you better get him this time. Amy was a real nice girl. She didn't deserve what happened to her. Poor Vern, I'm surprised it didn't kill him too."

Susan had a great deal more to say, but none of it pertinent to their investigation, so Erin got herself, Vic, and Rolf out of the apartment with its creepy stuffed cats as fast as she politely could.

Chapter 13

"Look up the Newman case," Erin said as soon as they got back to the Charger.

"Way ahead of you," Vic said, sliding into the passenger seat and setting his fingers to work on the computer. "Let's see here. Amy Newman, age thirty-six, found murdered in her apartment. No witnesses. Forced entry, nothing stolen. Cause of death: massive blunt-force trauma to the skull. Weapon never found. ME figured it was a tire iron from the impact marks. Got some pictures here... yeah. You can see where it hit her. Jesus. You were right about the door. Landlord must've replaced it after the guy kicked it in. The Homicide boys caught this one. Your basic home-invasion murder doesn't rate Major Crimes involvement."

"What about the ex-husband?" Erin asked.

"Earl Blackwell," Vic said. "Homicide checked his car and found out he was missing the tire iron from his trunk, plus they got a guy at a bar to testify Blackwell had blood on him later that night. But since they didn't pick Earl up until two days after the murder, he'd cleaned up in the meantime."

"DNA or fibers?" Erin suggested.

"Nothing conclusive. Blackwell may have been a drunken, abusive asshole, but apparently he was smart enough to ditch the clothes he'd been wearing and give himself a good scrubbing. Dunno how he didn't get blood all over his car, but CSU says it was clean."

"That's assuming he was guilty," she said.

"Yeah," Vic said in a flat voice. "As opposed to his ex-wife, who ran away from his physical abuse, getting killed by some other random punk who just happened to use a weapon matching the tool that should've been in his trunk, on a day he happened to be down from Pittsburgh. One hell of a chain of goddamn coincidences, if you ask me."

"And he got acquitted," Erin said heavily. "I suppose without a confession or any physical evidence, what they had was circumstantial."

"Goddamn Homicide dicks," Vic said. "They couldn't detect their way out of a wet paper bag. At least it wasn't those losers from your old house, Lyons and what's-his-name."

"Spinelli," she said. "The Brooklyn boys did the best they could with what they had. Sounds like it was a tough case to prove. But that's not the important thing. Where's Blackwell now?"

"Pittsburgh, I assume."

"Want to bet?"

"Ten bucks says he's in Pittsburgh."

"You're on," Erin said, fishing a tenner out of her wallet and laying it on the dashboard. Vic paired it with one of his own and went back to the computer.

"You think our mild-mannered court recorder offed him before he left town, don't you," he said as he typed.

"That's exactly what I think," she said. "I'd be surprised if he made it to the state line."

"Nope. Leastways, if he did, he covered his tracks so well they never found the body. Or it wasn't in any shape to be ID'd. I don't see an Earl Blackwell turning up dead anywhere in the Five Boroughs. Let me take a look at Pittsburgh now."

Erin waited. This took a little longer. The NYPD had access to police reports all over the country, but Vic had to get into another database. She reached across Vic to the glove compartment, retrieved a Milk Bone, and gave it to Rolf, who contentedly devoured it. Then she gave the dog a nice, long ear rub, which made his eyes go squinty and his mouth hang open in a happy pant.

"Aha," Vic said a few minutes later. "This is from our friends in the Pennsylvania State Patrol. Earl Blackwell, forty-one, of Pittsburgh, Pennsylvania, was found floating face down in the Monongahela River."

"When?" Erin asked.

"April 15th," he said. "Tax day. I hope he remembered to file. The IRS will come after you if you don't, dead or alive."

"How did he die?"

"The coroner ruled it accidental death," Vic said dryly. "But you could make a case for suicide, on account of his blood-alcohol level being through the friggin' roof and him falling in a river. Point-three-eight, if you can believe it."

Erin whistled. "I've never pulled over a DUI that high," she said. "I'm surprised he was able to make it to the river. That much booze in the blood can kill you even if you don't take a dive."

"Or if your skull isn't cracked," he added.

"His was?"

"Yeah. Just a sec, these autopsy reports are a bitch. We're lucky we have Levine. I can actually read her handwriting. Why didn't somebody type this up instead of scanning the doc's goddamn chicken-scratch? Okay, here we are, I think I got it.

The deceased suffered a depressed-skull fracture, likely from striking a rock or other piece of debris. Jesus Christ, it looks like the coroner's the one who was drinking. Levine would never fall for this bullshit."

"Was there an autopsy?"

"Yeah. Like I said, they ruled it accidental."

"Get on the horn with the Pennsylvania Staties. Ask them to send the autopsy report to Dr. Levine ASAP. I want her opinion."

"We don't have jurisdiction. Hell, this didn't even happen in our state."

"I know my geography, Vic. Speaking of which..."

Erin scooped the ten-dollar bills off the dash.

"Hey!" Vic said. "Those are mine!"

"How do you figure? You said Blackwell was in Pittsburgh. If the State Patrol scooped him out of the water, that means the body was outside city limits."

"Look at the friggin' map," Vic retorted, calling it up on the computer screen and tilting it toward her. "The Monongahela runs straight through Pittsburgh. They found Blackwell at the river bend here, by Whitaker. That's less than a mile outside Pittsburgh, and the first bridge upstream is Homestead Grays, here. That's in Pittsburgh. That's where he fell in, guaranteed. Gimme my twenty bucks."

"Fine," Erin said, handing over the bills. "You win. But I still think Lefkowitz killed him."

"That wasn't the bet," he said, pocketing the money. "You gotta be specific and pay attention to details. Hey, you ever hear that Dixie Chicks song?"

She stared at him in disbelief. "*You* know the Dixie Chicks? Isn't that a little off-brand?"

"Back in high school I was trying to score with a girl who was into them," he said. *Goodbye Earl*, that's the song. Real catchy. It's about this girl who gets beat up by her ex, so she and this other girl get together—"

"I know the song," Erin said. "Earl had to die, huh?"

"You're damn right," Vic said. "You know, the closer we get to nailing this vigilante, the worse I feel about doing it. Earl Blackwell was a real piece of shit."

"So was Wendell Stone," she replied. "And I assume Kamal Lobert probably was, too. But murder is murder. Cops don't get to decide which crimes are okay and which ones aren't."

"Bullshit," he said. "We make those decisions all the time. Take speed limits. Everybody speeds. *Everybody*. But Patrol cops don't pull everyone over. We use our discretion. Five over the limit? No biggie, let it slide. Ten over? Depends on the situation, and on whether they're being a jerk about it. But twenty? Then we nail their ass. And suppose we've got a homeless bum panhandling on the corner. Do we really haul all of them in for vagrancy? Or do we let them move on and live their lives, if you can call it living?"

"We're not talking about speeding, Vic," Erin said. "Or vagrancy. Three people are dead. Maybe more."

"More," he said grimly. "Amy Newman, for one. And LaRayne Shaw. And let's not forget Sarah Devers in that hotel fishtank. I still have nightmares about her."

"Really?"

He nodded. "Yeah. In the dreams, she opens her eyes and they're pure black. You know, on account of eightball hemorrhages. And she looks at me and I feel like I'm in there with her. I can't breathe. I'm drowning. Then I wake up gasping. It sucks."

"You ever talk to anyone about that?" Erin asked.

"I'm talking to you about it right now."

"I meant a professional. Doc Evans at the Eightball is okay. I've talked to him."

"I don't need a goddamn shrink," he said angrily. "What I need is to catch a bad guy. I mean a *real* bad guy."

"It looks like Lefkowitz is our guy," she said. "And we have to bring him in. Can you do that?"

"Yeah," he sighed. "I just feel like *I'm* the bad guy for doing it."

"We're not in a comic book," she reminded him. "Remember how mad you were at Ian when you said he was playing vigilante?"

"Yeah," he repeated. "Tell you what. If Levine says Blackwell got murdered, I'm convinced. Oh, shit."

"What?"

"If Lefkowitz really did whack Blackwell, that means he's on a multi-state killing spree. You know what that means."

Erin closed her eyes. "The FBI," she said.

"That's right. The goddamn Feebies. So let's get this thing put to bed before they hear about it. Remember who they sent last time we had a multiple murderer?"

"Don't remind me. None of us liked that jerk."

"I punched him in the face."

"No, you didn't."

"I'm pretty sure I did. And I enjoyed it."

"I was there," Erin said with slow emphasis. "I saw Agent Rockwell slip and fall. So did Zofia and so did you. And that's what I'll tell anyone who asks."

Vic grinned. "Oh, right," he said, winking. "I forgot."

* * *

"We've got our guy," Erin announced to the Major Crimes office by way of greeting.

"Excellent!" Webb said, standing up. "Which one is it?"

"Lefkowitz," she said. "The stenographer."

"The pudgy guy with the glasses?" Zofia asked. "You're kidding. He looks about as dangerous as my Uncle Frank."

"Is your Uncle Frank a serial killer?" Vic asked.

Zofia wrinkled her nose at him. "He's a sweet old man. Back when I was a kid, he always used to smuggle me candy when he came to visit."

"I could tell you stories about sweet old men giving candy to little girls," Vic said.

"Uncle Frank isn't a pervert!" she snapped.

"Uncle Frank also isn't our killer," Webb said. "But Vernon Lefkowitz is? How do you figure?"

Erin laid out what they knew. The others listened attentively, including Rolf, who didn't understand but figured his partner knew what she was talking about. She usually did. Even when she was talking nonsense, you never knew when that treasured "bite" command might come out of her mouth, so it was best to pay close attention and be ready.

"It's a compelling theory," Webb said when she'd finished. "But a little thin. You know what we need?"

"Evidence?" Erin suggested.

"Evidence," he said.

"We're having the Pennsylvania boys send the autopsy on Earl Blackwell to Dr. Levine," Erin said.

"She probably won't find anything," Webb said. "Sounds like the body was a floater that was in the water a while before it got scooped out. Most of the evidence would've been washed away."

"This is Levine we're talking about," Erin said.

"Hmm, good point," Webb said. "I suppose if anyone can find anything useful, she's the one. If she can tie Blackwell's death to the other two, that should be enough to get a warrant on Lefkowitz. I hope so, because otherwise this is a hundred percent circumstantial. It makes a good story, but that won't be enough to convince a jury."

"It'll be pretty ironic if we arrest this guy and he gets acquitted at trial," Vic said. "Do you think he'd feel compelled to beat his own head in if that happened?"

"Let's not find out," Webb said. "On the subject of catch-and-release, we're letting Micheal Shaw go. There's no reason to hold him. The DA was already planning to drop the charges. I just hope he won't sue the city."

"He's still a punk," Vic said. "I bet he'll be back in prison within six months. Ten bucks. Anybody?"

"That's my ten bucks he's risking," Erin said.

"*Was* your ten bucks," Vic replied.

He found no takers. Everyone in the room knew that most gang members were repeat offenders who usually found their way back behind bars, no matter how good their intentions between convictions.

"Now, as far as the mystery man who tried to kill you outside the hospital, O'Reilly," Webb said.

"What about him, sir?" Erin replied.

"Was it Lefkowitz?"

"Not a chance. He was working at the courthouse when it happened. I guarantee their security cameras will give him an alibi. Anyway, I don't think he'd want to kill me. He only goes after people he thinks are perps."

"Then who was it?"

"I didn't get a good look at him," she said. "There was some glare on the windshield and he was wearing sunglasses. He was a white guy, smaller than Vic."

"That narrows it down to ninety-eight percent of Caucasians," Webb said dryly. "Hair?"

"Dark."

"And you're sure you didn't recognize him?"

Erin paused. "I thought for a second, maybe..." she began.

"Who?" Webb pressed.

"It could've been Richard O'Malley," she said slowly.

"Could've been?" Webb asked. "Or was?"

She shook her head. "I might be imagining it. I couldn't put it at better than fifty-fifty."

"You sure?" Vic asked. "Because if we could put that weaselly little mope in jail, it'd make all of us feel a lot better."

"Me, too," Erin said. "But I can't lie about an ID."

"Of course not," Webb said. "And we wouldn't ask you to. But the O'Malley kid certainly has plenty of reasons to want you dead."

"Yeah," Vic said. "I'm just surprised he'd have the balls to go for you himself. The only reason he's not locked up with his old man is that he was never into anything heavy with the O'Malleys. Nobody trusted him to do wetwork, or even any of the serious moneymaking crap they were up to."

"Evan never wanted his kid involved," Erin said. "He was considering putting Richie in charge of the drug trade, but that was only right at the end, and only because he was running short of associates."

"And we moved on the gang before the kid got his promotion," Webb said. "So little Richard stayed clean. But he had to watch his dad and all his friends get locked up. Not to mention having his trust fund frozen, along with all the other O'Malley assets. Does he have *any* money at all?"

"Not much," Erin said. "And he doesn't have muscle, either."

"He threatened you at your engagement party," Vic said, remembering. "He walked right in there and threatened you to your face, in front of a roomful of cops. I should've kicked his scrawny ass then and there."

"Do you really think he tried to kill you?" Webb asked Erin, narrowing his eyes.

She shrugged. "Maybe. But if the car isn't registered to him, and he didn't leave prints, we'll never prove it."

"Not without compelling eyewitness testimony," Vic said.

"And I told you, I'm not going to lie about that!" Erin snapped.

"Not even to save your life?" Vic shot back.

"Neshenko, that's enough!"

Webb's angry voice split the air like a pistol shot. Everyone else froze.

"This is a police station," Webb went on angrily. "And you're a sworn officer of the law. If I ever hear you encourage anyone to commit perjury again, even as a joke, I'll have your shield. Is that clear?"

"That wasn't what I meant," Vic said sulkily.

"We all know damn well what you meant," Webb said. "Remember Andrew Keane? Remember what happens when cops start thinking the law doesn't apply to them? Not in my squad. Not in the Eightball. *Never again.*"

"Yes, sir," Vic muttered.

"What was that?" Webb demanded.

"Yes, sir," Vic said louder. Erin and Zofia joined in.

"Good," Webb said. "As a favor to everyone here, I'm going to pretend the last two minutes didn't happen. Now, just to be on the safe side, let's keep an eye on Richard O'Malley. If he does step out of line, I want to know about it. Then we'll come down on him so hard he'll think a skyscraper landed on his head. But until then, it's business as usual. In pursuit of which, O'Reilly, I'd like you to go downstairs and talk to our resident vampire. Let her know to expect the Blackwell autopsy."

"Copy that, sir," Erin said. After the way Webb had just cut Vic off at the knees, she was only too glad to get out of the office again, even if it meant a trip down to the morgue.

Chapter 14

Sarah Levine probably wasn't a vampire. Erin figured the odds to be about ninety-eight percent against it. However, that theory would explain a lot of things. Nobody could remember seeing Levine sleep. She spent most of her time underground, in the company of the dead. Her complexion was very pale. Erin couldn't recall having seen her eat, either. And she reacted to social cues like someone who'd read a book about being human but hadn't quite internalized how to do it. If she wasn't a vampire, she might possibly be some sort of space alien.

Levine was at her computer when Erin entered the morgue. The Medical Examiner was in the middle of typing up a report. She took no notice of Erin's arrival, nor Rolf's.

Erin cleared her throat. The K-9 wrinkled his muzzle and snorted to clear the formaldehyde stench out of his nostrils.

"This year's influenza vaccination efficacy is estimated at approximately forty percent," Levine said without turning. "It's still worthwhile to receive the vaccine, as it can diminish symptoms. However, we're nearing the end of the flu season, so you'll want to balance the costs and benefits."

"I don't have the flu," Erin said.

"Common cold, then?" Levine guessed.

"No, I was just trying to get your attention."

"Words would be more efficient and effective. Why are you here?"

"Did you get a report forwarded from a coroner in Pennsylvania?"

"Yes."

"Have you had a chance to look at it?"

"Yes."

"Really?" Erin was surprised. "It must have arrived just a few minutes ago."

"Correct," Levine said. "Approximately eleven minutes."

"What do you think about it?"

"I haven't examined it."

"But you said..."

"I said I'd had the chance," Levine said. "I haven't chosen to read it yet. I was in the middle of this report when it arrived. I am still in the middle of this report, and will continue to be as long as I am interrupted."

"Sorry, Doc," Erin said. "But I need to know your opinion of the autopsy as quickly as possible."

Levine immediately saved her document and closed it. She opened her e-mail and went to the autopsy. A series of scanned image files came up on her monitor. Levine's eyes moved rapidly from side to side, taking in the data.

"Please let me know as soon as you have a conclusion," Erin said. "This is important."

Levine, engrossed in her studies, didn't answer.

After a moment, Erin shrugged and flicked Rolf's leash. *"Fuss,"* she told him. He pivoted and took up position at her hip, walking beside her as she pushed open the morgue's door.

"This was a homicide," Levine said.

Erin pulled up short. "Really?" she said, hurrying back into the room. "How do you know?"

Levine pointed to a photograph of the back of Earl Blackwell's head. "Depressed-skull fracture," she said. "This impact was premortem, as indicated by the bruising pattern on and around it. If the fracture had resulted from striking a rock or other solid structure, it would have either a linear pattern, if he had struck the edge; an eggshell fracture, if the skull had struck a roughly flat surface; or it would show a single impact, if it had struck a jagged outcropping. Instead, it shows a similar semi-rigid pattern to that of Kamal Lobert's body."

"Similar?" Erin said. "Or identical?"

"No two impacts are identical," Levine said. "However, this wound was inflicted by a very similar weapon, most likely a pouch or bag of small metallic spheres."

"Ball bearings," Erin said.

"This victim drowned," Levine continued, pointing to the coroner's report. "However, the blow to the back of the head would have severely disrupted both consciousness and brainstem functionality. In all likelihood he was unconscious, and probably paralyzed, when he entered the water. He involuntarily inhaled water with fatal results."

"So somebody smacked him on the back of the head and he fell in the river?"

"That is my initial conclusion. However, my definitive answer will require a lengthier examination."

"Of course," Erin said. "Take your time on that."

"As opposed to whose?" Levine replied. "I am only taking your time as long as you choose to spend it here."

"I'll just be on my way, then," Erin said.

* * *

"I admit, I did not anticipate the pleasure of your company again so soon," Judge Ferris said.

"We need a search warrant, your Honor," Erin said.

"And an arrest warrant," Webb added.

"I will be glad to review your requests," the Judge said. "And I will expedite them. But I do not entirely understand. Were you in the neighborhood? You normally file these requests in writing. There was no need to come in person. Unless, of course, you wish to bend your departmental rules and have a taste of my white lightning. That offer is always open."

He patted the desk drawer where he kept a jar of his personal moonshine.

"Thank you, but no," Webb said with visible regret. "This business is best conducted sober."

Ferris's eyes narrowed slightly. The old man leaned forward, focusing all his attention on the detectives. "I feel you are about to make an unusual request," he said. "Perhaps an awkward or delicate one. Who is the subject of these warrants?"

"One of the court's employees," Erin said. "A stenographer, Vernon Lefkowitz."

There was a momentary pause. Ferris cocked his head, reminding Erin very much of the way Rolf tilted his head when confused. All the Judge needed, she thought, was a gigantic pair of ears. The man studied them for five seconds, which stretched into ten.

"I see," Ferris finally said. "You appear entirely serious."

"This isn't a joke, your Honor," Webb said. "We have reason to believe Mr. Lefkowitz has murdered at least three individuals: Wendell Stone at Grand Central Station, Kamal Lobert outside his tattoo parlor, and Earl Blackwell in Pittsburgh back in April."

"You lack jurisdiction for a murder committed in Pennsylvania," Ferris observed.

"We know, your Honor," Webb said. "And that death will need to be reclassified as a homicide. We will be communicating with the appropriate authorities regarding it. In the meantime, we're requesting arrest warrants for the other two."

"Your probable cause?" Ferris asked.

"Lefkowitz was a harmless guy," Erin said. "Shy, polite, kept to himself. A little guy. He lived alone. No wife, no family, just a cat. And he was okay with that. One day a woman moved in next door. Her name was Amy Newman. She'd come from Pittsburgh to start a new life, away from her abusive ex-husband. She was a friendly woman, outgoing, cheerful; all the things Lefkowitz wished he was. She gradually befriended him and drew him out of his shell over the next couple of years.

"I don't know whether he fell in love with her, or just valued her as a friend. It doesn't matter which. He was several years older, a lot shyer, and didn't really think of himself as boyfriend material. They never went out, never hooked up. But she lit up his life, right up until her ex-husband Earl broke into her apartment and beat her to death with a tire iron."

"Allegedly," Webb interjected.

"Right," Erin said. "Allegedly. Earl was arrested and put on trial, but the case relied on circumstantial evidence. No physical evidence, no eyewitnesses. The jury didn't think there was enough to convict him, so Earl went free. Lefkowitz had been brokenhearted by Amy's death, but Earl getting away with it was the last straw. He'd been sad; now he was angry.

"Lefkowitz's job put him in courtrooms every day. He'd had plenty of chances to see how the system worked—and how it failed. I think frustration had been building up in him for years as he saw injustices being done, day after day, month after month. But Amy was different. She'd been personally important to him.

"I don't know whether he intended to kill Earl when he tracked him to Pittsburgh, but he went there with a blackjack and a whole lot of rage. Earl never saw it coming. Lefkowitz might be an angry vigilante, but he was stuck in the body of a pudgy middle-aged clerk. He knew better than to give Earl a chance. He crushed the guy's head from behind and dropped him into the river."

"Allegedly," Webb said again.

"Allegedly," Erin agreed. "Then Lefkowitz came back to New York and went back to his quiet life. But something had changed. He'd found a larger purpose. He started paying closer attention in court. The next time he came across a case in which a young woman had been killed, and her killer went free, he took action. He had access to the court documents that told where he lived, his relatives, his routine. The legal system had already done his reconnaissance for him. He followed his targets and bludgeoned him from behind. He liked it, so he did it again.

"Vernon Lefkowitz thinks he's doing the right thing. He believes it's his job to punish these guys when the courts fail. And he's going to keep doing it until we stop him."

Ferris settled back in his leather swivel chair and nodded slowly.

"I begin to understand how you felt when you discovered corrupt members within your own organization," he said. "We always like to think our own people are above reproach. And I can certainly sympathize with this man's motives, but not his methods. How certain are you of the truth of these allegations?"

"We know Blackwell was murdered," Erin said. "Dr. Levine is completing her examination of his autopsy as we speak, but she was convinced in a matter of moments. And we know he was killed the same way as the other two. We have a witness who established the connection between Blackwell's ex-wife and Lefkowitz, so we have a firm motive for that first killing."

"Is that all?" Ferris asked.

"We know he was the court recorder in both other trials," Zofia said. When Ferris turned his attention to her, she flinched slightly. She wasn't used to speaking so directly to judges.

"And?" Ferris said, not unkindly.

"He was familiar with their case details, your Honor," she said. "We've verified from security footage that he left the courthouse just after Mr. Stone was released. We have an image of him exiting the building, wearing a coat and hat that match those of the suspect who was in position to assault Stone on the platform at Grand Central about an hour later."

Webb nodded approvingly at Zofia. She was the one who'd picked out the image from the courthouse cameras just before they'd called on the Judge. Vic grinned at her and turned his body so Ferris wouldn't see the unprofessional but enthusiastic thumbs-up he flashed in her direction.

Ferris nodded again. "Very well," he said. "What items are you seeking with your search warrant?"

"The blackjack," Vic said. "He's using a black sock full of ball bearings, so we're gonna grab all his black socks and check them for blood, hair, and fibers. If we find one full of metal, that's a bonus. He likes to leave a calling card, so we'll be looking for incomplete decks of cards. Bicycles, red-backed."

"We also want his coat and hat," Erin added. "For comparison with security footage from the train station. And we'll be checking his clothes for blood spatter from any of the victims."

"And, of course, any courthouse materials pertaining to any of the victims," Webb said. "He may have made copies of court documents and brought them home."

"You have the forms, I presume?" Ferris asked.

Webb slid the papers across the Judge's desk. Ferris picked them up and examined them. Thirty years as a judge, Erin thought; the man knew better than to sign anything he hadn't read, even from people he trusted.

Ferris picked up his pen. It was an impressive pen; hefty and solid, with what looked to Erin like genuine gold accents. Ferris's signature had a flourish as impressive as John Hancock's. His signature looked like it carried the full weight of the law.

"There," Ferris said. "Julia will make copies. I should thank you, ladies and gentlemen, for bringing this to me and allowing me to participate in the cleansing of the judiciary. But I fear at the moment, I find the entire subject depressing."

"I'm sorry, your Honor," Erin said.

He waved a dismissive hand. "Not your fault, Miss O'Reilly. Merely the maunderings of an old man. A slight depression of the spirits is nothing that cannot be elevated by the proper application of more uplifting spirits."

Translation, Erin thought: *I need a freaking drink.*

Webb stood up. "We'll leave you to it, your Honor. Thank you for your time."

Ferris, ever the old-school gentleman, insisted on shaking hands with each of them before they left. He actually bowed his head and lightly kissed the backs of Erin and Zofia's hands, to Zofia's consternation.

"I didn't know they still had guys like that," she said to Erin in an undertone as they left the Judge's office.

"He's one of a kind," Erin replied. "I love that old guy."

"Me too," Vic said. "One of these days I'm gonna kiss *his* hand, just to see what he does."

"He'll throw you in jail," Webb said. "Contempt of court."

"It'd be worth it," Vic said.

Chapter 15

"I really don't think we need these glory boys," Vic said.

"I heard that," ESU Officer Parker growled.

"You were supposed to," Vic replied.

Half a dozen Emergency Services Unit officers were stacked up in the hallway outside Lefkowitz's apartment. They were clad in full tactical gear, complete with helmets and riot shields. The men carried enough firepower to storm Omaha Beach. Seeing all that hardware, Vic hadn't even bothered with his own rifle, opting for his sidearm. Webb's little .38 revolver looked pathetic.

"If we'd been a little quicker, we could've scooped him up at the courthouse," Vic went on. "No muss, no fuss. It would've been easy. It's not like we're hunting bin Laden or the Unabomber. But the little weasel took off early, so now we've gotta go through all this hassle."

"I don't think he had your convenience in mind," Webb said.

"Everyone shut up," Lieutenant Lewis said in a low voice. "We're going now."

The tactical team was standing against the wall just to the left of the door. They'd make entry first, followed by the detectives. Lewis nodded to Parker, who was toting a sledgehammer.

The big man was polite, Erin thought. He always knocked when serving a warrant. But he knocked hard, and he only did it once.

The door flew open in an expanding cloud of splinters and sawdust. Parker took a step to one side as two other ESU guys, Carnes and Hopper, sprang into the room, assault rifles tight against their shoulders.

"NYPD!" they shouted. "Hands! Show me your hands!"

"I miss flashbangs," Vic muttered. The NYPD hadn't been allowed to use those ever since one too many accidental deaths from the supposedly non-lethal devices. He, Zofia, and Rolf were stewing impatiently while ESU flowed into Apartment 211. Webb waited more philosophically.

Erin thought the whole thing was stupid. Lefkowitz wasn't going to go down in some last-ditch, blaze-of-glory gunfight. As far as anyone knew, he didn't even own a gun. Any one of the Major Crimes detectives probably could've made a solo arrest with less drama and property damage. But Lefkowitz was also a suspected multiple murderer and Webb had been adamant. They weren't going to cut corners or take chances.

Fifteen seconds of shouting and tightly-controlled chaos followed. ESU knew their business, clearing room after room, keeping the initiative, moving fast. Vic clearly wanted to follow them in, but Webb held his people back. They'd just get in the way.

"One in custody!" Hopper called from the bedroom.

"Clear!" several other men yelled in response as they checked the rest of the apartment and sounded off.

Webb holstered his revolver. Vic grudgingly put away his Sig-Sauer. Erin had already returned her Glock to its usual resting place. They went in, Rolf tugging eagerly at the leash.

"*Fuss*," Erin murmured to him. The K-9 subsided, disappointed, to his customary place at her hip. There'd been no chase and no biting, which meant no rubber Kong ball either. And things had looked so promising a moment before. He still wagged, but it was a low, sulky motion.

They found Lefkowitz in his bedroom, face down on the mattress. His hands were cuffed behind him. Hopper knelt next to the prone man, keeping one hand between his shoulder blades to control him in case he tried anything silly.

"Going somewhere, Mr. Lefkowitz?" Webb asked, nodding to an open suitcase that lay beside him, partially packed.

"I suppose not," Lefkowitz said in muffled tones. His head was planted in the middle of his pillow.

"Help him up," Webb said to Hopper. "Let's go to the living room."

The ESU man marched the prisoner out and deposited him in his threadbare armchair. Hopper and Parker flanked the chair, making sure to keep their guns well out of Lefkowitz's reach. Webb pulled in a wooden chair from the small dining area and sat down opposite Lefkowitz. Erin got another dining chair and took her place next to Webb. The others were already searching the apartment for the evidence they knew they'd need.

"You know why we're here, Vern," Webb said. He spoke calmly, quietly.

Lefkowitz said nothing.

"We know about Amy Newman," Erin said. "And we know about Earl Blackwell."

"And Wendell Stone," Webb said. "And Kamal Lobert."

"We know what you did," Erin said. "And we know why. God knows, we understand. Hell, I've killed bad guys in the line of duty. It had to be done."

Her heart twinged a little as she said it. Try as she might, she just couldn't quite convince herself this hapless little stenographer was a true villain. It was all too easy to empathize with him. The easiest way to fake rapport was not to fake it.

"Am I under arrest?" Lefkowitz asked softly.

"Yes," Webb said.

"On what charge?"

"Two counts of murder."

"Two?" He seemed perplexed.

"You'll be extradited to Pennsylvania for the third one," Webb explained. "After the state of New York is done with you and the Pennsylvania boys reclassify Blackwell's death correctly. Of course, since you crossed state lines, you might be tried in Federal court instead. And you'd better hope not."

"Why not?" Lefkowitz asked. He blinked his watery eyes. Hopper had knocked off his glasses when the ESU man had tackled him, but Parker had retrieved them and balanced them back on his face. The frames had gotten bent in the brief struggle, giving him an off-kilter look.

"Because New York doesn't have the death penalty," Webb said with calculated brutality. "But the Feds do."

"You don't deserve to die for what you did, Vern," Erin said, leaning into her "good cop" persona. "And we don't want you to. We just need you to tell us what happened. So we can understand."

Lefkowitz was silent.

Zofia whistled sharply. She held up a pack of playing cards in one gloved hand. She opened the box and spread the cards on the dining table. "Jacks are missing," she reported. "Spades and clubs. I have a couple more decks here, too. Looks like they've been opened."

"Still nothing to say for yourself?" Webb asked.

Lefkowitz blinked at him and shifted, trying to find a more comfortable position for his wrists.

"Black jacks missing from this deck, too," Zofia said.

"I found one of them," Vic said from the front closet. He came into the living room with a trench coat in one hand and a jack of clubs in the other. "This was in a pocket. Want to guess what's in the other pocket?"

"A sock full of ball bearings?" Webb guessed.

"Give the man a cigarette," Vic said. "He could use one."

"You don't understand," Lefkowitz said.

"I want to," Erin said, leaning forward to catch his eye. "Tell me."

"Amy was so *nice*," Lefkowitz said. His eyes were filling up, swimming with unshed tears. "She was the nicest woman I've ever met. She'd never hurt anybody. Even Judy liked her."

"Judy?" Erin didn't understand.

"Judge Judy," Lefkowitz said. "She's a blue Persian. She's probably hiding under the bed ever since you knocked the door down. She doesn't like loud noises."

"You named your cat Judge Judy?" Vic said incredulously.

"Not the point, Neshenko," Webb said without bothering to look at him.

"I guess it makes sense," Vic added. "Cats are grouchy and judgmental, too."

"Shut up, Neshenko."

"Amy sounds wonderful," Erin said, pretending Vic hadn't spoken. "I'm glad you got the chance to know her."

"That man, that... *thing* tried to break her," Lefkowitz said. "He tried to stamp the light out of her eyes, but he couldn't. She had the most beautiful spirit. She never gave up hope. She got away from him and left him behind. But he followed her. And when he couldn't break her spirit, he broke her body. I saw what he did to her. I was in that courtroom. I saw the photos. I heard the lawyers. He was guilty! And he got away with it!"

"That must've hurt," Erin murmured.

"I thought I'd go crazy," Lefkowitz said. Tears were rolling down his cheeks now. "Maybe I did go a little crazy. I was just so *angry*. Nothing I did made it go away. It was this hot ball in my belly. I felt it all the time, day and night. I couldn't stand him walking around like nothing had happened, not after what he'd done. I didn't really plan anything. I just couldn't stop thinking about him. So I took a Greyhound to Pittsburgh."

"How did you know where to find him?" Erin asked.

"Court documents," Lefkowitz said. "He had a criminal record, of course. He'd committed assault six times that they knew of. But they didn't know all the times he beat Amy, because she never went to the police. And everyone just let him keep hurting more people. He never served more than a week or two in jail.

"I followed him to a bar and watched him get drunk. He drank so much he could hardly walk straight. The bartender wouldn't give him his keys. He got mad. He wouldn't wait for a taxi. When he walked out alone, I knew God was giving me my chance."

Lefkowitz's eyes were distant now, recalling. "It was easier than I expected," he said. "He was such a big, strong man, I thought maybe he'd kill me. But he fell over so easily."

"Did you put a playing card on him?" Erin asked.

"I was going to," Lefkowitz said. "I had it with me, in my pocket. But he fell over the bridge railing. So I and dropped the card in after him. It floated a little while. Then it sank. Just like him."

"Why the jacks?" Erin asked.

"I wanted people to know," Lefkowitz said. "That it wasn't random. That he was getting what he deserved. The jacks in a deck of cards represent knights, you know. The jack of clubs is Sir Lancelot in the French tradition. The jack of spades is Sir Ogier, one of Charlemagne's Peers. They fought for justice."

"A calling card," Erin said. "You saw yourself as a knight?"

"There's an old idea," Lefkowitz said. "Courtly love. From the Middle Ages. A knight was expected to do brave deeds for the lady he loved, without any reward for himself. He might never attain the lady. She might even be married to another man. It's a pure, holy love. It's not filthy or selfish. That's what makes it noble."

"So you were already planning to do it again?" Webb asked.

"I wasn't sure," Lefkowitz said. "Not until it was over. I'd been having nightmares, terrible dreams, ever since what happened to Amy. That night, at the hotel in Pittsburgh, I slept better than I had in months."

"How did you pick your next target?" Erin asked.

"He was another evil man," Lefkowitz said, and the calm certainty in his voice gave Erin a little shiver. "A gang member who'd killed an innocent girl out of sheer recklessness. I wouldn't have done it if he'd gotten what he deserved in court. But the jury let him go. They didn't care about LaRayne! But I did."

"You were Amy's champion," Erin said. "And LaRayne's."

He nodded. "Don't you understand now? Haven't you ever wanted to do something really brave? Something noble?"

"Yeah," Erin said. "That's one of the reasons I became a cop."

"You used your courtroom access to choose your victims?" Webb pressed.

"They weren't victims!" Lefkowitz said with a flare of sudden anger. "They were criminals! Perpetrators! Killers!"

"Wendell Stone, too?" Erin asked.

"You should know," Lefkowitz said. "You're the one who arrested him. If you'd done it right, I wouldn't have had to clean up your mistake."

"You little piece of shit," Vic growled, taking a step toward him. "Don't you dare put that on us."

Zofia put a hand on his arm and shook her head. He reluctantly subsided, quietly fuming.

"You were doing the Lord's work," Erin said. "Avenging innocent women who'd been killed."

"That's right," Lefkowitz said.

"You're being very forthright about this," Webb said.

"Why not?" the little man replied. "You have everything you need. Plenty of evidence. And I'm not ashamed. I'm proud of what I did. If more people dared, the evil men would be afraid of us."

"Where were you planning on going?" Webb asked.

"I knew you were suspicious," Lefkowitz said to Erin. "When you came to the courthouse today. I didn't think I had much time. I was going to take care of one more piece of business on my way out of town, but I thought after that I'd go to another state, another city. I'd find a way to keep doing my good work."

"What piece of business was that?" Erin asked.

"Arlen Ulrich," Lefkowitz said coolly. "He raped and murdered his own niece. One of your detectives was too eager to get an indictment. He falsified evidence and the case was dismissed. Fruit of the poisoned tree, the judge called it. Mr. Ulrich lives in the Bronx. For the moment."

"We'll look into Mr. Ulrich," Webb said. "That's a promise. I think we have everything we need for now. Mr. Lefkowitz, we'll need you to come downtown with us, obviously. You know how this works, I think."

"What was I supposed to do?" Lefkowitz asked as Parker took hold of his upper arm and hoisted him to his feet. "I couldn't let it go."

Webb didn't answer. Neither did Erin.

"Hey, buddy?" Vic said as the officers steered their suspect toward the door. "Can I ask you a question?"

"I've answered all your questions so far," Lefkowitz said. "What else do you want to know?"

"Your name," Vic said. "What is it, Polish?"

"Yiddish," Lefkowitz said. "My family came over from Romania in the 1930s because of persecution."

"Oh." Vic was clearly disappointed.

"Why on Earth did you want to know that?" Erin asked in an undertone, after Lefkowitz had been led away.

"I remembered the old Street Narcotics tradition," Vic said. "Remember Firelli and Logan? Wopstat and Mickstat?"

"Oh, right," Erin said. "If they arrested an Italian perp, Firelli had to buy the first round of drinks. If they got an Irishman, Logan was buying."

"I just figured, since we've got a Polack on the team..." Vic said, grinning at Zofia.

"Well, you're out of luck," Zofia replied. "Because he's not Polish. You can pay for your own damn liquor."

"Can I ask a favor, please?" Lefkowitz asked from the hallway.

"What is it?" Webb asked.

"Judge Judy," Lefkowitz said. "She doesn't have anyone to take care of her. I'd hate to think of her going into the system. She's used to being pampered. She's really very sweet, once you get to know her. If you could find someone to look after her, I'd be very grateful. She's innocent and shouldn't have to suffer."

Erin thought of Susan Rawdon across the hall, with her cat slippers and weird taxidermy. "I think I know just the person," she said.

Chapter 16

"We could've gone to the Barley Corner," Erin said.

"You're only saying that because you drink for free there," Vic said.

"Well, yeah," Erin said. "So?"

"But then you'd miss out on our charming company," Sergeant Logan said. "Not to mention the ambience."

"Ambience," Vic said. "I know that one. It's French for 'bad smell,' right?"

"Har har," Zofia said. "Listen to the funny man, making the funny jokes."

The Major Crimes squad had, at Zofia's suggestion, headed to the Final Countdown at the end of their shift. She'd made a couple of calls and her old team, the Street Narcotics Enforcement Unit from Precinct 5, had met them there. It was the end of the day for Major Crimes, but SNEU was just getting started. They'd be working all night.

Erin was fond of the Narcotics guys. There was Roberto Firelli, Bobby the Blade, the street punk turned straight-arrow cop, with his dorky mustache; little Marek Landa, the pint-sized Hungarian; and lean, street-smart Paul Logan. They were Zofia's other family and welcomed her back as such, which meant lots of good-natured insults and trash talk.

"You guys really shouldn't be drinking at the start of your shift," Webb said.

"We don't go on the clock for an hour and a half," Logan said. "And we're having a beer each. It won't even register on a breathalyzer by the time we start running vertical patrols."

"Me, I'm just glad I'm allowed to drink again," Zofia said. "Pregnancy sucks, guys."

"Thanks for the warning," Landa said. "I'll make sure to never get pregnant."

"Sandy agrees with you," Firelli said to Zofia.

She nodded. "See? The women know what's up. You dumbass guys don't have the first—wait a second! What did you say?"

Firelli was beaming. "I said, Sandy agrees. She's been throwing up a lot, but the doc says that should stop before long."

"Oh my God!" Zofia exclaimed, flinging her arms around the startled Firelli and giving him a big hug. "Congratulations! How far along is she?"

"Thirteen weeks," Firelli said. "Everything's going good so far."

"This calls for a celebration," Zofia announced.

"We're already drinking," Vic said.

"Then we're drinking more," Zofia said.

"I guess one more won't kill us," Logan said. "But that's the limit, guys. I want clear heads by the time we're streetside."

"This round's on me," Zofia said. "Even though the guy we caught was Romanian, not Polish."

"Eastern Europe," Vic said. "It's all the same."

"Hey!" Landa said indignantly. "Hungary and Poland are totally different. So is Romania."

"What's everyone drinking?" Zofia asked.

"Stoli," Vic said.

"Jim Beam," Webb said.

"Whiskey," Erin said. "Jameson, I guess." The Final Countdown didn't stock Glen D.

"I'll have a Bud Lite," Firelli said.

"This is a bar," Zofia said. "If you're not drinking alcohol, you should leave."

"There's alcohol in it!" he protested.

"If I spit in a glass after drinking vodka, it'll have alcohol in it," Vic said. "But that doesn't mean I'm gonna drink it and call it beer."

"I'll have a Heineken," Logan said.

"Me, too," Landa said.

"I'm glad we have something to celebrate," Erin said while they waited for Zofia to come back with the drinks.

"What are you talking about?" Webb replied. "We already had plenty. We closed two homicides, not even counting the out-of-state one."

"I don't feel too good about it," she said.

"Because Lefkowitz thinks he's one of the good guys?" Webb asked.

"I guess."

"O'Reilly, the 9/11 hijackers thought they were the good guys, too," the Lieutenant said gently.

"I know," she said. "It's just... Wendell Stone was guilty, damn it all! We know that for a fact. And if Lefkowitz hadn't nailed him, he would've gotten away clean!"

"From the perspective of the legal system, he did get away clean," Webb said. "Lefkowitz wasn't acting in an official capacity. He was committing murder. Don't ever forget that."

"I know," Erin repeated. "That's my point. The system failed."

"In our legal system, the burden of proof is on the prosecution," he reminded her. "That means guilty guys sometimes walk."

"Some innocent guys still get locked up," Firelli added. "We don't like to think so, but it happens. Especially minorities and guys with records. Just think how much worse it'd be if the DA didn't have to live up to a high standard. Which scares you more? A murderer on the loose, or knowing the Federal stormtroopers might kick down your door when you haven't done a damn thing to deserve it?"

"It's broken," Erin muttered. "The whole thing. All of it. That's why Lefkowitz snapped."

"Not all of it," Webb said. "Look around you."

"I can't see anything," she said. "This place should really get some brighter lights. Those fixtures can't be up to code."

"The dim light is part of the ambience," Logan said.

"There's that word again," Vic said.

"I'm serious," Webb said. "Look at the people at this table. What do you see?"

"A whole lot of ugly SOBs," Erin said, earning a good-natured laugh.

"She's not wrong," Vic said.

"I see one hell of a bunch of men and women," Webb said. "You know what they say about the Five's SNEU squad?"

"They say we can't be bought," Firelli said with quiet pride. "They say we're a hundred percent legit, straight as they come."

"Exactly," Webb said. "I see the best goddamn cops in New York. You go out there every day, rain or shine, snow or sleet, and you get the Job done. You're on the street enforcing the law. It's a thankless job that wears you down. I know it and you know it. We see bad guys getting away with things and good people getting hurt. But you keep showing up, and without you, this crummy world would be a whole lot crummier."

"Hear, hear!" someone said from the next table.

The voice was familiar. Erin turned, the hairs on the back of her neck prickling. She saw a skinny man with dark, slightly unkempt hair. His eyes were bloodshot. He didn't look like he'd been sleeping well.

"Richie," she said quietly, fighting the urge to reach for her Glock. "Richie O'Malley."

Richie began a slow, sarcastic clap. "That's right, boys and girls," he said. "Let's hear it for New York's Finest, the NYPD! The very best of the best, pure and fucking spotless! That's right! What a fine bunch of folks! They'll never kill, lie, or steal; just ask them. They'll tell you to trust them and then they'll stab you in the back the second you look away."

"Who is this punk?" Logan asked Erin. "A drunken idiot, or do we need to do something about him?"

Vic was already on his feet. "Forget about him," he said. "He's leaving, and if he does it before I get to his table, he's using the door. Otherwise he's going through the friggin' window."

Richie grinned. "I'd love to see you do it," he said. "A big thug like you chucking an unarmed man through plate glass. I bet that'd play real well on the ten o'clock news."

"Leave him, Vic," Erin said. "He's drunk."

"And you're a treacherous bitch who'd screw anybody to get what you want," Richie said. "But in the morning all I'll have is a hangover. You'll still be you. For a little while, at least."

"What the hell are you talking about?" she snapped. But Richie was already on his feet, walking toward the back of the room.

"I oughta kick his ass," Vic growled.

"He's not worth it," Erin said. "He's headed for the restrooms, probably to puke his lousy guts out."

"I'm wondering what he's doing here," Webb said quietly. "It strains coincidence that he'd just happen to be in this bar at the same time as the woman he hates. He's stalking you, O'Reilly."

"Yeah," she said, thinking back to the half-glimpsed sight of the driver of the car that had tried to smear her across the pavement. It could have been Richard O'Malley, but it also could have been any of a hundred other guys. She just wasn't sure. It would be so easy to point the finger at him and throw him behind bars, but what would that say about her?

"We gotta deal with this guy," Vic said. "He tried to kill you, for Christ's sake!"

"We don't know that," Erin said. "Not for sure."

"So he goes off to do it again? Just like that?!"

"And there's our legal system in a nutshell," Webb said dryly. "The part that *is* broken."

Zofia came back to the table, accompanied by a waitress. "What'd I miss?" she asked brightly.

"Your boyfriend wanted to start a bar fight," Erin said.

"That's not true," Vic said. "It wouldn't have been a fight. A fight implies there would've been two guys hitting each other. He wouldn't have got a single shot in on me. I would've left his friggin' teeth all over the floor. We're talking soup and milkshakes for the rest of his damn life. Speaking of which, what in God's name are you drinking? It smells like Pine-Sol. That lemon-scented crap you clean the floor with. I can smell it from here."

"This?" Zofia held up a glass with a dark amber liquid. "I asked the bartender what he recommended. It's Scotch, Kahlua, orange liqueur, and lemon juice. A little sweet, a little sour. Just like me. Don't change the subject. Who were you fighting with?"

"Evan O'Malley's brat," Vic said. "He tried to kill Erin, and now Erin doesn't want me to beat some manners into him."

"For the last time, Vic, we can't just go hitting people if we don't like them," Erin said. "He's my problem and I'll deal with him. And in the meantime, I'll keep checking under my car."

"You'd better," Vic said. "If he kills you, I'll crack open your casket at the funeral and kill you again."

"You wouldn't," Erin said.

"I'd be in my dress blues," he said. "Wearing gloves. I wouldn't leave prints. They'd never prove it was me."

Zofia passed out the other drinks. They toasted Firelli, Firelli's wife, and their soon-to-be baby. The mood lightened a little, but Webb caught Erin's eye.

"You need to take this more seriously," he said quietly. "If he's following you around, I don't think he's just trying to intimidate you."

"Good," she said. "Because intimidation won't work. I'm not scared of him."

"Maybe you should be," Webb said. "Richard hates you. He holds you personally responsible for throwing his father in jail and wiping out his inheritance."

"That's because I *did* throw his father in jail and wipe out his inheritance. But that's on Evan, not on me."

"You really think you can convince Richard of that? You think just because he's a screwup, he's not dangerous."

Erin shrugged. "I've handled worse guys than him plenty of times."

"Vinnie the Oil Man might have said the same thing about some punk kid named Alfredo Madonna. Remember how that turned out?"

"It's fine, sir," Erin insisted. "Vinnie was an arrogant bastard who got careless. I've got this."

Webb nodded doubtfully, but he didn't say anything else.

*   *   *

Erin left the Final Countdown an hour later, sober enough to drive—and to have Rolf check the Charger for bombs, just as she'd promised Vic. Richard O'Malley hadn't come out of the bathroom by the time they left. He really must have been smashed, Erin thought.

Rolf sniffed the undercarriage and wheel wells happily enough; it was all just a game to him. He found nothing, so Erin loaded him up and headed for home. It was a little after eight and the sun was just going down. The Manhattan skyscrapers cast their concrete canyons into deep shadow.

Erin was trying to sort through her thoughts. She knew, on a fundamental level, that it was okay by her for Vic to punch an incompetent, egomaniacal FBI agent, but it wasn't okay for Lefkowitz to knock off a couple of scumbags. Both were a form of street justice, so why was one acceptable and the other wasn't?

"Is it because Vic's my friend?" she asked Rolf. "Or is it because he's a cop? Or something else? Am I just a damn hypocrite?"

Rolf cracked his jaws in an enormous yawn.

"You're right," she told him. "I'm overthinking this. We've had too long a day to waste the rest of it on philosophy. Vic wasn't going to kill Agent Rockwell, no matter how big an asshole he was. Rockwell, not Vic. Vic's an asshole too, I know that. You know what I mean."

Rolf didn't, but he kept listening anyway.

"But we have to deal with that O'Malley brat," she went on. "Because Webb's got him pegged. Maybe I should bite the bullet and fat-finger his mugshot for the car thing. I could, you know. I'm pretty good at lying these days."

Just saying it out loud made her feel dirty. She recalled another night behind the wheel of her car, months ago, contemplating ending a mobster's life. She hadn't done it, but the way she'd been planning it had shaken her right down to her soul. That was the night Erin O'Reilly had found out she was capable of murder.

"I can't," she said to Rolf. "Because if I do, then I really am just the same as Vern. I was frustrated that we couldn't get Vinnie the Oil Man the right way, so I wanted to get him the wrong way. And you know what? I could've done it. Hell, maybe I should've. How many people died because of him, before Alfie Madonna did what I wouldn't?"

Rolf yawned again and blinked sleepily. He really did want to pay attention, but Erin was losing him. She hadn't used a single one of his command words, and she didn't sound excited or angry. He decided she was just doing that human thing again, making pointless sounds. He lay down in his compartment and rested his chin on his paws, but kept looking at her. He liked looking at Erin. It felt good, no matter what she was doing.

"Damn it," Erin said quietly. It was a problem without a good solution. She thought of Lefkowitz saying, "What was I supposed to do?" She didn't have an answer for him, either. So she drove the rest of the way home in silent thought.

"We can't save the whole world," she said at last, as she turned into the parking garage opposite the Barley Corner. "Dad always used to say that when he'd had a rough day on the Job. We just have to deal with what comes our way, one thing at a time. I'm not responsible for anybody's soul but my own, so I better take care of it."

She nodded to the guy on the gate, recognizing him as Stephen Denver, one of Ken Mason's people. Mason was running security at the Corner, now that Ian Thompson was working for FDNY. Mason wasn't a match for Ian—practically nobody was—but he was a solid, dependable former Marine, and employed guys like himself. Denver had come home from Iraq with a Bronze Star and Purple Heart, minus his right foot and two fingers on his left hand, courtesy of an IED. The prosthetic foot slowed him down a little, but didn't keep him from working a quiet security gig.

Denver returned the nod and worked the gate. She drove through and took the ramp up to the second floor.

"But I hope Richie steps out of line soon," she added. "So we can put him away. Webb's right. Maybe the kid's an incompetent ass, but a loser with nothing to lose is a dangerous guy. Here's what we'll do. First thing tomorrow, I'll get a file running on him and—"

The car came in from the side. Its headlights were dark and it was gray, the same color as the concrete. She had less than a second's warning before it T-boned her. There was no chance to get out of the way, or even to brace for impact.

The Charger lurched to the side, slamming against a support column with a crash of metal that sounded like an explosion. Erin's head was flung against the door, enveloped by the side-curtain airbag as it deployed. Rolf was tossed like a fluffy ragdoll, doing a half-somersault and smacking into the window with a startled yelp. The compartment's glass shattered. One of the back doors popped open, the latch broken on impact.

Five seconds might have passed, or thirty, or more. Erin had no idea. Her thoughts had gone mushy and confused. She fumbled at her seatbelt, her thumb finally finding the release, but the buckle didn't disengage. The mechanism was jammed. Crumpled metal pressed in on her from the side, pinning her legs. She tasted blood in her mouth. Her lip and cheek were puffy. Had she bitten them? She couldn't remember.

"Rolf," she mumbled, trying to turn her head. The airbag was in the way and her neck was killing her. The compartment was empty. Where was her dog?

She pawed at the airbag. It had been punctured by debris and air was whistling out of a dozen holes, but it was taking time to flatten out. Front airbags automatically deflated, but most side ones stayed inflated to protect passengers if a car rolled over. In this case, the feature was an impediment. She wrestled it partially out of her way. Her window was gone, obliterated. Little pebbles of safety glass were scattered like glittering confetti.

The other car was still there, nose jammed against the Charger's flank. It had crushed the door panel in on Erin. The driver's door of the car swung open. A man got out and began walking toward her. He had something in his hand; she dimly recognized it as a claw hammer.

"I did tell you about the lock on the service door," Black Jack McGraw said with an apologetic smile. "This is just a job. Nothing personal."

Chapter 17

"Wait," Erin said thickly, speaking through rapidly-swelling lips. "Just hold on a second."

She reached for her Glock. The gun wasn't easily accessible. Her car seat had been forced out of position by the impact and her body was awkwardly twisted. The door panel was pressing her legs sideways. She got hold of the pistol grip but couldn't clear the holster.

"Ah ah," McGraw said, shaking his head. He hooked the hammer's claw around the remnants of the airbag and yanked it to one side. "None of that, ma'am. Don't worry, this'll be over quick. I don't get off on pain. This is just an unpleasant job, nothing more. Hold still. One good tap and we're done."

He reversed the hammer and brought it back in a short, sharp arc, aimed at Erin's temple.

Somehow, operating on instinct and reflex, Erin's left hand jerked up into the way of the blow. The steel hammerhead hit her forearm with an awful shock of metal against bone. Sudden, incredible pain flashed up her arm like an exploding firecracker. She gave a choking cry. Her vision went dark for a moment from sheer sensory overload.

"Sorry," McGraw said with bizarre tenderness in his voice. "I told you to hold still. Quit making it hard on yourself. I can make the pain stop."

Erin knew another swing was coming. She ducked and leaned away, writhing in the seat, trying to free herself, or at least to get her gun out. The second hammer-blow caught her in the meat of her upper arm, just below the shoulder. Her whole arm was on fire now. She let go of the Glock's handle, grabbed at the hammer with her right hand, and curled her fingers around the head.

McGraw yanked it free. He was too strong. She didn't have any leverage. She put up her good hand to try to block the next stroke, wondering through a haze of pain and confusion what she could possibly do. Who could help her? Denver was downstairs, too far away. Rolf had been ejected from the car and might be dead or unconscious.

"*Fass!*" she yelled as loudly as she could.

"Shh," McGraw said. He nimbly knocked her hand aside with the hammer's claw and jabbed the top of the hammer into her face. Steel smashed against her cheek and her head snapped back against the headrest. A starburst exploded behind her left eye. She felt oddly disconnected from herself, dimly aware she was about to black out.

"You just don't quit," he said, sounding genuinely impressed. His voice seemed to come from much farther away, as if he was talking down a deep hole. "I really do feel bad about this. I think if the cards had been dealt different, we maybe could've been friends. Oh well, you know how it goes. Sometimes you just get a bad hand and you bust. It's okay. Shush now. Lights out, honey."

Erin screamed at herself to move, to keep fighting, but it was so hard to concentrate. There was a wet, meaty crunch, very close. Was it the sound of her own skull cracking? She hadn't felt anything hit her. They said you didn't hear the bullet that killed you. Maybe it was the same way with blunt force. Maybe this was it; she was dead.

Something landed on the hood of the Charger with a soft, heavy impact. Erin's vision was blurred by pain and tears, but she saw a pair of figures intertwined. Then they slid off the hood, down out of her field of view. She couldn't see McGraw anymore. Someone was growling. It was a feral, wild, savage sound, utterly out of place in a Manhattan parking garage.

"Ma'am? Ma'am!"

A man was running toward her, awkwardly, with a weird hitch in his step. Erin swiped at her streaming eyes with her right hand and blinked rapidly. The running blur resolved into Stephen Denver. He was coming as fast as his artificial foot would allow.

She waved weakly. "In here," she said. "Watch out! He's armed!"

Denver pulled up short, whipping out his sidearm and wrapping his other hand around the butt of the pistol. He was aiming at something out of Erin's field of view. He approached more cautiously. Then he stopped and relaxed.

"It's okay, ma'am," he said. "He's down."

"Down?" she repeated dully.

"Affirmative," Denver said. "Your dog got him."

"Rolf?" Erin's heart leaped. "Is he okay?"

"He's got blood all over him," Denver reported. "But he's still in the fight. Stay still, ma'am. I'll call 911."

"What about McGraw?" she asked.

"The guy on the ground?"

"Yeah."

"He's out," Denver said. "Think maybe he's dead. Dog has him by the back of the neck. Doesn't look like letting go, either."

"First aid kit," Erin said, gesturing toward the passenger side. "Glove compartment. Take care of Rolf first."

"Will do, ma'am," Denver said. He holstered his gun. "Don't worry. Reinforcements are on the way."

* * *

The NYPD's response time for south Manhattan was less than five minutes, but Carlyle arrived before the first patrol car showed up. Denver had already called his boss from his security booth, the moment he'd heard the crash upstairs. That was standard military and police protocol; before investigating, always let the higher-ups know something was happening. By the time the cops arrived, Denver was doing first aid on Rolf, Ken Mason was providing perimeter security, and Carlyle was tending to Erin as well as he could.

"I'm fine, really," she kept insisting. Now that the initial shock and fear had worn off, she was mostly sore and pissed off.

"Your dog's saying much the same," Carlyle said. "The two of you deserve one another. Good Christ, darling. Can't you even park your car without running afoul of some villain?"

"I told you to check the service door," she said.

Carlyle flinched like she'd slapped him. "I put in the work order," he said. "Through a couple of Corky's union lads. They scheduled it for next Monday. I'm sorry. Had I known that bastard would be back, I'd have found a way to rush the job."

"It's not your fault," she said. "Just get me out of here."

"Sorry, ma'am," one of the Patrolmen said. "The way this door is jammed, we'll need the Jaws to get you out. We're waiting on FDNY. They should be here any minute."

"Good thing I'm not claustrophobic," she muttered, which wasn't entirely true. Being trapped in a half-crushed car was making her frantic to get loose. It was taking a lot of her self-control to hold still and keep her voice calm.

"You'll have a grand shiner in the morning," Carlyle said, gently touching her cheek where McGraw's hammer had hit her. "How's the rest of you?"

"I told you, I'm fine. I don't think the arm's broken, but I'm going to have bruises like nobody's business. How's Rolf?"

"I think he's okay," Denver said. At Erin's command, Rolf had let go of McGraw and consented to lie down for the former Marine to tend him. But the Shepherd hadn't fully trusted him until Erin had somehow managed to extract his rubber ball from her pocket. Now Rolf lay happily on his side, chomping the hard black rubber while Denver carefully probed his bloodstained fur.

"A little more detail?" Erin suggested.

"Glass cuts, mostly," Denver said. "Did he really get chucked through the window?"

"The window's reinforced," she said. ".There's no way his body could've broken through on its own. The release catch popped when we took that hit. He got launched through the door. He's lucky he didn't hit anything hard."

"Missed the column by an inch or two," Denver confirmed. "I didn't see the crash, of course. Came as fast as I could. I caught the last couple seconds of the fight when I came up the ramp. Rolf came around the back of the other car and took the Tango from behind. Got his teeth around the back of his neck and *crunch.* Nailed the guy, one bite."

"This man's spine is broken," another Patrolman said. He was kneeling beside McGraw's body. "No pulse. Jesus. Can a dog's teeth really do that?"

"Rolf's can," Erin said with weary pride.

"What I can't figure is how he got his car in without me seeing it," Denver said. "I'm real sorry, boss. No excuse. I've got a little stuff in the back office. I can grab it and be out of your way, or I can finish out the shift if you want."

"Don't talk nonsense, lad," Carlyle said. "You're not sacked. He didn't sneak an automobile into the garage. He crept in on foot and used one that was already here."

"Not yours!" Erin gasped. Carlyle loved his Mercedes.

"Nay, darling," he said with a dry chuckle. "I go about in a top-of-the-line luxury sedan. It's said to be entirely theft-proof. Look a wee bit closer at the vehicle that struck you. I'm afraid you've been the instrument of destruction of Mr. Mason's transportation."

"Really?" Erin looked at Mason, who was surveying the scene with arms crossed.

"Affirmative, ma'am," Mason said. His expression was completely neutral.

"Shit, I'm sorry," she said.

"What for?" he replied. "He hit you. Wasn't your fault. It's not the first ride I've had totaled. Lost a couple Humvees in the Sandbox. One IED, one collision. Took a hit from a five-ton six-by-six just outside Baghdad. Army idiot blew through a blind intersection and took me out. This Accord was a piece of crap anyway. Folks gave it to me when I got back, on account of my dad getting a new CRV. I think it was a '95. Maybe a '96."

"That explains it," the first Patrolman said. "Those older sedans are easy to hotwire. I know a couple kids in my old neighborhood that could have this boy running in under a minute, and that's if you remembered to lock your doors."

Sirens and a deep-throated horn blast heralded the arrival of an FDNY fire engine and an ambulance. The ambulance parked a short distance from the crash and disgorged a couple of EMTs. The fire truck was too big to make it up the tight ramp to the second level of the garage, so its crew left it on the street and jogged up carrying their rescue gear.

"You boys can clear out," the FDNY Lieutenant said to the uniformed cops. "The grownups are here to take over."

"Late, as usual," one of the Patrolmen said. "Good thing there wasn't a fire. It would've taken out half the block by now."

One of the firemen was studying what was left of Erin's car. "Halligan's no good, sir," he reported. "We need a cutter."

"Probie!" the Lieutenant called. "Get the Jaws up!"

The youngest fireman immediately began setting up a hydraulic pump which was connected to a combination cutter/spreader. He moved with quick, calm competence, but not quite quickly enough for his commander's taste.

"Sometime this week, Thompson!" the Lieutenant barked.

"Ready, sir," the probie said.

"Ian!" Erin exclaimed.

The other firemen laughed. "We got us a damsel-in-distress scenario, boys!" one called. "They know each other! Love is in the air!"

"Better make sure that blonde babe doesn't find out about her!" another advised. "She's already way out of your league."

Ian Thompson ignored the ribbing. "You good?" he asked Erin.

"I'll be fine as soon as you get me the hell out of here," she said.

"Don't move," he said. "You might have spinal damage. Won't be a problem. Have you out in a minute."

The engine crew rolled the wrecked Accord away from the Charger and got to work. One of the more experienced firefighters did the cutting. The powerful hydraulic shears easily snipped through the doorframe on either side of Erin. They cut the whole door off and tossed it aside. Two more men laid out a backboard with a C-collar.

"Oh, no," Erin said. "Not that. There's nothing wrong with my spine."

"This isn't up for discussion, ma'am," the Lieutenant said. "You've been in a violent automobile accident. None of us know how badly you might be hurt, including you. Until we get you checked out at the hospital, we're not taking chances. If you start jumping around, you might end up permanently paralyzed, or even dead."

"God damn it," Erin muttered. But she let them carefully disentangle her from the wreckage and lay her out on the board.

Rolf got up, still holding his rubber ball, and padded over to her. He snuffled at her face and wagged his tail.

"Good boy," she told him. "*Sei brav*, kiddo."

He wagged harder.

"We'll get her to Bellevue," the head EMT said.

"I need to call my commander," Erin said.

"He'll already know about it," a Patrolman said. "I'll let Dispatch know your status and where you're going."

"I can ride along," Denver offered.

"Are you a family member?" the EMT asked.

"I'm security," Denver said.

"Then no," the medic said firmly. "I don't need any damn rent-a-cops getting in the way."

"I'm her fiancé," Carlyle said. "And I'll be escorting her."

Denver hovered, looking tense and unhappy.

"I need you here, Steve," Erin told Denver. "Look after Rolf. Get him to my vet. The name's on a tag on his collar. Rolf, you're with this guy. You got that?"

Rolf gave her a look even less happy than Denver's.

"You can hold onto the ball, though," she added. "Until I see you again."

He wagged sullenly, but consented to be led away by Denver.

Soon Erin was in the back of the ambulance, driving toward Bellevue Hospital. They weren't in any real hurry, so they went without lights or siren. One of the paramedics gave her a quick check, verifying her vital signs and making sure she didn't have any unnoticed wounds.

"Corky's going to tear himself up over this," Carlyle said. "If he hadn't looked McGraw up, this likely wouldn't have happened."

"It wasn't Corky," she said. "I think..."

"What?" Carlyle asked sharply.

"I'll tell you later," she said. The last thing she wanted was Carlyle angling for personal revenge. He was a calm man most of the time, but when his loved ones were threatened, he was capable of astonishing violence. He'd once beaten a man to death with a barstool in revenge for the death of his first wife.

Erin wondered again, as the ambulance rolled through the darkening streets, how she could forgive and love a man who could do something like that, but arrest Vernon Lefkowitz for doing practically the same thing. She might have to talk to Doc Evans at the Eightball and see what he said. Or maybe she'd better have a chat with her priest.

Chapter 18

"You're a very lucky woman," Dr. Nussbaum said.

"That's why I keep ending up in the ER," Erin said. "Because I'm so lucky. Lucky, lucky, lucky."

Nussbaum held up his clipboard. "I have your medical history here. It reads like science fiction. Multiple concussions, cracked ribs, bullet grazes, lacerations, blunt-force trauma... Oh yes, and that one time you got shot in the head point-blank."

"And your argument is that this makes me lucky?"

"You ought to be dead." Nussbaum shook his head. "Probably more than once. So yes, you should be thankful you're in the ER instead of the morgue. But when I said you were lucky, I was restricting my comment to your recent vehicular trauma. You seem to have escaped yet another concussion, thanks to your airbags and the partiality of whatever god owes you a favor. You have a bone bruise on your left ulna, but the hammer didn't fracture the bone, so you should have full use of the limb. And while you might have a hairline crack in your cheekbone, if you do, it will mend on its own."

"It hurts like a son of a bitch," Erin said, gingerly touching her cheek. It felt hot and swollen.

"Yes, I expect it would," Nussbaum said. "There's a major nerve cluster right about there. But here's some more good news. Since you don't have any serious head trauma, I can prescribe you a varied and exotic assortment of excellent painkillers."

"What happens if I mix them with booze?"

"Don't do that."

Erin scowled. "I thought you said it was good news."

"We don't have to keep you here," Nussbaum continued, ignoring her. "There's no reason you can't go home tonight."

"Except that I don't have a car anymore," she said.

"Our city is blessed with an excellent subway system," he replied. "One of whose advantages is that you won't be in any more automobile accidents."

"I can phone us a ride," Carlyle said. "We're not putting you on the subway. Not tonight."

Erin slid off the examining table. "Okay," she said. "I'll get out of your hair. Thanks, Doc."

"We really should get you a wheelchair," the doctor said. "It's hospital policy."

"I walked into this room as soon as they got me off that damn backboard," Erin said. "And I'm walking out of it. I've got your hospital policy right here."

"I know better than to try to stop you," Nussbaum said. "Oh, your brother just finished an appie. When he heard you were here, he wanted to come in and see you, but I told him to wait until we were done with the examination. I think you might stop by and let him know you're okay."

"Why'd you tell him I was here?" Erin asked indignantly. "He'll just worry."

"He's your emergency contact," Nussbaum said. "He's the person we're *supposed* to tell."

"Oh. Right." Erin had been meaning to get her information changed to show Carlyle as her contact, but hadn't gotten around to it.

They found Sean Junior sitting just down the hallway, trying and failing to lose himself in an old issue of the *New Yorker*. He looked tired, but when he saw Erin he jumped up and hurried over to her.

"What happened, kiddo?" he asked. He obviously wanted to give her a hug, but knew better than to grab hold of an accident victim. He settled for giving her an awkward pat on the shoulder.

"Some psycho crashed a car into me," she said, trying to shrug it off. "No big deal."

"Your face has a pretty sizable edema," he said. "Any TBI? What did the MRI show?"

"You worry too much, Junior. I'm fine. If I'd had my bell rung too hard, your buddy Nussbaum wouldn't have let me walk around. He wanted to put me in a wheelchair, but I wouldn't let him."

"No," Sean said, smiling sadly. "I imagine you wouldn't. Is Rolf okay?"

"I think so. He's at the vet right now, getting checked out. Seriously, I'm fine. Stop looking at me like that."

"Like what?"

"Like I'm missing both legs or something. Sheesh, you look like a sad puppy in a Disney cartoon."

"Sorry," he said. "I worry about you, kiddo. You're in here way too much."

"So are you."

"I work here."

"Yeah. Too much."

"What's that supposed to mean?"

"Are you hiding?"

"Erin!" Sean exclaimed, bristling. "I was just up to my knuckles in some poor guy's guts, snipping out his appendix before it could pop and kill him! It's an easy operation, but it's still a life in my hands. So I wanted a little pause before jumping into the next pile of organs. Is that a crime?"

"I'm not talking about that!" Erin shot back. "I'm talking about the hospital. You're here all the damn time! You hardly see your wife and kids."

"We're short-staffed," he said. "Everybody's pulling extra shifts."

"I'll see to getting that automobile, darling," Carlyle said quietly, taking his cue to give her some space to deal with her family crap.

"Junior?" She made her tone gentler, not wanting this to turn into a shouting match. "Are you avoiding Shelley?"

"What? Why would I do that?"

One of the advantages of being a detective was that after a few dozen interrogations, it was painfully easy to see when someone was dodging a question.

"Good question," she said. "Why would you?"

"Did she put you up to this?" he asked.

Erin snorted. "Of course not. Shelley would never ask me to. But when we were dress shopping earlier in the week, she told me you guys were seeing a marriage counselor."

"She shouldn't have said that."

"Is it true?"

"Yeah, but it's nobody else's business. This is our marriage, not yours."

"But you're my brother!" she said, taking hold of Sean's upper arm with her uninjured hand and giving him a firm shake. "I love you! I love Shelley, too! And I love Anna and Patrick. I don't want you to screw this up."

Sean opened his mouth to say something angry. Then his face deflated and his shoulders sagged. The look of helplessness on his face pulled at Erin's heart.

"It's already screwed up," he said. "It's broken and I don't know how to fix it. Why do you think I hang around the ER? It's full of problems I *can* fix. I can stitch a torn artery together. I can pin a shattered femur. I stuck a guy's thumb back on last week, you know that? His whole thumb! He cut it off with his bandsaw, but his wife was smart enough to pack it in ice and bring it with. But my marriage is broken and I don't know what to do."

"Junior," she said with rough affection. "You're a damn good doctor, and as far as medical crap goes you're a genius, but you can be a real moron. You don't have to fix your whole relationship."

"Erin, what the hell are you talking about?"

"You need to fix what's in here." She poked him in the chest, right over his heart. "The rest will take care of itself. Shelley screwed up. She betrayed you and she's been beating herself up for it ever since. You know why she's so guilty? Because she loves you, you big jerk! She knows she hurt you, and she'd do anything to take it back. Do you hate her?"

"What? No!"

"Are you trying to punish her?"

"No!" He hesitated. "I mean, maybe... a little. I was pretty mad. I guess I still am."

"That's what you need to deal with," Erin said. "Jesus Christ, I just arrested a guy because he couldn't let go of his anger. This revenge bullshit doesn't solve a damn thing, and I'm sick of it. This crap eats you up inside and then you break your own life and you think it's the same as getting even. You're hurting her, but you're hurting yourself just as bad. I don't even know why I'm telling you this. I'm not your damn counselor.

Maybe it's because some asshole tried to murder me, and that kind of shit puts things in perspective. You're beating the shit out of both of you. How's that working out for you?"

Sean backed away from her and leaned against the wall. Then he sank all the way to the floor. He put his head in his hands. Then Erin's big, tough, older brother started crying.

It had obviously been near the surface, looking for an outlet, because the tears came fast and hard. Erin walked over, knelt, and awkwardly put an arm around him. She waited, letting him get it out.

Rolf padded across the floor to join them. He sniffed at Sean curiously and cocked his head at Erin. Then he sat down next to Sean and laid his chin on the doctor's knee.

"I just want things back the way they were," Sean finally managed to say, sniffling loudly.

"Is that really what you want?" she replied. "To have Shelley feeling ignored and unhappy?"

"That's not what I meant," he said. "Damn it, this wasn't my fault, Erin!"

"None of it?" she asked gently.

He didn't answer.

"I'm not saying you deserved what happened," she said. "You didn't. But neither of you deserves to lose your marriage over it. Talk to each other. Make up. Go on a trip somewhere. Have a second honeymoon. For Christ's sake, have hot, steamy sex!"

He grimaced. "You're my kid sister, Erin!" he said. "You shouldn't be talking about that!"

"I'm thirty-six, dumbass," she replied. "I've had some great sex in my life, and I hope you have, too. You didn't buy your kids at a department store, right? God, I can't believe I have to tell you this. I've never even been married! But you need to put more into your marriage, not less. I don't know a damn thing about being hitched. But I do know a thing or two about revenge. You know what Carlyle told me about it?"

"What?" Sean said.

"He said it just made him feel hollow. The thing that made him come back to life was falling in love all over again. That's what you need to do. Fall in love again. Just do it with the same woman as before. Since you've done it once, you already know how."

"I *do* love her," he insisted.

"Then maybe you ought to start acting like it," she said.

"You're really into this whole 'tough love' thing, aren't you," he said sourly.

"I'm your sister," she said. "That means I have to kick your ass sometimes, especially when a girl's involved."

"That's fair," he said, smiling weakly. "I think maybe you're right. I guess I just haven't forgiven all the way."

"You really should forgive her," Erin said quietly.

"I meant myself," Sean said.

"You should do that, too."

"I don't know how. Do you?"

"I'm working on it."

There didn't seem to be anything else to say to that, so Erin didn't try. She sat next to him and held his hand. Rolf kept leaning on him, granting Sean the privilege of rubbing his ears. That was where Webb, Vic, and Zofia found them ten minutes later.

"You're fighting hitmen again," Vic said in accusing tones. "And you didn't bring me."

"Okay, first off, I didn't know it was going to happen," Erin said, standing up. "Second, Rolf did the actual fighting, not me; and third, you're drunk. I can smell the vodka from here."

"I was off duty," Vic retorted. "It's a free country. I'm over twenty-one. I can drink if I want to. And being drunk is an advantage in a fight. I thought the Irish knew that."

"Jesus, Erin, are you okay?" Zofia asked, staring at her discolored cheek.

"Now I know how a nail feels," Erin said. "A guy tuned me up with a hammer. What did you expect?"

"Good thing the wedding's not until September," Zofia said. "Those bruises will be long gone."

"Captain Holliday is at the garage," Webb said. "He's taken personal charge of the investigation. He seemed to think I might be too close to the intended victim."

"Aww, that's sweet," Erin said.

"But he's keeping me in the loop," Webb went on. "The would-be assassin has been identified as John McGraw, AKA Black Jack McGraw, handyman and freelance muscle."

"I know," Erin said. "I've met him before, remember?"

"Yes," Webb said dryly. "But he didn't try to kill you that time. What changed?"

"Someone hired him," she said. "He made a point of telling me it wasn't personal, right before he started playing Whac-a-Mole on my face."

"Whenever someone tries to kill me, I damn well hope it's personal," Vic said. "It feels pretty goddamn personal to me."

"People try to kill you all the time," Zofia said. "Are you saying they all hate you on a personal level?"

"Probably," Vic said. "But it's okay. I hate them right back."

"I won't ask you about McGraw's death," Webb said. "Because IAB will be talking to you very soon, and I don't want to prejudice your statement. Lieutenant McDowell is probably already on her way. But I do want to know whether he told you who put out the contract."

"I thought it was obvious," Vic said. "You should've let me chuck him through the window. We're all thinking it. That O'Malley brat is behind this whole thing."

"Good theory," Webb said. "What evidence supports it?"

"McGraw didn't say anything about who hired him," Erin said. "At least, I don't think so. I was a little loopy from the crash. Richie made a threat back at the bar."

"We heard him," Webb said. "Unfortunately, it was too vague to stand up in court."

"I thought the O'Malley kid was broke," Zofia said. "How would he afford a hit on a cop? That has to run at least ten grand, maybe more."

"More," Vic said. "Erin isn't your typical cop. She's a damn celebrity. I'm betting twenty large at least. Hell, I wouldn't do it for less than fifty."

"You'd kill me for fifty thousand dollars?" Erin asked.

"I said I wouldn't do it for less," Vic said, grinning. "Nobody likes a girl who comes cheap. Take it as a compliment. I'm probably only worth fifteen, max. Some folks would do me for free."

"And he wonders why Internal Affairs doesn't like him," Webb said. "That's a good point, though. We went over O'Malley's finances with a fine-toothed comb when we busted his father. The kid didn't have that kind of cash."

"Maybe he gave McGraw an IOU," Zofia said.

"Hitmen don't work that way," Vic said. "It's cash up front with them. Maybe the punk came into some money. Lottery tickets or some other crap."

"Who else wants you dead, O'Reilly?" Webb asked.

Erin started counting on her fingers. "Well, there's Valentino Vitelli for starters," she said. "Kingston Schultz, Kyle Finnegan, Evan O'Malley, the Heartbreaker Killer... damn. I'm out of fingers."

"Point taken," Webb said. "I'm putting a protection detail on you until we sort this out."

"Like hell you are," she said.

He raised an eyebrow. "I beg your pardon?"

"Like hell you are, *sir*," she corrected. "Carlyle has good people watching the Corner. When I'm working I have plenty of guys like Vic to watch my back. I've always got Rolf. And I carry a gun. *Two* guns."

"None of which protected you tonight," Webb said.

"I'm not dead," she said. "And Rolf did protect me."

"From where I'm standing, that's mainly on account of luck," he replied. "This makes two attempts on your life in the past two days."

"That car thing outside the hospital was nothing," Erin said. "I had closer calls waiting for the bus when I was a kid."

"Was McGraw driving the car that tried to hit you the first time?"

"No," she sighed. "I don't think so."

"Then the threat isn't neutralized," Webb said.

"Am I interrupting?"

Everyone turned to the newcomer. Lieutenant Fiona McDowell had a face that might have been pretty if she smiled more. It was cold, purposeful, determined; the kind of face Michelangelo might have sculpted on a day he was really angry. The Eightball's top Internal Affairs cop was clad, as always, in her dress blues, fully buttoned up and immaculate in spite of the late hour. She was carrying her hat under one arm.

"Am I wearing a homing beacon or something?" Erin demanded. "How does everybody know exactly where I am?"

"Are you trying to hide from us?" McDowell asked, straight-faced.

"This is a hospital," Sean said. "For people who are sick or injured. Can you all take your police business somewhere else?"

"Of course," McDowell said. "My apologies, Doctor. Detective O'Reilly, I need to talk to you about the incident this evening. I had heard you had been injured and were at the hospital. You appear to have been discharged. However, if you aren't prepared to make a statement at this time, or if you'd like a Union lawyer to be present, I'd be happy to postpone until tomorrow."

"I'd like to get it over with," Erin said. "But Dr. O'Reilly's right. This isn't the place for it. And I need to get my K-9 from the vet, but my car got trashed."

"I'm more than willing to provide transportation," McDowell said. "Then, after we've finished at the Eight, I can see that you're taken home safely."

"That's very generous," Erin said through clenched teeth. "Just let me talk to my fiancé and let him know he should go home without me."

"Thanks for stopping by, sis," Sean said. "I appreciate what you said. I'll think about it."

"You still have to think about it?" she retorted. "And you're the one who aced med school."

"You okay?" Sean asked.

"I keep saying it," Erin said. "Why doesn't anyone believe me?"

"Gee," Vic said. "I wonder."

Chapter 19

McDowell drove an unmarked Chevy Impala. Erin wasn't surprised to find it spotlessly clean and well maintained. McDowell steered it through the late-evening Manhattan traffic with calm competence.

"That was your brother back at the hospital?" she asked.

"One of them," Erin said.

"Everything all right with the family?"

"Nothing wrong that'll affect my job."

"I was asking as a human being, not as an IAB Lieutenant."

"And if I'd said it would wreck my job performance?" Erin couldn't resist asking.

"Then I would have asked some more questions," McDowell said. "As an IAB Lieutenant. Are you cleared for duty?"

"Yeah. No serious head trauma and no broken bones."

"I'm glad to hear it. And your K-9?"

"I think he's okay, but I won't know for sure until we get to the vet."

McDowell nodded.

"You weren't still on duty, were you, sir?" Erin asked.

"No. I clocked out a little before six."

"But you're still wearing your uniform."

"That's an incorrect assumption. I put it on again when I got the call about the officer-involved... biting."

"I've never seen you out of uniform, sir."

"That's because you've never seen me when I'm not working."

"You always wear it on duty?"

"Yes."

"Why, if you don't mind me asking?"

McDowell wasn't irritated by the question. "To remind myself I'm a member of the NYPD," she said. "If I'm judging cops, I can't forget that I am one. It reminds me to turn the lens around and take a good look at myself, too. It's important to keep up appearances. Also, it spares me the trouble of deciding what I'm going to wear to work."

Erin wasn't expecting those last words. She choked on a startled laugh.

"It's a legitimate concern," McDowell said. "Everyone is judged by what they wear, but women more than men. Take you and Detective Neshenko, for example. You dress much better than he does. Why?"

Because Vic's a slob who doesn't give a damn how he looks, Erin thought. "Vic isn't much of a believer in appearances," she said. "He gets good results by looking big and scary."

"Of course," McDowell said. "You'll want to put some ice on that cheek, by the way."

"I know."

They arrived at the veterinarian's office without incident. The receptionist knew Erin on sight, even with her swollen face.

"I'll have the Doctor bring your good boy right out," she said.

The vet emerged a few moments later with Rolf. The Shepherd was too well trained to fling himself on Erin, but his tail started lashing eagerly the moment he saw her. He trotted quickly toward her, brown eyes fixed on her. He made a soft, eager noise deep in his throat that was somewhere between a whine and a groan. He was still holding his rubber Kong ball in his jaws.

Erin went down on one knee to meet him, ignoring the pain from her scabbed kneecap. She put her arms around his neck and hugged him. Rolf accepted the embrace with slightly-embarrassed dignity. He didn't particularly love being hugged, but it was important to his partner so he tolerated it.

"What's the damage?" Erin asked the vet, staying at Rolf's level and rubbing the base of his ears.

"Surprisingly minor," the vet said. "He has a number of small abrasions, but nothing that required stitches. No fractures, no internal damage. He's one tough boy."

"Damn straight," Erin said, ruffling the dog's ears. She was trying not to cry in front of McDowell. Rolf, seeming to recognize her strained emotions, acted the part of the professional dog who was just doing his job. The effect was somewhat spoiled by the well-slobbered rubber ball, but he didn't want to let go of it.

"He did crack a tooth," the vet went on. "Not one of the main canines. Number thirteen incisor, on the left. We did an extraction, so if he's a little logy, it's just the aftereffects of the anesthetic. I couldn't tell what caused the breakage. He must've bitten down really hard on something. Do you know what?"

"Vertebrae," Erin said absently.

"Vertebrae," the vet repeated, blinking. "As in, human vertebrae?"

"The NYPD doesn't comment regarding ongoing investigations," McDowell interjected. "Detective O'Reilly has no further comment on the subject of her K-9's dentition."

*   *   *

Some people associated conference rooms with high-powered executives and important meetings. For Erin they meant unpleasant interviews, particularly the room on the third floor of Precinct 8. The attendees at this specific late-night interview were herself, Rolf, Lieutenant McDowell, and Captain Holliday. McDowell sat across the table from Erin. Holliday was at the head of the table, watching both women intently.

Rolf sat beside his partner. Normally the K-9 would have lain down for a meeting, and he was still slightly groggy from his dental procedure, but he could feel Erin's tension, so he stayed as alert as he could, staring at her with concern. Erin was starting to wish everyone would look at someone else.

McDowell hit a button on the recorder that lay between them. "Initial post-incident interview of Detective First Grade Erin O'Reilly," she said. "May Nineteenth. For the record, Detective O'Reilly has waived her right to an attorney. Also present: Captain Fenton Holliday.

"At approximately nine-fifteen this evening, Detective O'Reilly's NYPD-issued car was involved in a multi-vehicle collision on the second floor of a parking garage on Chambers Street, opposite the Barley Corner pub. Detective O'Reilly was admitted to Bellevue Hospital for minor injuries and released. The other vehicle, registered to Kenneth Mason, was driven by a man identified as John McGraw. Mr. McGraw was pronounced dead at the scene by EMTs. Investigation of the scene was conducted by Captain Holliday. Detective O'Reilly, please tell us, in your own words, what occurred."

Erin laid out what had happened as clearly as she could recall, including both her meetings with McGraw. Holliday and McDowell listened as she recounted the crash and McGraw's follow-up assault.

"I wasn't able to draw my sidearm," she said. "It was jammed under my ribs and I didn't have enough room to get it out of the holster. He attacked me with a claw hammer. I was pinned in the wreckage and tried to defend myself with my bare hands."

"Did you believe Mr. McGraw intended to kill you?" McDowell asked.

"Absolutely." Erin repeated what Black Jack had told her about it being nothing personal. She shivered slightly, recalling the almost friendly way he'd said it.

"What did you do then?" McDowell asked.

"Rolf had been ejected from the car when his compartment popped," she said. "So I ordered him to bite. I didn't know if he was conscious or... or even if he was alive, but I had to try something. I couldn't escape and I couldn't fight back from inside the car. Rolf was conscious and alert, in spite of minor injuries. He went for McGraw."

"When you say your K-9 'went for him,' what did that entail?"

"I issued his 'bite' command. He bit McGraw once."

"Where?"

"Just outside my window, within about three feet of me."

Holliday's mustache twitched slightly with suppressed amusement. McDowell didn't move a muscle.

"Clarification: where on the assailant's body did your K-9 bite?" the Lieutenant asked.

"On the back of the neck."

"Is your K-9 trained to go for the throat?"

Erin felt a chill. "No," she said, quickly and decisively.

"What part of the body is he trained to attack when ordered?"

"The forearm."

"Has he previously disregarded his training and bitten a suspect on any other part of the body?"

Erin really didn't like where this was going. "Yes," she admitted. Lying would be worse than useless. This information was in her case files and McDowell would certainly see it there. But what was McDowell implying? If the Lieutenant decided Rolf was vicious and uncontrollable, it wasn't just a question of retiring him. McDowell could order Rolf put down.

Erin tried to gauge the other woman's state of mind. It was hopeless. She might as well be trying to stare down a statue. It wasn't just a poker face; it was a whole poker body. And this marble woman held Rolf's life in her hands. Erin felt helpless, knowing her only recourse was the truth. She silently prayed it would be enough.

"On what occasions?" McDowell asked.

"Earlier this year, Vic Neshenko, Rolf, and I were at Riker's Island," Erin said. "We were attacked by a group of armed inmates. During the fight, Rolf bit a prisoner's face."

"Did that prisoner survive?"

"Yes. He needed some stitches, that was all."

"Was his action warranted?"

"Detective Neshenko and I were assaulted by seven armed inmates," Erin said. "We had turned in our firearms at the entrance and were unarmed. It was a desperate close-quarters fight, in which both Detective Neshenko and I received stab wounds. All three of us operated with restraint under the circumstances."

"How would you define restraint in that situation?"

"We didn't kill any of them. That incident has already been investigated and our use of force deemed appropriate."

"Any other incidents?" McDowell asked.

"Yes."

"Please elaborate."

"A little over a year ago, during a fight with a suspect who was resisting arrest, the perp got his hands on Detective Neshenko's sidearm. I ordered Rolf to bite and he wasn't able to reach the man's arms. He was a big guy and it was a confused situation. Rolf bit him on the ass—I mean, on one cheek of his buttocks."

Holliday's mustache shifted again. This time Erin was sure he was hiding a smile.

"Was Detective Neshenko negligent in allowing the suspect access to his sidearm?" McDowell asked.

"No," Erin said. "The suspect headbutted him, breaking his nose. He was temporarily incapacitated by pain."

"Has your K-9 ever attacked anyone without you ordering him to?" McDowell asked.

"Yes," Erin said, suppressing a sigh. Rolf was staring up at her with complete trust and devotion in his eyes. Right now, she didn't feel she deserved it. She felt like a rat.

"When?"

"We were arresting the perp who stole the Raphael painting from the Queens art gala. The perp was using the painting as a shield. I hesitated to shoot, since it was worth millions of dollars and I didn't want to damage it. He had me at gunpoint. A civilian who was present told Rolf to bite and he did."

"Is that a typical response from your K-9? To take orders from random bystanders?"

"Absolutely not."

"Why did he obey that civilian?"

"Two reasons. One is that Rolf only follows German commands, and this particular civilian was a native German-speaker. He knew the correct command. The other is that Rolf recognized I was in danger and he already wanted to bite the bad guy."

"You seem very confident of your K-9's ability to assess a situation."

Erin met McDowell's eyes without flinching. "I am," she said.

"Why?"

"Because he's been right every time it's mattered," Erin said. "And he's saved my life more than once. He's the smartest dog I've ever met." *Smarter than a lot of humans,* she silently added. *Including maybe some in this room.*

"In your opinion, did he deploy an appropriate level of force against your assailant tonight?"

"Yes."

"He could have bitten his target's arm."

"McGraw's arms were partially inside my car at the time," Erin said. "Rolf would have had trouble reaching them, coming from behind at ground level."

"So you consider his use of lethal force appropriate?"

"Yes," Erin said again, without hesitation.

"You seem very sure of your answer," McDowell observed.

"If I could've cleared my Glock, I would have killed McGraw myself," Erin said. "My life was in imminent danger. Rolf saved it—again."

Erin tried to keep the defensiveness out of her voice and mostly succeeded. She looked defiantly at the Lieutenant, silently daring her to keep hammering away.

McDowell stared at her for several very long moments. Then she turned to Holliday.

"Captain, you have analyzed the scene, is that correct?"

"Yes," Holliday said.

"Are K-9 compartments designed to open automatically in the event of collisions?"

"No."

"What was the condition of Detective O'Reilly's K-9 compartment?"

"The window glass was shattered," Holliday said. "The reinforcing screen over the glass remained intact, so in theory the compartment's integrity should not have been compromised. However, the compartment door was open. It is the initial opinion of CSU that the side impact jarred the release mechanism and it failed, resulting in the K-9's ejection from the vehicle."

"Whose responsibility is the maintenance of said compartment?"

"O'Reilly's Charger is part of the Precinct 8 motor pool," Holliday said. "It is subject to standard maintenance procedures, and had been cleared for Departmental use. I will interview the motor pool mechanics tomorrow, but it is CSU's opinion that the latch's failure could not have been reasonably foreseen by Detective O'Reilly, nor by a qualified mechanic."

"I see," McDowell said. "What is the initial coroner's report regarding McGraw's cause of death?"

"His third and fourth cervical vertebrae were crushed," Holliday said. "His spinal cord was fully severed. It was a nearly perfect hangman's fracture. Death was instantaneous."

"To be clear, this damage was not caused by the collision?"

"It was the result of a single bite by a large dog. The ME will have a cast of the bite pattern to match to the dog."

"Nobody's debating which dog bit him," Erin burst out.

"True," McDowell said. "But this is the second fatal incident in which your K-9 has been directly implicated. This raises troubling questions, so Captain Holliday is being very thorough, as he should. What have you determined about Mr. McGraw, Captain?"

"He was muscle for hire," Holliday said. "No firm affiliations. He has a thick jacket with numerous assault charges."

"Is he known to have killed anyone?"

"Nothing proven," the Captain said. "But we have two unsolved homicides in Queens which are a possible match for his MO."

Erin hadn't known that. "Really?" she said. "Who?"

"That is not pertinent to the current interview," McDowell said. "What possible motive would Mr. McGraw have to harm Detective O'Reilly?"

"I believe he was hired to do it," Holliday said. "It appears he made entry to the garage by picking the lock on a basement-level service door. We found lockpicks on his person and scratch marks on the lock. CSU is working on matching particles on the picks to the tumblers in the lock. McGraw then used a slimjim to open the lock on Mr. Mason's Honda Accord, hotwired the car, and waited for Detective O'Reilly. We found the slimjim on the floor of the passenger side of the crashed Honda. The car's steering column shows evidence of the hotwiring."

"Did you get a statement from Mr. Mason?" McDowell asked.

"Yes," Holliday said. "The vehicle had not yet been reported stolen, because it had not been removed from the garage in which it had been parked. Mr. Mason is a decorated combat veteran and is employed by Morton Carlyle."

"Detective O'Reilly's fiancé?" McDowell asked.

"Correct," Holliday said. "He is a bouncer and security guard at the Barley Corner and has a reserved space in the garage. That space has a direct line of sight to the location of the collision. I believe Mr. Mason is not personally involved in the incident."

"Did Mr. McGraw have any other weapons on his person?"

"He had a number of hand tools which could be easily used as close-quarters weapons," Holliday said. "These included a hacksaw, a short-handled crowbar, a pair of pliers, and a box cutter."

Erin swallowed and tried not to think about some of the options McGraw had been prepared to employ.

"Do you have any idea who might have been responsible for hiring Mr. McGraw?" McDowell asked.

"Our best suspect at this time is Richard O'Malley," Holliday said. "However, we have not yet established a direct connection. We're very early in our investigation."

"Of course," McDowell said. "Detective O'Reilly, do you have anything to add?"

Erin considered her answer for a moment. "I support my K-9 a hundred percent," she said, speaking slowly and clearly. "I didn't want McGraw dead. I would have preferred him to be taken alive, so we could find out who he was working for. But he was trying to kill me. Rolf did what any good partner would do. I'm alive and mostly intact because of his quick, effective action. He's a well-trained and discerning K-9. He understands how to assess threats and is no danger to civilians. I trust him around my brother's children without hesitation."

"Do you think he will bite any throats in the future?"

"I plan on giving him reinforcement training in bite work," Erin said. "We'll focus on the fundamental technique to ensure he goes for the arm whenever practical."

"What if it isn't practical?" McDowell asked.

"Then he'll go for whatever he can reach," Erin said levelly. "I don't tell Rolf to bite every bad guy we run into. His teeth are a weapon and I treat them the way I would my gun or my Taser. I never deploy him lightly."

"Is your K-9 dangerous?"

"Of course he is," Erin said. "So is my gun. But the gun's a lot more likely to kill than the dog. Rolf's bitten dozens of bad guys. Two of them have died. One of those died because he fell, not because he was bitten. The reason McGraw is dead is because of McGraw, not because of Rolf."

McDowell nodded once. "All right," she said. "I think that's everything for tonight. Thank you for your cooperation, Detective O'Reilly, Captain Holliday. We're done here."

Erin tried not to sag with relief. She held her stiff, professional posture all the way out of the conference room and down the stairs to Major Crimes. Holliday followed her down.

Chapter 20

"That could have gone much worse," Holliday said quietly.

"Yeah," Erin said bitterly. "She could've ordered my dog killed."

Major Crimes was deserted except for the two of them and Rolf. The Shepherd cocked his head curiously at her. He wasn't sure what she was talking about.

"If you wouldn't mind, could you step into my office for a minute?" Holliday asked.

"Yes, sir," she sighed. She was exhausted. Her arm and face pulsed with pain in time with her heartbeat. She didn't want to talk to anyone. She wanted to go home and try to sleep. But she led Rolf into Holliday's office behind the Captain and closed the door.

Holliday opened a desk drawer and took out a chemical ice pack. He crushed it and handed it to Erin, who gingerly held it against her cheek.

"Have a seat," he said.

"*Sitz*," she murmured to Rolf, who sat beside her. Without being asked, he settled his chin across her knee like he had with her brother.

"Lieutenant McDowell isn't one of the bad guys, O'Reilly," Holliday said.

"Neither am I," she retorted.

"I know," he said. "And so does McDowell. But she didn't get her nickname for nothing."

"The Cast-Iron Bitch," Erin said. "They got that right."

"Precisely." Holliday opened another drawer. This time he came up with a bottle of Glenlivet and a pair of shot glasses. "You're not pulling overtime tonight, O'Reilly. Neither am I. That means we're off duty, as of the moment your interview ended. Would you share a drink with me?"

"Gladly, sir."

He poured a shot and handed it to her, then poured another for himself. They sipped.

"It's not that Glen Docherty-whatever your fiancé stocks, I'm afraid," he said. "That stuff's practically impossible to find this side of the Atlantic. But this is twenty-year Scotch. A friend gave it to me when I became a twenty-year man with the NYPD. He said the whiskey and I had aged together, so we deserved one another."

"It's good," she said truthfully.

"You have to understand something about McDowell," he said. "She holds absolutely everybody to the exact same standard. If she believed she'd stepped out of line, she'd discipline herself. Have you ever read *Les Misérables*?"

"I've heard some of the songs," she said. "From the musical."

"She's like Inspector Javert," he said. "If Javert was on the right side, instead of a puppet of the *ancien regime*. She's not out to get you and she's certainly not out to get Rolf. But she is concerned about public safety. She doesn't know Rolf the way you do and she doesn't take anything on faith. The bad thing about her is, she takes every situation on its merits. You can't carry a credit balance with her. But that's the good thing, too. She doesn't hold a grudge."

"That's because she wrecks anybody who steps out of line," Erin said.

"Then it's a good thing you didn't," Holliday countered. "If Rolf was a human who'd shot McGraw dead, it would have been ruled a clean shooting. From where I'm sitting, you and he didn't do a single thing that wasn't necessary. And it's thanks to your partner here that I still have my top detective."

Erin felt a rush of pride, both in Rolf and in what Holliday had just said about her. "Thank you, sir," she said.

"I don't think you need to worry about McDowell," Holliday continued. "She's not out to get every cop; just the bad ones. I'd be lying if I said she didn't make me a little nervous every time I'm in the same room with her, but that's not such a bad thing. It's the way civilians feel when we pull them over. It's an important reminder that we're as human as the people we protect, and we're not above the law. Nor should we be."

"Yes, sir," Erin said.

"But that's not why I asked you in here," Holliday said.

"It's not, sir?"

"Let's talk about Richard O'Malley," he said. "And how we're going to get him."

"I thought we hadn't proved it was him," she said.

"We haven't," he said. "Yet. But he's been keeping tabs on your movements. He wasn't anywhere near the parking garage tonight. After he left the Final Countdown, he went to a club in the Village. As far as I know, he's still there. Plenty of witnesses to verify it."

"That's convenient for him," Erin said.

"Isn't it?" Holliday said dryly.

"Hold on," she said. "You checked him out already?"

He nodded. "I wasn't always a desk jockey, Detective," he said. "I have a gold shield of my own. I know this business. And I can call on a lot of resources in a hurry if I need to. Besides, the NYPD has had Richard O'Malley on its radar ever since Christmas."

"What?" Erin exclaimed, springing to her feet and dislodging Rolf's head from her lap. The Shepherd bounced to his paws, ready for action. "Why didn't I know about this?"

"It's a separate operation," he said. "In point of fact, I didn't know about it myself until this evening. It's a Narcotics op, long-running."

"He's dealing drugs?"

"I haven't fully familiarized myself with the investigation," Holliday said. "I'll be bringing some late-night reading home from the office with me. But from what little I know so far, it appears he's suspected of involvement with a major fentanyl operation."

"I guess that explains where he got the money to have me whacked," Erin said. "He's an ambitious little bastard. I didn't think he had it in him."

"It seems he's a fairly small fish in this particular pond," Holliday said. "He's just one of a regular rogue's gallery of scumbags. I don't know the particulars, but I can tell you the Narco boys are watching dozens of targets. As far as O'Malley goes, they're hoping he'll lead them to someone bigger up the chain. But if he's coming after cops, we can forget the big picture. I'm going to take him down."

"How are we going to prove it?" she asked.

"The same way we prove everything," he said. "We build the case, a piece at a time. We get names and dates, photographs and recordings. I don't know what we can prove so far on the drug angle. We did find a burner phone on McGraw's body. He took a call from someone about the same time you left the Final

Countdown. Unfortunately, it came from another burner number and we haven't been able to trace it."

"You won't," Erin predicted. "Richie's kind of an idiot, but he's smart enough to have ditched it by now."

"I agree," Holliday said. "That means we're unlikely to be able to pin the hit on him. My question is, are you willing to accept O'Malley going down on narcotics charges but not for attempted murder? It may be the best we can get."

"If it takes him off the street, I'll accept whatever's on offer," she said. "But we might be able to stick him with the rest of this, too. If we get audio surveillance, maybe he'll say the wrong thing. He's going to try again."

"Probably," he agreed. "But I don't want you on the sharp end of this one, O'Reilly."

"Why not?" she demanded. "I'm the one he wants to kill!"

"That's exactly why not. You're too close to this. You're emotionally compromised."

"I was emotionally compromised by the whole damn operation against the O'Malleys!" she exclaimed. "That didn't stop me going through with it. And this isn't just about me. He'll try for Carlyle too, and maybe Corky while he's at it, which means Teresa Tommasino's in danger too. And—"

Holliday held up a hand. "I understand your concerns," he said. "And I promise to keep you in the loop. But you're not going to be leading the charge. Think about it. He's watching you. If he finds out you're watching him, it could jeopardize the Narcotics investigation."

"What do you need me to do?" Erin asked resignedly, feeling the short-lived burst of energy seeping out of her.

"Just keep doing your job," he said. "And try not to worry, but keep your eyes open."

"I thought this was over," she said. "The O'Malleys were done. That was *months* ago! There wasn't supposed to be any blowback. We were supposed to get all of them!"

"Revenge is very good eaten cold," Holliday said.

"Are you quoting *Star Trek* at me, sir?" Erin asked, surprised.

"Eugène Sue, actually," he said. "*Mathilde*. Published in the mid-19th Century. Like revenge itself, the proverb is older than it appears to be."

"Never heard of it," Erin said. "Do you read a lot of French literature, sir?"

"I had an interest in it in college," Holliday said. "Particularly the stuff from the mid-1800s. Victor Hugo, mostly. What do you read?"

"These days, it's mostly DD-5s and Departmental reports," Erin said.

Holliday chuckled. "Me, too. I'm looking forward to retirement, so I can get back to reading books again. Relax, O'Reilly. This is all going to blow over soon. If Richard O'Malley is as dumb as you've led me to believe, he won't last long. Either we'll get him or he'll do something stupid and his new business associates will take care of him. Regardless, I have him on my radar now, and I won't stop until he's out of the picture, one way or another. Any questions?"

"No, sir," she said.

"I've already approved a replacement vehicle for you," he added. "It'll take a few days, but I understand the motor pool has a spare Charger equipped for K-9 use. They just need to repaint it in street colors. Do you have a color preference?"

"Black is fine, sir," she said.

"Do you need a lift home?"

"I'll call Carlyle. He'll have someone pick me up."

"Good. And O'Reilly?"

"Sir?"

"Excellent work on the courthouse murders. As usual."

"Thank you, sir."

"I meant what I said, about you being my top detective. Goodnight."

Carlyle's Mercedes pulled up in front of the Eightball a few minutes after Erin's call. Ken Mason was driving. Carlyle himself was riding in back. Erin saw the bulge of a concealed handgun under Mason's coat when he twisted around to make sure she'd gotten in okay. He was expecting trouble. She slid into the back seat beside her fiancé, taking the middle position. Rolf settled on her right.

"Sorry I didn't ride with you from the hospital," she said. "Lieutenant McDowell needed to talk about what happened. You know how it goes. The thin blue line goes through a lot of red tape."

"No apology necessary, darling," Carlyle said. How are you feeling?"

"Like I got in a car crash. Sorry about your ride, Mason."

"Not a problem, ma'am," Mason said. "I've been thinking about upgrading for a while now. You just gave me a good reason. I should apologize. If I'd gotten a newer car sooner, that tango might not have been able to hotwire it."

"He'd have found some other way to come at me," Erin said. "Forget about it."

The ride to the Barley Corner was short and uneventful. Mason dropped them off at the front door.

"Move quick and get under cover," he advised as Carlyle took hold of the car door handle. "Could be snipers."

"I'd rate that as unlikely," Carlyle said.

"Don't bet on it," Erin said.

He gave her a quick, searching look, but said nothing. They walked briskly across the sidewalk and into the pub. Light and cheerful noise enveloped them. The customers seemed entirely innocuous, but Erin found herself scanning every face and watching every pair of hands, looking for threats. She'd fallen back into her old paranoid mindset so easily, it was practically a reflex.

All she saw was a redheaded Irishman sitting at a side booth in the company of a pleasant-faced woman of Italian extraction. When the redhead spotted the new arrivals, he waved them over.

"Corky," Erin said, nodding to him. "Ms. Tommasino."

"The two of you fought off an assassin together," James Corcoran said. "At my very bedside, no less. I think you ought to be on a first-name basis."

"Fair enough," Erin said. "Evening, Teresa. I hope Corky's showing you a good time."

"Always," Teresa said, giving Corky a warm smile. "Will you be joining us?"

"I've had a pretty long day—" Erin began.

"Which is why she needs a drink," Corky interjected, sliding over to make room. "Whatever you're drinking, this round's on me."

"I own this pub," Carlyle observed. "And Erin drinks for free. But we'll join you for a few minutes."

"So much the better," Corky said. He signaled the waitress. "Caitlyn! Another glass of red for the light of my life here, and I'll have another pint of Guinness."

"Glen D for me," Erin said. "Straight up. Better make it a double. It's been that kind of night."

"Ought you to be drinking, darling?" Carlyle asked. "Given your medication?"

"I already had one with the Captain," she said. "The doc said I'm not supposed to mix the pain pills with booze. Given the choice, I'll take the booze. Forget the damn pills."

"I'll have a shot of Docherty-Kinlochewe as well," Carlyle said to Caitlyn. "Thank you, darling."

As the waitress slipped through the crowd, Corky gave Erin a look.

"Perhaps you oughtn't to be celebrating quite so much, love," he said. "From the look of it, you've already had more than your share. Been having a wee donnybrook, I'd say."

"You should see the other guy," Erin said, rubbing Rolf's head.

"So I heard," Corky said. "Listen, Erin, I'm owing you an apology. I'm the one who went asking questions about Black Jack and put you on his map. I've brought trouble to you without intending it, and I'm sorry. How can I make things right?"

"Forget about it, Corky," she said. "Sheesh. Everyone's apologizing to me tonight. This wasn't your fault. You might have actually helped."

"Really?" His face brightened.

"Yeah. If I hadn't already met him, he would've taken me even more by surprise. At least when he came at me with that hammer, I knew what to expect."

"He did what?" Teresa asked, eyes widening. "With *what?!*"

"Jack McGraw tried to crack my skull with a hammer," Erin said, gesturing to her cheek.

"I could've told him that was a right fool's errand," Corky said. "All the Irish have hard heads, and Miss O'Reilly's is harder than most. This lass bounces bullets off her noggin. A wee carpentry tool hadn't a prayer."

"Have your lads any idea who sent him?" Carlyle asked. "Is it who we're suspecting?"

"Probably," Erin said. "Our best guess is Richie."

"That gobshite!" Corky spat disgustedly. "I've a mind to teach him some manners on the tip of my blade."

"James!" Teresa exclaimed.

"Sorry, love," he said. "Old habits, aye?"

"You are not to go stabbing anyone," Teresa said severely. "Not with any of your knives, nor any other implements. Put that fork down! You're reformed."

"*Mostly* reformed," Corky said, winking at her. But he laid the dinner fork back on the table, somewhat reluctantly.

"Don't go looking for trouble," Erin said. "Either of you. Richie may try something and he may not. He hates everyone at this table, except maybe you, Teresa. And I can see where he's coming from. We ruined his life, after all."

"It wasn't his to begin with," Corky said. "He never earned a single thing for himself. His da gave it all to him on a platter. He was born with a silver spoon shoved so far up his... well, we needn't say where he keeps his silverware, but I'll wager the sun's never shone on it. What's he ever done to deserve wealth or power? He's naught but a spoiled brat, throwing a tantrum on account of losing his sweeties."

"None of us can help where we come from," Teresa said, laying a hand on Corky's.

"It doesn't much matter whether his feelings are justified," Carlyle said. "What matters is whether he'll act on them. From what Erin's saying, he's already made two tries for her. I think he'll likely try again."

"Then it's self-defense," Corky said. His hand strayed to the fork again.

"James, no," Teresa said.

"You can't be thinking to just sit by and let this happen!" Corky insisted, looking at Carlyle.

"Erin can take care of herself," Carlyle said mildly. "I trust her judgment and her experience."

They were interrupted by the arrival of their drinks. As Corky said, hoisting his glass, alcohol took precedence over business.

"I just love what you've done with this place," Teresa said to Carlyle. "You'd hardly know it was renovated. Everything looks so well-established."

"We used distressed lumber," Carlyle said, glowing with pride. "The lads did the best they could to integrate the new stuff with what could be salvaged from the old furnishings after the fire."

"I can see why you love it so much," Teresa said. "Tell me, Detective—Erin, I mean—how much danger is there, really?"

"Richie won't be in the picture long," Erin promised. "We'll get him, and we'll do it through completely legal means."

"Of course you will," Corky said, rolling his eyes theatrically.

"We're done going through back channels," Erin said. "No more shady deals, no more car bombings, none of that crap. And no knifings! I just talked to the Captain and he's got things in hand."

"How are you planning to get him?" Carlyle asked.

"Through the drugs," she said. "He's dealing fentanyl with some pretty bad guys. That's how he's financing himself these days. Narcotics has a bead on him. They should be ready to move soon. And that information doesn't leave this table, got it?"

"Nod's as good as a wink, love," Corky said and winked. "Mum's the word and sharp's the action. He'll not hear a peep from me. I'm the very soul of discretion."

"The more you talk about it, the less convincing you are," Erin said.

He just grinned, laid a finger alongside his nose, and winked again.

"How do you stand him?" Erin asked Teresa. "He's like a perpetual twelve-year-old."

"I teach elementary school, remember?" Teresa laughed. "I also know why some boys act out in class. It's not because they're bad at heart. It's because they're not getting enough love and attention, usually at home."

"That's not my problem these days," Corky said, giving Teresa a look that made her cheeks flush.

"James!" she said again. "You are impossible!"

"The main thing is to watch your step," Erin said. "I'm pretty sure Richie won't come after you until he's gotten us, Corky. But if he's made a list, I'll bet you're on it."

"His da's trial is coming up," Carlyle said. "Along with the rest of the O'Malleys. I understand the date's been set?"

"Yeah," Erin said. "It's starting the first week in October."

"Grand," Corky said. "You can have your wedding first, and even a bit of a honeymoon, and be back in time to see Evan and Company get their just deserts."

"If he's trying to influence the trial, Richard will move before then," Carlyle said. "That's five months from now. I hope your lads are ready to take him by the time you make an honest lad of me."

"Holliday said he'd keep me posted," Erin said. "God, I hate playing defense."

"Then you shouldn't have become a copper," Corky said. "Your lot often can't move before something dreadful's been done. Whereas my people can do whatever we want, whenever we want, to whomever we want. My former people, that is. Lads with whom I'm no longer the least bit affiliated."

"Right," Erin said, resisting the urge to roll her own eyes. "Are you keeping him out of trouble, Teresa?"

"I'm trying," Teresa said. "But he's less trouble than he'd have you think. He's really very sweet on the inside."

"One of these days I might believe that," Erin said. "Right now, what I want to do is get some rest. Sorry, but being nearly murdered tires me out. I'm going to call it a night."

"That's your own affair," Corky said. "But if I were you, I'd ride that feeling of cheating the Reaper. No sensation quite like it. Cars, take it from me; some of the best nights of a lad's life come from near-death experiences. Don't go missing out, and don't go letting her fall asleep on you."

"I'll keep that in mind, lad," Carlyle said.

Chapter 21

"I don't want to hurt your feelings," Erin said. "But I really don't feel like following Corky's advice. I hurt all over."

"I've been ignoring the lad's romantic advice for better than thirty years," Carlyle said, smiling. "I'll be happy to take a rain check."

"Thanks," she said, unbuttoning her blouse and gingerly easing it off her shoulders. "Jesus. This is as bad as when Mickey Connor tuned me up."

"Jack McGraw had recourse to a hammer and Mr. Mason's Honda," Carlyle said. "Mickey only made use of his bare hands. All things considered, I'd say you got off lightly."

"Easy for you to say," she grumbled. "Can you see my shoulder? How's it look?"

"You've the makings of a grand bruise," he said. "On your cheek as well. Your eye's rather blackened into the bargain."

"If it wasn't for Rolf, it would've been a lot worse," she said.

Rolf, sitting at the foot of the bed, stretched and cracked his jaws in a mighty yawn. His tongue uncurled like a pink party streamer. Erin had given him a late dinner and he was still enjoying the full feeling in his belly.

"Are you on modified assignment?" Carlyle asked, unknotting his tie and hanging it on its rack.

"Yeah," Erin said. "I didn't kill him directly, but a guy died from my dog. Until IAB officially clears the both of us, it's desk duty for me."

"Is that such a terrible fate?"

"Not at the moment." Erin went into the kitchen and came back with a bag of frozen peas pressed against her upper arm.

"Do you anticipate any trouble on the internal front?" Carlyle asked.

She thought about it for a moment. "No," she decided. "McDowell grilled me pretty hard, but I think I gave her the right answers. If she really thought Rolf was some sort of public menace, she wouldn't have let me walk out of the Eightball with him."

"*Is* the lad a public menace?" Carlyle asked, looking down at the Shepherd.

Rolf gave him an ambiguous stare.

"K-9s hardly ever kill anyone," Erin said. "Cops fatally shoot about a thousand people a year, give or take."

"That's rather a lot," Carlyle said.

"Maybe," she said. "That's spread around six hundred thousand law-enforcement officers. That means five hundred ninety-nine cops didn't kill somebody this past year for every one who did. But dogs? I think there were two K-9s that killed people last year, not counting Rolf. And twenty-seven K-9s died in the line of duty."

"I didn't know you possessed such a wealth of statistics," Carlyle said.

"I pay attention to the numbers when it comes to K9s," she said. "But here's the thing. I've killed more bad guys than Rolf has. If anyone's going to be taken off the street, it ought to be me."

"You're no killer, Erin," he said, laying a hand on her uninjured shoulder.

"The scoreboard doesn't agree with you," she said. "I killed that Russian human-trafficking scumbag. I helped kill Hans Rüdel and Siobhan Finneran. I blew Mickey Connor's brains out. And I wasted Gordon Pritchard in Corky's hospital room. For a woman who's not a killer, I sure pile up a lot of bodies."

"None of those gave you any choice," he said. "You don't go looking for people to kill, nor does your dog. I'm glad Lieutenant McDowell recognizes it."

"She's just doing her job," Erin said. "She doesn't take anything personally."

"That's a good thing, surely?"

"You'd think so. But it's actually kind of scary."

"Justice is certainly more frightening than mercy," he agreed. "How many of us truly want to get what we deserve? In my experience, it's the lads who think they deserve nothing but good who are the greatest bastards, while us tormented souls may be decent enough underneath."

"Maybe that's why we need God," Erin said. "We can't deliver justice *or* mercy, so we have to leave it up to Him in the end."

"For myself, I'm rather hoping He's in a merciful mood when I come before Him," Carlyle said. "Do you ever worry about your soul?"

Erin thought about the time she'd planned to kill Vinnie the Oil Man, how easy it had seemed. She could have done it. Then she thought of Richard O'Malley and what she might be willing to do to protect herself from him.

"Yeah," she said, almost in a whisper.

"How are you feeling about the lad Rolf killed?" Carlyle asked gently.

"Rolf's soul is fine," she said. "He doesn't struggle with guilt. Just look at him."

Rolf cocked his head. His tongue was still hanging out. He looked like he was smiling a big, doggy grin.

"Do dogs have souls?" Carlyle wondered.

"Of course they do," she said. "If we do, so do they. All you have to do is look in their eyes. Dogs automatically go to heaven. We're the ones who have to earn it."

"Jack McGraw deserved to die, did he?" Carlyle pressed.

"Everybody dies," Erin said. "And we didn't execute him. Webb's right. Cops can't be executioners. What happened in that garage wasn't punishment and it wasn't justice. It was self-defense. Maybe Black Jack deserved to die, but I can't be the judge of that. If we start thinking it's our job to hand out street justice, then we really are just the same as Vern Lefkowitz. Rolf killed McGraw because that jerk was trying to kill me. That's consequences, not justice. It's like the law of gravity kicking in when you jump out of an airplane."

"You're a fountain of philosophy at the moment," Carlyle said with a smile.

"I hurt too much to sleep," she said. "So I'm talking."

"Corky has a point," Carlyle said after a moment. "Richard O'Malley is a threat. Time was, he and I would have been seriously discussing permanent measures to neutralize the lad."

"Yeah," Erin said. "And time was, you two would've been planting bombs to blow up British soldiers. But you're not doing it now. Jesus Christ, I just got done saying we can't pull shit like that! We have to leave it to the courts."

"What if they can't be trusted?" Carlyle asked. "What if the system itself is broken?"

"Then Lefkowitz was right," she said. "And it all comes down to personal revenge. Has that worked very well for you? Or for Northern Ireland, come to that?"

"Not particularly," he admitted. "I trust you, darling. But Corky's right about one other thing, too. You can't seriously expect me to stand aside and watch Richard kill you. I've lost one wife to senseless violence. I'll not lose another."

She leaned her back against him. He wrapped his arms around her stomach and held her.

"You won't have to," she said. "We're not talking about some combat veteran like Ian Thompson, or even a hardened killer like Mickey Connor or Snake Pritchard. This is Richard O'Malley. The best he can do is hire some other chump to do his dirty work, and maybe try to run me down in the road. He's an amateur, a wannabe. It's going to be fine, you'll see."

"If Richard does kill you, I'll end his miserable life," Carlyle promised. "No matter what it does to my soul. I'll send him screaming to hell, and he'd best hope I don't end up down there with him, because I'll remember him when I get there."

"Damn it, enough with the revenge!" Erin snapped, twisting around to face him. "I don't want you to avenge me and I don't want you to die for me! You think it's romantic, but I've seen too many bodies, so I know better."

"Then what would you have me do, darling?"

"Well, for starters, I'm going to try pretty hard not to die."

"Grand plan. I approve. But then, most lasses don't precisely intend to perish."

She put her hand over his heart. "Keep the faith," she said. "We've been through worse. You know I have a dangerous job. But I also have good people watching my back and a good dog standing next to me. I know you're worried about going through the same stuff you did before. But I'm not Rose."

"Aye, darling," he said, jaw clenched. "I know."

"Revenge just goes round and round," she said. "If we get on that carousel, we'll never get off it. I know you love me, but there's better ways to show it than blowing up an idiot. Rose wouldn't have wanted you to kill that jerk in that bar twenty years ago. You know why you still feel guilty about that?"

"Because murder's a mortal sin?" Carlyle replied with a wry half-smile.

"No. Well, yeah, there's that. But you feel it because you know in here," she poked his sternum, "it was a pretty shitty way to honor your wife's memory. If I do die, and to repeat, I don't plan on it, I don't want some damn stupid revenge tainting your memory of me. Don't let Richie spoil what we have. You keep saying I saved you. If that's true, don't go throwing it away on that loser. He's not worth it."

"You've a grand way with words, darling," he said. "Have you ever considered becoming a poet?"

"No."

"You win, Erin." He bent forward and kissed her lightly on her uninjured cheek. "I promise not to go desecrating our love through unspeakable violence, no matter what happens. All I'm asking in return is your promise it won't come up as a possibility."

"I'll do my very best," she said.

"Grand. Do you think you can sleep?"

"I'm going to try," she said. "Lord knows I'm tired enough."

*   *   *

But sleep proved elusive. At first Erin couldn't get comfortable. Her left arm ached all the way from the shoulder to the fingertips. Her face throbbed. She discovered other, lesser pains she hadn't even suspected. A car accident gave the whole body quite a jolt. Her skeleton had been rattled like a bony tambourine. She couldn't lie on her side or stomach. Even stretching out on her back was no good.

Then, once the pain had really sunk in, she couldn't stop thinking. Richard O'Malley's face blended into his father's, then her own dad's. She thought of Carlyle beating a man to death for murdering his wife, and that led her to Lefkowitz crushing Earl's skull on a Pittsburgh bridge. Then her thoughts spun to Black Jack McGraw and his courteous, friendly words as he'd tried to smash her head with his hammer. Adrenaline spiked through her at the recollection and she was suddenly completely awake, heart pounding.

She lay on her back, listening to Carlyle's quiet breathing, and tried to calm herself. She couldn't. Residual fear and anger chased each other through her brain. The body's acute stress reaction, she bitterly reflected, was a hell of a thing. This wasn't the first time it had happened. At least this time she hadn't pulled a gun on Rolf.

She stuck it out for another fifteen endless minutes in the dark bedroom, watching the digital clock crawl from one minute to the next, seeing if she could relax. She couldn't.

Finally, around midnight, she got up, moving as slowly and stealthily as she could so as not to disturb her fiancé. She opened her dresser by feel and got a sweatshirt, which she pulled on over the long T-shirt she slept in. Then she went bare-legged out to the kitchen to Carlyle's liquor cabinet.

She got out the Glen D and poured herself a stiff shot. She started to put the bottle back in the cabinet, paused, and kept it in one hand. When she turned toward the study, Rolf was standing in the kitchen doorway staring at her.

"Shut up," she told him in an undertone. "This is medicinal booze. Maybe I should've taken those damn pain pills instead."

He didn't reply, didn't judge. He just padded along the hallway beside her.

She kept her own laptop next to Carlyle's computer. She flipped hers open and switched it on. She sipped whiskey while the computer powered up. Rolf circled, arranging his legs, and curled into a ball at her feet, tucking his snout under his tail.

Her computer was securely encrypted and connected to the NYPD database. She logged in and called up Richard O'Malley's record.

She'd been conditioned by undercover work and the paranoia it had fostered, so she was expecting not to find anything. To her surprise, she saw a treasure trove of information: known associates, video clips, financial records, the works. Every piece of a major ongoing investigation was right there at her fingertips.

"Why didn't they tell me?" she asked Rolf, who raised his head, blinked sleepily, and immediately re-curled.

She went through Richie's records file by file, drinking more than she should and forgetting the time. The evidence might not be enough for a slam-dunk in court, but the pattern was clear; Richie had become a drug middleman for some very dangerous guys. Russian Mafia, from the look of them.

"Fentanyl," she murmured. It was more dangerous than heroin, more addictive, easier to overdose on. And it was synthetic. People made it right in New York City. It didn't have to be smuggled in. Richie was making a lot of money. It wasn't beyond the realm of possibility that he'd earmarked some of his newfound wealth to pay back a certain NYPD detective and her traitorous fiancé.

"Can't let it go, darling?"

Carlyle stood in the doorway, clad in his silk bathrobe.

"Sorry," Erin said. "I didn't mean to wake you."

"I've worked nights longer than you," he said, coming in and pulling another chair over. "I often find myself wakeful in the wee hours if I try to sleep like normal folk. Is it the pain of your injuries, or something else that's troubling you?"

"Richie O'Malley," she said.

"Unless I'm mistaken, that lad's being investigated by others," he said.

"I can't help it. I need to know what's going on. They've got some stuff on him, and it's pretty incriminating, but the Narcotics guys aren't going to move hard against him. They'll lean on him to give up his bosses."

"Naturally," Carlyle said. "That's common practice when dismantling organized crime, or so I'm told."

"Yeah," she said. "But if he does flip, and if we can't prove he was behind McGraw's hit, he gets off easy. Maybe he even walks. Holliday said he won't, but it isn't Holliday's investigation."

"What can your lads do about it?"

"That's what I'm trying to figure. We need to pin something big on him, something that convinces the DA he's worth nailing. The problem is, if I didn't know better, I'd think he was nobody special myself. He looks so damn pathetic, it's hard to take him seriously."

"Corky's the same way," Carlyle said. "He told me once that the best way to keep the coppers off your back is to keep them laughing at you. Do you think Richard's putting up a front?"

"No," she said. "I think he really is a dumb spoiled brat who's in over his head. That's why we didn't scoop him up when we took in the rest of his dad's gang. Nobody ever trusted the kid with anything big enough to stick. Even Evan knew his son was worthless. That's why he wanted you to take over from him one day."

"I suppose I'll take that as a compliment," Carlyle said. "What is it you're intending?"

"I'm going to drill down on him," Erin said grimly. "He's careless enough that he let something slip, I know it. I'll find it and I'll use it to bury him. Then it'll finally be over."

"Pardon my asking," he said. "But isn't that precisely the opposite of what you've been ordered to do?"

"What Holliday doesn't know won't come back on me," she said. "Don't worry. I'll be careful. I managed to fool everyone in the O'Malleys and the Lucarellis for months, remember? Plus Keane and the rest of his bunch of slimy dirty cops. Relax. It's not like I'm going to be kicking down doors. This is surveillance. It's safe enough. Besides, if he's gunning for me, it's not like sitting at home would be any better."

"I'd feel more comfortable if Ian could be watching over you," he murmured.

"He is watching over me," she said. "He was one of the firefighters who cut me out of my car. Didn't you know?"

"Nay," he said, surprised and pleased. "How did the lad handle himself?"

"He did fine," she said. "It was a little weird hearing them calling him 'probie,' though. He's so competent, it's easy to forget he's a rookie when it comes to firefighting."

"I'm sure the lad will earn their trust soon enough," Carlyle said. "And speaking of that, I'll continue to trust you. Kindly don't make me regret it."

Erin kissed him. "Have you ever?" she asked.

He brushed back a trailing strand of hair from her forehead. "Not yet."

"And after we get Richie, it's over," she promised.

"Nay, darling," he said. "That's no ending. It's a beginning."

Chapter 2

Coventry took her usual precautions on the way to her bolt-hole, asking the cabbie to drop her a fair distance away, reversing direction several times, and crossing the street twice. Content that she was not being followed, she eased into the alley, up a rickety back stair, and into the foul smell and smoke of a gambling hall. She nodded a cheery greeting to Nick, the burly man who watched the door. She crossed the room, playfully slapping away the hands of a couple of the lads as she danced past them.

"You're in a right rare mood, Cov," Slinky McGee observed. "Good night?"

"Best of 'em, Slinky," she said, winking.

"If you're wanting, we could deal you in," he said. "Or you can sit on my lap and play my cards for me."

"You'd like that, you old goat," she said. "I may be just a wee scrap of a girl, but I'm more woman than the likes of you'll ever manage."

Slinky put his hand over his heart in mock distress. Coventry saw only smiles on familiar faces. She knew every man in the room. They were bad men, she supposed, but really decent enough chaps if one scraped away the surface dirt. She'd been rooming here nearly three months, longer than she'd rested in any one place in years, and she was starting to feel almost at home.

With a flirty wave to her admirers, she swirled her skirt and walked down the back hall to her room, snatching up a candle as she went.

"You'll be paying for that bit of wax, love!" Slinky called after her.

"I'll toss a farthing in with my rent come Monday, you penny-pinching flapdoodle," she tossed over her shoulder.

She made certain to lock the door and shoot the bolt the moment she was inside. There was a difference between feeling at home and being a fool.

The room wasn't much to look at, but by Whitechapel standards it was a right treat. To start with, it was hers and hers alone, with a real solid door. No mere ragged curtain separated her from a consumptive neighbor or a litter of squalling brats. The ceiling was sloped low on one side, so she could only stand up near the door, but she had a mattress stuffed with rags, only slightly verminous, a tub for laundry and bathing so she needn't go to the shared washroom, and a few pegs for her clothes. There was even a small, grimy window. In spite of the cold, it was propped open a hands-breadth.

"Whisper?" she called quietly.

After a brief, breathless pause, a faint meow answered her.

"There you are, you precious wee thing," Coventry said, kneeling down and extending a hand. A rangy black cat materialized out of the shadows in the corner of the room, green eyes glowing in the candlelight. Whisper stalked slowly to meet the girl, sniffed her hand, and rubbed his cheek against her knuckles.

Coventry stroked the cat's neck and back. "I've not brought you anything," she said. "But I promise we'll take a stroll down to the market tomorrow and find some fresh fish. I've had a brilliant night and we'll not be wanting for vittles today, nor tomorrow, and who's to say fairer than that?"

Whisper purred, his tail rising at every stroke of her hand.

Now that she knew the cat was in for the night, Coventry closed the window. Whisper got in and out that way, running across the rooftops as easily as the lads came and went by door and stair. He was hardly her cat. It was fairer to say, she was his girl. He'd announced himself the first night she'd spent in this place, proving that the room was not, as Slinky had promised, unoccupied. The two of them got on famously. Coventry left the window open for him, no matter the cold, and gave him little tidbits as occasion and income allowed. In return, Whisper kept the room free of rats and mice and provided a warm, undemanding bed-mate.

Coventry took up a loose floorboard under a corner of her mattress, revealing the little hiding-place she'd worked out for herself. She took out all the loot she'd pilfered from Mr. Horrocks and gave it a quick once-over, then deposited it in the hole and replaced the board. The banknotes were the best, of course, but the very size of the denominations promised to be difficult to dispose of. Perhaps they'd be best as a nest egg, something to save for a rainy day. But she'd do well to sell the traceable goods to Fergie as quick as she could, come morning.

She took off her red dress, stripping down to her chemise and sighing with relief once she'd rid herself of the corset. Then, already shivering a little with the cold, she pulled on her plain, ragged nightgown and rolled herself in her woolen blanket. Her pillow was a bundle of rags, faintly moldy but really not bad, and she shared the bed with only a few fleas. On the whole, things could be a great deal worse.

Whisper curled in beside her. Coventry put an arm around the cat, bundling him close, enjoying the throaty rumble of his contented purring. Soon she was asleep.

*   *   *

The fog had lifted and the sun was well up by the time Coventry reluctantly abandoned the nest of warmth she and Whisper had made for themselves. The London sky was faintly visible through the grimy window, clouds of coal-smoke from the chimneys blotting out most of the blue. Still, it didn't look likely to rain, and that was something to be thankful for.

While Whisper luxuriously stretched and saw to his morning toilet, daintily licking his paws, Coventry washed her own face, using a polished tin plate for a mirror. She made certain to remove all trace of her tart's makeup. What was left was a young woman who could pass for a girl. She sometimes cursed her fresh-faced beauty. If she'd not been such a looker, she'd not likely have come to this pass. Still, once the gin was spilt in the gutter, there was precious little use crying over it. She put on her other dress, her everyday dress. This was pale blue, stained a bit at the hem, darkened with coal-dust, and starting to fray at the cuffs. And, of course, it went over the thrice-damned corset and petticoats.

Inside a quarter of an hour, her hair tucked back in a braid, looped and pinned around her head, Coventry looked like any young woman of modest means. She had a wicker shopping-basket to hold on her arm and a plain narrow-brimmed hat that matched the dress. Unable to resist, she gave the hat a saucy tilt. In the bottom of the basket, under a folded cloth, were the jewelry and knickknacks formerly belonging to Bartleby Horrocks. Tucked up the right sleeve of the dress, clipped to her forearm, was her stiletto. Thus fortified, Coventry Adams emerged to meet the day.

She'd gone only two paces down the hall when she saw Whisper frisking about her ankles. Apparently he thought it best to accompany her to market to protect his investment in her.

"As you will, you wee dark lump," she said with an affectionate smile. "But don't you come crying if a cart runs over that tail you're waving so proud."

Whisper looked up at her and blinked as if to suggest he was affronted by the mere suggestion of such clumsiness.

Daylight revealed, in unflinching clarity, all the dingy ugliness of Whitechapel. The name, Coventry thought, had never suited the neighborhood. The colors of Whitechapel were dirty brick and dingy grey. Not even the linens on the clotheslines were white, not once the coal-smoke got to them. When she'd been a girl, Coventry had learned about the peppered moths. In 1811, the moths had been white with dark grey spots. Less than forty years later, a field collection in Manchester had revealed they were being rapidly replaced by their cousins, black-bodied with wings the color of soot.

The Darwinians, of course, had seized on this as evidence of their radical theory of natural selection. Coventry took the more practical lesson to heart. If one wanted to survive in a dark world, one had best learn how to blend with the shadows.

How she missed books! She dreamed, sometimes, of her father's library. To have a whole room devoted to nothing but the storage of knowledge! It was a silly, girlish dream, she knew, but sometimes she wept for it.

But dreams were for slumber. Now that she was awake, she had best keep her wits about her. The air was sharp and cold, the wind whipping color into her cheeks. She glided through the crowds, avoiding contact whenever possible, making a path when she must. She was small, but she knew how to command her space, to project herself into her environs. And she had a knack with words, particularly the sort of vicious abuse the fishwives slung about the market. Coventry could fair blister the ears of even the most debauched rowdy.

Her first stop this day was Fergie's rag and bottle shop, a dilapidated little store a stone's throw from the market. She pushed the door open, hearing the tinkle of the little bell that hung from the ceiling, and stepped into the dark interior. Whisper scuttled in on her heels.

The shop was very dark, for the windows were so dusty they might almost have been bricked up. Sagging shelves groaned and creaked under the weight of countless piles of worthless detritus. The place was a veritable maze, but Coventry had been here many times before and knew her way about. She walked confidently along the serpentine path that led to the counter, catching a glimpse of a skittering little creature out of the corner of her eye.

Whisper saw it too. The cat crouched, tail lashing. Then he pounced, a brief scuffle and a muffled squeak heralding the end of a mouse's short, sad life. Whisper rejoined Coventry, tail waving like a triumphant flag, a limp grey body dangling from his mouth.

"Fergie!" Coventry called.

"That you, Cov?" called a reedy Irish-accented voice.

"Now who else would I bloomin' well be?" she retorted. She had reached the counter, which was likewise piled with junk, but saw no sign of the proprietor.

"Can't be too careful," Fergie replied, popping into view like a jack-in-the-box. He was an odd-looking little man, all skinny limbs and bony joints, tufts of hair thrusting haphazardly from all points of his skull. He grinned lopsidedly when he saw her. His whole face was slightly off-kilter, which made one want to tilt one's head when looking at him.

"Got something I thought you'd want a butcher's at," she said. It had taken her some time to catch the knack of the Cockney rhyming slang. In this case, "butcher's" was short for "butcher's hook," rhyming with "look," which was what she was actually saying. It was an almost impenetrable dialect, which was precisely the point. Cockneys had no interest in speaking clearly to outsiders. Knowing the slang was a shibboleth, a gateway to lower-class London.

"Well, let's have a gander," Fergie said. "Always a pleasure to see you, Cov. You're lookin' lovely as ever."

Coventry, after a quick look over her shoulder to ensure they were alone, spread out her offerings on a small space of open countertop. Fergie fumbled in his pocket for an eyeglass. He screwed it into his right eye, making his face even more lopsided than before. He picked up the items one by one and squinted at them.

How the fence could see anything in this light was a mystery to Coventry. Perhaps he never went outside, and so remained acclimated to the shadows. Certainly she had never seen him anywhere but this shop. Whisper might have better night-vision than Fergie, but she would place no wager on it.

"Hmm, very nice, very nice," Fergie murmured. Some fences pretended disinterest in their wares, figuring they could drive a cheaper bargain, but Fergie valued his long-running relationship with Coventry. He knew if he tried to skin her, he might get away with it once, but if she found out, she'd take her business elsewhere. Besides, Coventry had a better eye for jewelry than many street girls and was hard to cheat.

"I'm guessing you didn't buy these from Asprey or Garrard," he said, speaking of two of the posher jewelers in London.

"Got them off a gentleman," she said with a bland smile.

"Presents, were they?"

"Not precisely."

Fergie nodded. He didn't need to know the details, nor did he wish to. He only needed to know whether the articles were stolen. Coventry had just told him that, though not in so many words.

"I'll give you fifty quid for the lot," he said.

"You'll sell them for five hundred," she said. "I'll be wanting a hundred."

"They're fair scorching," he argued. "I'll not get anything close to market price. Sixty, and that's taking bread out of the mouths of my wee ones."

"If you're a father, I'm the Archbishop of bloody Canterbury," she retorted. "Eighty and they're yours."

"Enough haggling," he said. "We both know you'll settle for sixty-five."

"Don't be putting words in my mouth, when what we both know is we'll meet at seventy-five."

"Done." Fergie grinned and offered his hand. Coventry shook with him, almost managing to avoid thinking about where his hand might have been or what it might have been doing. "Half a moment, I'll fetch your coin."

He bustled into his back room and returned a few moments later with a cigar-box that rattled enticingly. He opened the box so the lid was between them and counted out an odd collection of well-worn coinage. Coventry didn't mind. Old coins raised no eyebrows and would be easy to spend.

"Be seeing you, Fergie," she said. "This world or a better."

"If you wind up waiting in heaven, you'll be waiting for me a long time," he cackled, ending in a dusty coughing fit. "Mind your step, Cov. A hundred perfect jobs won't make up for the one you botch."

Back on the street again, Whisper still proudly carrying his kill, they made their way to the market. There Coventry bought a loaf of bread, a wedge of cheese, two bottles of cheap red wine, two cabbages, and some salt beef. True to her word, she then went to the fishmongers to see about a nice bit of fish for Whisper.

The fishwives were the best gossips in the market. Coventry always put her ear to the ground when she visited. One never knew when one might hear something of interest, or of possible value. As she perused the day's catch, she heard one of the women reading from the newspaper. Few of these women could read, so a knot of them had clustered around the reader, hungry for news.

"...found murdered in his hotel room," the woman was saying, sounding out the critical word with morbid delight.

"Murdered?" one of the listeners echoed, to the accompaniment of a chorus of theatrical gasps.

"Just think of it!" another said. "Such a great man, too!"

"Hush!" a third said. "Go on, Nora, tell us what it says!"

"Au-thor-i-tees are in-ves-ti-gay-ting," Nora said, getting over the long words with difficulty. "They suspect the victim had an... an..."

"Yes?" several breathless voices asked.

But the word "assignation" was beyond Nora's literary grasp. "He was entertaining a tart in his room," she guessed.

Heads bobbed knowingly. Even the toffs were only human, after all. Serve him right if he was done in by one of those women. Still, it was hard to imagine.

"The Met-ro-pol-i-tan Police expect to solve the case quickly," Nora said. "Scotland Yard has placed one of its rising stars on the job."

"'Ere, Nora, what's a rising star?" a woman inquired.

"It means a lad who's not on top yet, but he'll get there," her companion explained.

"Detective Farrell declined to comment," Nora recited. "But this reporter is sure this grisly and brutal murder will not go long un-avenged, and Minister Horrocks will have justice."

All the blood drained out of Coventry's face. Perhaps it was the squeeze of her corset, but she could scarcely draw breath. She never fainted, never, but for a moment the fishmarket spun about her.

"'Ere, madam, you all right?"

A rough but friendly pair of hands caught her just under the shoulders. Coventry blinked and saw the mustached face of a fisherman. He had weather-beaten cheeks but bright eyes. Coventry had learned to pay close attention to what could be seen in a man's eyes. She saw nothing here but kindness and concern.

"I'm all right," she said. "Just got taken a bit funny is all."

"Sit down for a spell," he suggested, gesturing to a nearby wooden crate. "You'll feel better in a bit."

"No, thank you, sir," she said, waving him off. "I... I must be going."

She extricated herself from her would-be helper and fled the market. Her head was awhirl with horror. Dear God, she thought. Bartleby Horrocks, dead! The opium? Surely not!

But opium had killed many a healthy lad before Mr. Horrocks. What if she had administered too much of the stuff?

What if the mixture had been bad? Good Lord, she had killed the poor man! Granted, he was a filthy womanizing beast, but murder?

She was a murderer. The full force of law and society would be turned against her, determined to run her to earth like a fox. Then a trial, prison, and... and the gallows. But that was not the worst of it. Coventry Adams had sworn never to take a human life, no matter the reason. And now, for the sake of a few pretty trinkets, she had lost all that was left of her soul.

She fled almost blindly, rushing she knew not where, hot tears burning in her eyes. She thrust through crowds of Londoners, heedless of their indignant cries. Where could she go? She had nowhere, no one. She was utterly lost.

*   *   *

Panic was well enough, in its way, while it lasted. But sooner or later, sanity always prevailed. Coventry's wits drifted back after perhaps half an hour. She had been weeping. Her eyes were red and sore. Her head ached, as did her feet, punished by the cobblestones. She did not immediately know where she was.

As her fear subsided a little, anger flooded in to replace it. She was angry principally with herself. She knew better than to rush off like some little fool, headlong into whatever dangers might surround her. There would be time enough to punish herself for what she had done. For now, she had to think.

"Go back," she whispered to herself. "Fetch your bits of things. Then away." A ship, perhaps. Across the Channel to France? That might serve. She knew enough French to get on with. A new city would be dangerous, surely, but how much worse could it be?

She looked about her, taking in her surroundings, and quickly recognized the street. Even in her panic, she had been thinking better than she knew. She was five minutes' walk from Slinky's gambling hall.

An anxious meow, coupled with a furry pressure against her ankle, made her glance down. There was Whisper. He had dropped his mouse somewhere along the way, but he had kept near her. Now he stared up at her and cocked his head quizzically.

Coventry gulped at the sudden lump in her throat. She was not, after all, completely alone. The thought gave her more strength than she would have thought possible. She still had her basket on her arm, containing the food she had bought. She had money hidden in her dress, with a great deal more under the floorboards. It was a slight risk, going back to fetch it, but one worth taking.

She hurried, not quite running, into the familiar alley and up the stairs. Slinky's establishment was deserted at this early hour. She unlocked her room, went in, and gathered up her things. She nearly left the red satin dress behind. It had been expensive, but it was bulky. Nonetheless, after a moment's thought, she folded it as best she could into her one piece of luggage, a battered portmanteau almost too large for her. She ate a few quick bites of food, thrust the remainder of the bread, cheese, and beef into the suitcase, and took her leave, dropping a few coins on the mattress to pay her rent. She might be a thief, but she would never cheat her landlord. She laid the key beside the coins. The door she'd leave unlocked.

"Well, lad?" she asked Whisper. "Is this goodbye? If you're wanting to keep to your cove, good luck to you. I can't promise much, but I'll miss you."

The cat licked a paw and brushed it over one of his ears. Then, seeing Coventry stepping out of the room, suitcase in hand, he meowed and trotted to join her.

Coventry closed the door to Slinky's place behind her and started down the steps, wrestling with the portmanteau. She was thinking what dock to make for, and what time the next ship might sail. Her plans were falling into place. At the back of her mind, shock and dismay still clamored for her attention, but she ignored those thoughts. Time enough later, she thought.

"Carry that for you, lass?"

The voice was young and pleasant, with the unmistakable lilt of Ireland. That was no surprise. The Irish were common enough in Whitechapel.

"No fear, lad," she replied. "I've got it." There wasn't a chance she'd trust her luggage to a complete stranger.

"A hand, then," he said as she neared the bottom of the stairs.

Coventry looked him over. He was only a few years older than she and quite a looker. His hair was dark and wavy, his mustache well-trimmed, his smooth cheeks showing he had managed to escape smallpox. He was dressed as a workingman, but something in his clothes looked just a trifle wrong. He held out a hand to assist her down the last few steps, smiling in a friendly fashion.

"And who'd you be, then?" she challenged.

"My mum called me Finbar," he said. "But that's a bit much. Most folk call me Finn. How's about you, madam?"

She hesitated. Her instincts, clouded by the emotional upheaval of the past moments, cried a sudden warning. The young man's eyes were a remarkable dark blue, very intense. She saw no cruelty in them, but she did see grim purpose.

"What's your business here, Finn?" she asked, putting her back against the alley wall and starting to sidle past him. She was suddenly, terribly afraid.

"I'm hoping to find a wee lass," he said. "I've heard she stays hereabouts. A bonnie lass, so they say, quite young, reddish-brown hair. Looks a fair bit like yourself, come to that."

Then, too late, Coventry identified him. Copper, she thought, and with that one word she panicked again. Dropping her portmanteau, she spun on her heel and started for the alley entrance.

Finn was too swift for her. Before she had gone more than three running paces he was on her, gripping her wrist with a terribly strong hand. Coventry twisted, instinctively fighting the trap. He had her right hand, the one with the stiletto. She clawed at his face with her left, gouging at his eyes.

He turned his head aside, her nails raking his cheek. Then he had her other wrist, holding both hands. Coventry kicked at his shin, then stomped on his foot, grinding down with her heel. Finn flinched but did not let go. She thrashed wildly, trying to drive her forehead into his face, but he was clearly no stranger to street brawls and drew back out of her reach. He forced her hands down and spun her about, twisting her right arm up behind her back and slamming her into the brickwork.

The breath left her in a gasp, but Coventry still tried to fight. The feel of his body against her back called up awful memories of sordid alleyway trysts. She struggled wildly, desperately. But she was no match for his size and strength. He kicked her feet apart, making her totter. Then she felt cold steel against her skin, heard the clink of an adjustable wrist-bar.

"Forgive me," Finn said through clenched teeth. "I'd hoped not to need these, but you're giving me no choice, you wee wildcat." By his strained tone, she knew she'd caused him some pain, at least.

Her left hand was free for a second. Coventry squirmed frantically, but her case was hopeless. Soon that hand, too, was pinioned behind her back, the cuffs clicking shut.

"Now," Finn said. "Let's step inside and catch our breath, shall we? I think we've a few things to discuss, you and I."

Get a reminder when the new series is out

Join Steven's list at
clickworkspress.com/join/steven

Here's a sneak peek from Book 30: Last Round

Coming 12/15/2025

"You know why they call it a stakeout, right?"

Vic Neshenko was grinning. Erin O'Reilly didn't need to look at him to know; she could hear it in his voice.

"I'm sure you're about to tell me," she said.

"Back in the old days, when a wolf was eating their sheep, farmers would lay an ambush," he said. "They'd get all their pitchforks and sickles, and they'd take a goat and tie it to a stake on the edge of the woods. Then they'd hide just over the hill and wait. When the wolf came after the goat, they'd jump him and stab the shit out of him."

"Thanks for that charming piece of agricultural history," she said. "So who's the goat in this scenario?"

"You could be," he said. "We could tie you out, alone and unarmed. When that punk came out to kill you, I'd bust his ass."

"That's a great plan, Vic."

"Really?"

"No. It's crap."

"I guess from the goat's point of view, that's true," he said, still grinning. "It beats sitting in this car all night."

He stretched as much as the passenger seat in Erin's Charger allowed. Vic was a big guy, six-foot-three and broad-shouldered, and some of his space was taken up by Erin's onboard computer. He also had a regular buffet of snacks and drinks at his feet, none of them healthy.

"You know the other way shepherds got rid of wolves?" Erin asked from the driver's seat.

"How's that?"

"They bred great big dogs to rip the wolves to shreds."

Rolf, as if recognizing his cue, chose that moment to stick his furry head through the opening between the seats. The German Shepherd's tongue was hanging out in a doggy smile.

Vic handed the K-9 a pork rind and was lucky enough to keep all his fingers. "I can see the value of that," he admitted. "I remember that hitman a couple months ago. Rolf practically bit his friggin' head off. That's why we're out here babysitting the O'Malley brat. If he hadn't tried to have you whacked, I'd be getting a decent night's sleep, sharing a bed with a girl who's a lot prettier than either of you two. No offense."

"None taken," Erin said. "The only way I'd share a bed with you is if I got so drunk I passed out and tripped over something."

"I'm just saying, this would work better if we had some decent bait," Vic said. "The little jerk's out drinking with his buddies, having a good time, and we're sitting in this car like a couple of assholes. We're not even pulling overtime, since this isn't a sanctioned operation."

"You don't have to be here," she reminded him.

"Like I'm gonna let you follow Richie O'Malley around on your own," he retorted. "You'd screw it up and I'd have to ride in like the goddamn cavalry to rescue you. And I don't even know how to ride a horse."

"I appreciate it, Vic," Erin said, and she meant it. Cops risked their lives every time they went out on the street. That was the Job and they all accepted it. But when the shit went down, they could count on thirty-five thousand other officers having their backs. Here and now, Erin and Vic were disobeying orders. They were putting their jobs and reputations, as well as their lives, on the line.

Erin's instructions were to leave Richard O'Malley alone. According to Captain Holliday, Richie was one suspect in a sprawling Narcotics investigation. He was helping move fentanyl for the Russian Mob. But Erin believed Richie was also behind two attempts on her own life. Richie was pissed because Erin had betrayed his dad's trust, thrown Evan O'Malley and all his associates in jail, and stripped Richie's inheritance away. Plenty of less desperate men had killed for much less. Erin wasn't about to stand back and let the wheels of justice roll slowly over Richie. She needed him off the street, before he sent another assassin.

"Yeah, whatever," Vic muttered. "Eight weeks we've been doing this. And what've we got to show for it? This guy's the lamest criminal in the history of lame criminals. We don't have a single thing we can use that Narcotics doesn't already have. We can't see anything the Narco boys aren't seeing, because we have to hide or we'll get made by our own damn people!"

"What's your point, Vic?"

"My point is we're wasting our time. I get it, I don't want this asshole popping off rounds at you either. But the vory are nasty SOBs. Did it occur to you that hanging around the Russian Mafia might be putting you in more danger, not less? These guys tried to kill me once."

"I remember."

He sighed. "Don't you think it might be better if we actually did what we were supposed to for a change?"

"Who are you?" she demanded. "And what've you done with Vic?"

He snickered. "Okay, okay. Sorry. I haven't been getting any damn sleep and it's making me grumpy. I have a day job, you know."

"So do I," Erin said. She sat back and rubbed her face. "I'm sorry too. We're all tired. I thought this would be easier."

"Because Richie's a moron?"

"Something like that, yeah."

"But he's clever enough to hide from us," he said. "So what's that make us?"

"Chumps," she said. "Maybe Holliday was right. This cowboy crap isn't doing anyone any good. Richie hasn't made a move on me since that thing in the parking garage. Maybe he's given up. We should concentrate on our normal cases. It isn't like I don't have other things on my mind, too."

"Yeah," Vic said. "Like the wedding. How's the planning going?"

"Like you care."

"I don't. But Zofia keeps asking about it. She's got a calendar. A real paper one, like people used to use a hundred years ago. She's actually putting Xs in the days, counting them down. I gotta be careful. Weddings are like the flu."

"Miserable and exhausting?" Erin guessed.

"Contagious," he said. "Between Ian Thompson and that rehab nurse getting hitched, and you and Carlyle, next thing you know, Zofia's gonna want me to put a ring on her."

"And you don't want to?"

"I don't want to do it just because everybody else is doing it. If I ever do get married, it's gonna be for the right reasons."

"Which are?"

"Tax breaks and regular sex."

"You're a real romantic, Vic."

"I know. I'm a softy. So what do you want to do?"

Erin shook her head and turned the key in the ignition. The Charger's engine rumbled to life. "Let's call it a night," she said.

"Are we giving up on Little Richard?"

"I have no idea. We'll see."

*　*　*

Erin's fiancé was waiting up for her, even though it was after midnight. That wasn't surprising; Morton Carlyle had been, at various points in his life, a pub owner, a gangster, and a bomb maker for the IRA. All these occupations lent themselves to a nocturnal existence. The Barley Corner, Carlyle's pride and joy, was still open when Erin got there, and Carlyle was sitting in his usual spot at the bar. He was having a drink with James Corcoran.

"Evening, darling," Carlyle said, standing up to greet her.

"And a grand night it is," Corky added, bouncing to his feet. "It's scarcely begun. Have a pint with us, love!"

"How many has he already had?" Erin asked Carlyle in an undertone as she slid onto the barstool on the other side from Corky.

"Six," Carlyle said. "Unless he started drinking before he got here."

"I'm offended," Corky said with a display of wounded innocence that fooled nobody. "Everyone knows the Corner's the place to get the finest Guinness and whiskey this side of the pond. I'd never pollute myself with cheap rotgut before passing your doors, Cars. Have I really had six?"

"Aye," Carlyle said. "Three shots of Glen D and three pints."

"I could've sworn it was only five," Corky said. "But then, I never was much good at maths. How's about you, Erin?"

"I'm good," she said.

"Grand," Corky said. "We were just talking about you, if you'll believe it."

"Only good things, I hope."

"What else is there to tell?" he replied. "In point of fact, we're discussing the wedding. Just round the corner, so it is."

Erin sighed. "I'm getting enough of that from my mom," she said. "And even Vic, if you believe it. You'd think Mom hadn't gone through this whole thing twice before, with my big brothers."

"It's different with a daughter," Carlyle said.

"Aye," Corky agreed cheerfully. "There's likely to be more female guests, so there's better chances for the unattached lads."

"I'm a cop, Corky," Erin said. "That means half the guests on my side are going to be male police officers. Some of them will be armed. And you'll be attending with your girlfriend, unless I'm very much mistaken. That doesn't really sound like good chances to me."

"Force of habit, love," he said, winking. "No fear. Terry's more than enough woman for me. Speaking of which, I've a responsibility to discharge."

"And that is?" Erin asked, feeling a twinge of dread.

"As best man, the stag party's mine to organize," he said. Seeing the look on Erin's face, he held up a hand. "Now, before you say anything, remember I've known Cars my whole life. I know what sort of lad he is, and the sort of revelry he'll enjoy. I'd not go planning anything of which he'd disapprove, nor yourself, come to that."

"I'm surprised at you," Erin said. "I'm starting to think Teresa really has reformed you."

His bright green eyes twinkled. "So I've a list of possibilities here, for your approval. The first thing I'd like to do is—"

"No," Erin said flatly.

Corky blinked. "But Erin, love, you've not even heard what it is."

"It's strippers, isn't it," Erin replied. It wasn't a question.

"Well, aye, but that's not the point."

"What is the point?"

"You didn't trust me enough to hear me out."

"But I was right. That means I trusted you exactly the right amount. Trust doesn't mean giving people the chance to screw you over, Corky. It means knowing people well enough that you know how they're going to react in a given situation."

"Well, by that measure, everyone ought to trust me," Corky said. "I'm an open book. But I can't deny I'm a bit hurt. I had it all planned out. It would've been very tasteful. A religious experience, you might say."

Erin put her face in her palm. "Oh God," she said. "They were going to be dressed as nuns?! What the matter with you, Corky?"

"I can see why they made you a detective," Corky said with undisguised admiration. "It's a wonder any crimes go unsolved in this great city of ours."

"And on that subject," Carlyle interjected. "What's our mutual friend been up to?"

"Nothing," Erin said. "I mean, Richie's meeting with bad guys. He's making phone calls. He goes to skeezy bars and hangs out with lowlifes."

"That's not a crime," Corky observed. "Else you'd have to arrest yourself, love."

"What, exactly, are you saying about my pub?" Carlyle demanded.

"Only one of you is a lowlife, anyway," Erin said.

"Which one?" Corky asked. The twinkle was back in his eye. "I'll have you know, those stripper nuns come highly recommended. I talked to a couple of lads who said seeing them was like seeing the face of God Himself."

"No strippers," Erin said. "Also no whores, drugs, gunfights, or explosives."

"A fine stag party this'll be," Corky muttered. "There go the next four things on my list. I might as well start over from scratch."

Carlyle smiled and nodded his approval to Erin. "Nothing incriminating?" he asked her.

"Not outside of what the Narco boys have," she said. "He's involved with the Russians, all right. Vic says it's part of the same vory we tangled with a couple years ago. You remember Peter Vlasov?"

"Quite an unpleasant lad," Carlyle said. "But he wasn't a drug smuggler. His traffic was young women. As I recall, he's a guest of the state now."

"Yeah," she said. "He lost a chunk of his guts when I shot him at the airport, but he's still alive. He'll be about ninety years old when he finally gets out of prison, assuming he gets time off for good behavior, which we shouldn't."

"With Vlasov out of the picture, who's running their business these days?" Carlyle asked. "My contacts on the street aren't what they used to be, I fear, since you threw most of them behind bars."

"One of his cousins," Erin said. "Gennady Vlasov. According to the Narcotics file, he's branched out into hard drugs in a big way lately, filling the hole in the market we made when we took apart the O'Malley and Lucarelli narcotics operations."

"The more things change, the more they stay the same," Carlyle said quietly. "What do you know about this Gennady?"

Erin shrugged. "He's a nasty piece of work, too," she said. "What do you expect? We don't think he's even in the country, though. He has lieutenants doing his legwork over here. He's in Russia, as far as anyone knows."

"Too bad," Corky said. "Extradition's near impossible from that godforsaken place."

"Narcotics is trying to set up a sting," Erin said. "They're hoping to lure Gennady over here, so they can grab him on American soil. He's the big fish. Nobody but me gives a damn about Richie O'Malley."

"I assume Mr. Vlasov has quite the host of hardened killers about him," Carlyle said. "Which begs the question, why Richard would employ outside talent to do away with you. One would think he could task a few Russian thugs to waylay you."

"I've been thinking about that," Erin said. "And my guess is the Narcs are right when they say Richie's just not that important to them. They're just getting their fentanyl business established and they don't want extra police attention. If their people start offing cops, the NYPD's going to come down on them like the wrath of God and they know it. I think Richie probably asked to use some of their people and they refused."

"That's some consolation," Carlyle said. "Those Russian lads are nothing to sneeze at. They're cold, violent, and as tough as they come. At least the Irish have some rules. The Russians have none."

"So what are we doing about Richie?" Corky asked.

Erin spread her hands. "What can we do?" she replied. "I've been cranking out unpaid overtime for weeks now. Vic's been helping out when he can, but we don't want to get Lieutenant Webb or the rest of the squad involved. We're lucky this hasn't gotten back to Captain Holliday as it stands. I'd hoped to get this taken care of before the wedding, but it doesn't look like happening."

"It'll all come right," Carlyle said. "There's no percentage in spending lives and resources on you, darling. Sooner or later Richie's going to give up. And perhaps in the meantime we'll get lucky and someone else will solve the problem for us. He's chosen a particularly dangerous line of work, and if he doesn't watch himself, his wife's going to be widowed and his lad will grow up fatherless."

"Yeah," Erin said. "I'm going to skip the drink."

"Why?" Corky asked. "Don't you want one?"

"I want three," she said. "But I don't think I should have them. I'm tired. I'm going up to bed."

"I'll be up shortly," Carlyle said. He kissed her cheek.

Erin said goodnight to Corky, for which she received another kiss on her opposite cheek. Then she went upstairs. She stripped off her work clothes and pulled on the old T-shirt she slept in. She brushed her teeth, but skipped the shower. She hadn't gotten too dirty, and she'd be taking Rolf for a run in the morning and getting sweaty, so she'd shower then. She climbed into bed, taking a moment to check her e-mail one last time for any urgent messages.

She froze, staring at the screen. "What the hell?" she murmured.

Rolf, hearing the strange tone in her voice, clambered up on the mattress next to her and thrust his muzzle in close, trying to see what was going on. He'd never understood the fixation those little black boxes had for humans. Strange sounds came out of them sometimes, but they didn't smell interesting, you couldn't eat them, and they didn't make good chew-toys. There was no accounting for human behavior.

Erin hesitated. But the message still sat in her inbox. It wasn't going anywhere. Finally, she jabbed it with a finger, opening it.

The e-mail was short, clipped, and formal. It was an official notification from Riker's Island Prison, informing her that an inmate, one Kyle Finnegan, had filed a request for her to visit him at her earliest convenience.

"Finnegan," she said softly. "That crazy son of a bitch. What on Earth does he want to talk to me for?"

She had no answer. Neither did Rolf. It shouldn't have bothered her. Finnegan was crazy, all right; Vic liked to recall how he'd once eaten a piece of a man's face, raw, with hot sauce. He was also clever and completely ruthless. But he was caged now, safely behind bars. He couldn't do anything to her.

That was what she kept telling herself as she tried to go to sleep. But she couldn't quite make herself believe it.

Ready for more?

Join the Clickworks Press email list
for the latest on new releases, upcoming books and
series, behind-the-scenes details, events, and more.

Be the first to know about
new releases from Steven Henry
by signing up at
clickworkspress.com/join/steven

About the Author

Steven Henry learned how to read almost before he learned how to walk. Ever since he began reading stories, he wanted to put his own on the page. He lives a very quiet and ordinary life in Minnesota with his wife and dog.

Also by Steven Henry

Fathers
A Modern Christmas Story

When you strip away everything else, what's left is the truth

Life taught Joe Davidson not to believe in miracles. A blue-collar wood-worker, Joe is trying to build a future. His father drank himself to death and his mother succumbed to cancer, leaving a broken, struggling family. He and his brother and sisters are faced with failed marriages, growing pains, and lingering trauma.

Then a chance meeting at his local diner brings Mary Elizabeth Reynolds into his life. Suddenly, Joe finds himself reaching for something more, a dream of happiness. The wood-worker and the poor girl from a trailer park connect and fall in love, and for a little while, everything is right with their world.

But suddenly Joe is confronted with a situation he never imagined. What do you do if your fiancée is expecting a child you know isn't yours? Torn between betrayal and love, trying to do the right thing when nothing seems right anymore, Joe has to strip life down to its truth and learn that, in spite of the pain, love can be the greatest miracle of all.

Learn more at clickworkspress.com/fathers.

www.ingramcontent.com/pod-product-compliance
Lightning Source LLC
Chambersburg PA
CBHW030002010826
48973CB00007B/2119